His thumb brushed her chin. "I see you were able to clean up."

"You, too." She smiled, quite aware that he was still touching her. She stood motionless so as not to break the connection.

"You're awful pretty." His gaze moved from the flat plane of her chest bared by her neckline to her mouth. His eyes darkened.

She remembered that look! And the answering flutter in her stomach. Before she realized it, she had taken a step toward him.

"Damn." He shifted closer too, muttering, "Ought to kiss you and see if you remember that."

His voice was so low she barely caught his words, but when she did a wave of heat flushed her body. Nervous now, she let her tongue come out to moisten her lips and a nearly pained look came over his face.

For a split second she thought he might kiss her. She wanted him to because she suddenly, shockingly, recalled the feel of his mouth on hers. She wanted to feel it again....

AUTHOR NOTE

This is the eighth and final book in my *Whirlwind, Texas* series. As such, I had a difficult time writing this letter. It took me a while to realise that the reason I had so much trouble knowing what to say is because I've 'lived' in Whirlwind for almost ten years.

The series was originally conceived as three books, but I soon discovered there were other characters with stories to be told. Over the last couple of years I've had quite a lot of mail about the romance of Bram Ross and Deborah Blue, so it seems fitting to end the series with their story. These two are destined to be together, but before they can have a future they have to deal with their past, and Deborah doesn't remember it—or Bram—at all. I hope you find their story as special as I did.

This series has been a delight, and these people have become like family to me. It is my wish that they have brought you a fraction of the joy they brought to me.

Happy Trails!

WHIRLWIND COWBOY

Debra Cowan

First published in Great Britain 2012
by Mills & Boon, an imprint of Harlequin (UK) I
Harlequin (UK) Limited, Eton House, 18-24 Para
Richmond, Surrey TW9 1SR

ROM
Pbk

© Debra S. Cowan 2012

ISBN: 978 0 263 89269 7

Printed and bound in Spain
by Blackprint CPI, Barcelona

Like many writers, **Debra Cowan** made up stories in her head as a child. Her BA in English was obtained with the intention of following family tradition and becoming a schoolteacher, but after she wrote her first novel there was no looking back. An avid history buff, Debra writes both historical and contemporary romances. Born in the foothills of the Kiamichi Mountains, Debra still lives in her native Oklahoma with her husband.

Debra invites her readers to contact her at PO Box 30123, Coffee Creek Station, Edmond, OK 73003-0003, USA, or visit her website at: www.debracowan.net

Previous novels by this author:

WHIRLWIND BABY
WHIRLWIND BRIDE

To all the readers who love Westerns
as much as I do and so enthusiastically embraced
the *Whirlwind* series—this one's for you.

Prologue

West Texas
May 1886

The sharp crack of gunshots still echoed in Bram Ross's ears as he urged his horse away from the shoot-out at the Eight of Hearts ranch. Wincing, he wiped at the blood running down his right cheek. He could smell it on the warm May air.

Only minutes ago Bram and his friends had been in a confrontation with a band of cattle rustlers and the man who had given them their orders. Dr. Annalise Fine had been smack in the middle of it. Thankfully, she was unhurt and safe now with Matt Baldwin.

The sheriff and two other men were taking

the dead bodies of the outlaws and their boss back to Whirlwind.

Only one man had gotten away.

Now Bram rode hell-for-leather after Cosgrove, the snake who had slithered off in a hail of bullets after one of his shots had plowed a furrow in one side of Bram's face. He barely kept his fury in check as he followed Cosgrove's tracks southwest across the prairie from Eight of Hearts land and onto the Baldwins' property.

Considering how many men had been firing weapons, it was lucky only the outlaws had been killed.

Bram was beyond angry that Cosgrove had escaped. He had more than one score to settle with the rustling bastard. The skunk hadn't only injured Bram, he had stolen so many Circle R cattle that Bram's family had come close to losing their ranch.

In moments he reached Ross land, passing the small cabin his brother had spruced up last year before his wedding. Grass and dirt flew from under his gelding's hooves as they thundered across the prairie. Bram realized Cosgrove was headed toward the west edge of Circle R property.

And the house where Deborah Blue lived with her mother and three sisters.

Why was the lowlife going this way? Foreboding snaked up Bram's spine. Did it have anything to do with Deborah? It was no secret that Cosgrove was interested in her, but to come here on the run from the law and Bram? The closer he got to the house, the harder his gut churned.

Though the tracks stopped a good distance from the roomy log house, Bram urged his mount there anyway. If Cosgrove was fool enough to stop here, he wasn't leaving. Bram quietly dismounted, pulled his rifle from his scabbard and slipped carefully to the corner of the house. No sign of anyone in the garden at the side of the house or in the corral or barn. No one riding through the tall prairie grass behind. There was no sound from inside and no one answered his knock.

If Cosgrove had stopped here, maybe no one had been home. The tightness across Bram's chest eased slightly—until he heard the rattle of an approaching wagon. He raised his rifle, then quickly lowered it when he saw Mrs. Blue in her wagon with three of her four daughters. No sign of Deborah among them.

His gut knotted. Instead of waiting for the women to reach him, Bram strode toward them.

Recalling the row he'd had with Deborah

last night, he wondered if perhaps she hadn't answered his knock because she was still angry.

"Hello, Bram." Deborah's mother, a tall, thin woman, gave him a wobbly smile. Seeing his bloody cheek, she drew in a sharp breath. "Are you all right? What happened?"

"I'm fine, ma'am." He yanked off his hat, quickly explaining that there had been trouble at one of the neighboring ranches.

There was no sign Cosgrove had been here, no sign that Deborah had left with the bastard. So where was she? "Deborah isn't with you?"

"No," Jessamine Blue said. "She stayed here while the girls and I went to town."

Apprehension drummed through him. "I knocked, but got no answer."

Mrs. Blue frowned, touching the knee of the raven-haired daughter beside her. "Jordan, go check the house."

The sister closest to Deborah in age, with the same black hair and blue eyes, allowed Bram to help her from the wagon, then hurried inside.

He had just handed down the older woman when Jordan returned with a piece of paper. She sent Bram an uncertain look before reaching her mother. "She's gone! She left a note."

Gone? For a moment Bram's thoughts stalled. Gone where?

Mrs. Blue quickly scanned the note, shaking her head, sounding bewildered. "She's gone to Abilene to meet with the school board about her new teaching job."

The words hit him like a kick to the head. "Why? Why would she do that now? School doesn't start until September."

After their heated argument last night, she had agreed to think about turning down the job and staying here with him.

The job was for only two school terms. She'd sworn she would return to Whirlwind. And him.

His ma had said the same thing one day when he was four and Jake was five. Bram hadn't seen her again until he managed to track her down eleven years later. She had refused to come back to Whirlwind with him. He'd never told Jake about that—who needed to hear that their own mother wanted nothing to do with them? Bram had lived that minute over enough for both of them.

And now Deborah had left Bram, too. That cut too close to the bone. He had asked her to consider staying here, with him. She had considered it all of thirteen hours. He had her answer.

Nothing and no one meant enough to her for her to stay.

Her mother's blue eyes, faded from age and

illness, filled with tears. "I don't understand why she felt the need to leave now."

Neither did Bram. He might want to go after her, but what was the point? Besides, he couldn't lose Cosgrove's trail.

Cold, sharp fury sliced through Bram. Fine. He was done with her. And he was wasting daylight.

He vaulted into his saddle and bid the Blues goodbye as he rode off. After promising to give his proposal some thought, Deborah had up and left instead.

That hurt every bit as much as the searing pain in his cheek.

Bram could forget her. He *would* forget. But he wouldn't forget Cosgrove. He would hunt down that lying, thieving thug and have his revenge, no matter what he had to do to get it.

Chapter One

West Texas
June 1886

Where was she? The ground was hard beneath her back. Her head pounded as she stared up at a gray sky and the sun hidden behind red-tinted clouds. Carefully pushing herself up on her elbows, she winced as sharp pain speared through her skull. Her shoulder ached, too. She was behind a two-story white brick building she didn't recognize.

She touched her temple, and her fingers came away bloody. She inhaled sharply. Blood also streaked her pale blue floral bodice. What had happened?

A creaking sound had her looking over her

shoulder. A saddled black horse watched her with dark eyes. Then she saw a wet stain a couple of feet away.

She eased over and touched it, startled to realize it was more blood.

Cold, savage fear ripped through her and she got unsteadily to her feet, fighting back panic. Whatever had happened here had been deadly. She couldn't remember it, but she *knew* it.

Her head throbbed as she looked around wildly, trying to identify something, anything. Not the building hiding her or the store across a dusty street or the railroad tracks beyond. Nothing was familiar.

Alarmed and confused, she felt tears sting her eyes.

From the front of the building she heard the heavy thud of boots. A man muttered in a low, vicious voice. The hairs on her arms stood up and fear rushed through her.

There was no thought, only instinct. She gathered her skirts and hurriedly mounted the waiting horse, riding astride. Her skull felt as though it was being cracked open and she thought she might pass out from the pain.

Urging the animal into motion, she rode hard away from the unfamiliar buildings and headed for the open prairie. Someone yelled after her. She wasn't sure what he said, but she didn't stop.

Gripping the pommel with sweat-slick hands, she kept the horse at a full-out run until she was assured no one was behind her.

Then she slowed the horse to an easy pace. As far as she could see there was an endless sea of golden-brown prairie grass, dotted here and there with a few evergreen trees. The landscape looked familiar, but she didn't know why. She didn't know anything.

A forceful gust of wind had her grabbing the pommel. Bits of dirt and grass pelted her face as well as her mount's. The animal slowed, but kept moving.

Dust whirled across the prairie. The horse's hooves pounded in a steady lope. On and on. Daylight turned to gray. They crossed a dry creek bed, then topped a small rise. Through the swirling light and dirt, she spied a small cabin and a barn. As she rode up to the front of the house, she called out, but no one answered. There was no sign of anyone at all.

Glancing over her shoulder, she frowned at a boiling mass of clouds sweeping across the ground. The first stirrings of a dust storm. Being caught out in it could be deadly.

Fighting back panic, she decided to take shel-

ter in the small cabin. She wasted no time settling the horse in the barn. After filling the
trough with water from the pump just outside,
she closed the animal inside and ran to the cabin,
praying she would be able to get in. When she
tried the door, it opened and she slipped inside
with a big sigh of relief.

Shaking out her skirts then brushing off her
hair and bodice, she took stock. A Franklin stove
sat in the corner to her left, along with a sink
and a pump and a short work cabinet. There was
a small but sturdy-looking table, and straight
ahead an open door revealed the foot of a bed.

The windows, real pane glass, shook as the
wind gathered force. Her shoulders and neck
throbbed, but she searched for candles or a lamp
in case she needed light later.

Though small, the cabin was solid and would
offer protection from the storm. Looking down,
she stared at the bloodstains on her bodice. Her
mind was empty. Why couldn't she remember
anything?

A shiver rippled up her spine. Not only was
she completely alone and lost—she had no idea
who she was.

After a week of tracking Cosgrove, Bram had
lost him and returned home. Whirlwind's sher-

iff, Davis Lee Holt, had wired every lawman in the state and promised to send word to Bram if he received any news.

Bram had duties at the ranch, but he still checked with Davis Lee every day about Cosgrove. Two weeks after the trail had gone cold, Bram got news. Surprisingly it was from his uncle, not the sheriff. Uncle Ike had witnessed Cosgrove robbing a bank in Monaco.

Bram had ridden straight to the small town located northwest of Whirlwind, where he discovered Cosgrove had murdered a man during that robbery.

Bram had picked up the outlaw's trail again, this time headed east toward Whirlwind. Cosgrove would be a fool to go back there and probably hadn't, but the approaching dust storm had erased any sign that he might have changed direction.

The past three weeks had been hell, and Bram laid that on Deborah as much as the outlaw he chased. He hadn't spoken to her mother or sisters again, though Bram's brother, Jake, had. He had felt it his duty to let Bram know Deborah still hadn't returned home.

Bram tried to tell himself he didn't care. She'd made her choice and it wasn't him.

The spiraling wind swirled across the prairie, flaying his face and body with sharp bits of dirt and grit. The gunshot graze on his cheek was healing. Dragging his dark bandanna up to cover his nose and mouth, he knotted it tightly.

He was worn slick, dirty and madder than hell that this dust storm would force him to briefly suspend his search for Cosgrove, but he would find the low-down dog again. He wouldn't stop until he did. In addition to being a rustler, Cosgrove was now a murderer. Bram wouldn't be the only one out for the bastard's blood. If possible, he hated the cattle thief even more than he had three weeks ago.

The wind swept around him and he barely caught his hat before it blew off. The small cabin on the edge of Circle R property was less than a mile away, so Bram directed his mount there.

By the time they reached the building, the red dust was thickening, spreading. At the barn behind the cabin, he dismounted and slid open the door. When his mount balked at entering, Bram grabbed the bridle to lead the animal inside. He understood the dun's wariness. This storm made him uneasy, too.

The dust swirled inside, the wind noise escalating to a steady hollow hum. Bram quickly pulled off his saddlebags, unsaddled his horse, then removed the bridle.

Scout stomped, shifting nervously. Bram spoke softly, trying to calm the gelding. A clothesline stretched from the barn to the cabin and would enable Bram to find his way if the dust became too thick to see the house. Just as he bent to pick up his saddlebag, the horse backed up, almost pinning Bram to the wall.

"Whoa." He laid a calming hand on the animal's hindquarters and edged away from the weathered wall. That was when he saw another horse deep in the shadows.

Not just any horse. He blinked.

That looked like Cosgrove's black mare.

No way in hell. Bram couldn't be seeing what he thought he was.

He eased closer, noting that the animal was unsaddled and had been brushed down. Speaking softly to the horse, he lifted its left front leg, then the back one. A *C* had been crudely carved into the top of the mare's rear shoe. It was slyly done, the top of the *C* coming out of the tack's head, but this *was* Cosgrove's horse!

The damn brand blotter had been forced to take shelter, too. Here!

Bram's lips twisted. This was too good to be true, and he wasn't going to waste the opportunity to catch the bastard. Or kill him. After the murder committed by Cosgrove during that bank robbery, Bram would have no qualms about taking in a dead man.

Satisfied that there was enough water in the trough near Cosgrove's animal for both horses, Bram returned to his things in the corner and slid his Spencer rifle out of its scabbard.

After checking his gun, he stepped outside. The wind nearly shoved him to his knees as he shouldered the door shut. Gripping the clothesline for support, he slowly made his way to the cabin's back stoop.

He had the advantage of surprise, but because both the front and back doors opened into the large main room, he wouldn't have the drop on Cosgrove for long. Once Bram opened the door, the wind would sweep in, alerting anyone in the cabin.

He slowly turned the knob, then flung open the door. He leveled his weapon, aiming straight at…a woman!

She screamed, stumbling back against the dining table and folding her arms protectively around herself.

"Sweet mercy." Bram froze, his mind trying to catch up to what he was seeing.

There in the flickering lamplight stood a half-naked Deborah.

Deborah.

What the hell?

Chapter Two

Struggling to recover from the shock of seeing her, Bram kicked the door shut and advanced. Had Deborah been with the outlaw since she had left her home? During the whole time Bram had been tracking the bastard?

She looked terrified, her gaze darting around for an escape. That blistered him up even more. "Cosgrove, show yourself!"

Visibly trembling, Deborah eased back, putting the small dining table between them. She hit the corner, jolting the burning lamp there as she did so.

"Don't move!" he ordered, shoving down the gritty bandanna.

She froze, looking as though she might cry.

Closed inside as they were, the wind had

faded to a low vibrating hum. Keeping his gun trained on her, Bram yelled again, "Cosgrove!"

In the hazy yellow light he could see Deborah go pale. That wasn't all he could see. Thanks to the soft amber light, the sleek lines of her body were plain through the thin fabric of her summer chemise. The undergarment and a pair of sturdy brown shoes were all she wore. Where the hell were her clothes?

Just the thought that the man who had taken so much from him might have seen her half-naked or more had Bram's finger twitching on the trigger.

His gaze leveled on hers. "Where is he?"

"Where is who?" she asked shakily.

"You know who."

Inching away, she shook her head. "I don't."

Her delicate features were pinched with fear and her raven-black hair slid around her bare shoulders like a cloud of midnight. Looking at her made Bram hurt. And filled him with cold fury.

She reached for the nearest chair.

"I said don't move."

"I need to get my dress." Her voice quivered.

Considering how his traitorous body was re-acting to the sweet curve of her hip and the fullness of her breasts visible through her chemise, he saw the merit in letting her put on her clothes.

"Stay put. I'll get it." He walked toward her, keeping his back to the cabin wall and one eye on her. Bits of grass and rock pelted the front window.

The dress hung over the back of a chair, a pale blue floral he recognized. He tossed it to her, dust drifting from the garment as she spread it protectively over her front, covering most of herself.

He dragged his gaze from her. "Cosgrove!" he called again.

"There's no one else here," she said quietly.

He gave her a withering look. "I saw the bastard's horse in the barn."

"I'm the one who rode that horse." Her voice shook.

Rifle trained on her, Bram motioned her out from behind the table, keeping her in his sights. He herded her to the corner then looked into the bedroom, where a fine silt covered every surface. The room was empty.

He knew Cosgrove hadn't gone out the front while Bram was coming in the back. The horse Bram had tracked also hadn't been carrying two people. Deborah was telling the truth. About that, anyway. He still couldn't believe she had been with Cosgrove.

Sheer terror darkened her blue eyes. She was probably afraid of what he would do or say about her running off with the man he hated.

The force of his anger when he thought she'd left to take the job in Abilene had been strong enough to sear his insides. But learning she'd been with Cosgrove drove a hole right through Bram's chest.

His gaze swept over her and she clutched the dress more tightly to her. The strap of her chemise had slipped down, baring the silky skin of one shoulder. Skin he knew tasted as sweet as cream and felt that way, too.

The heat he always felt around her burned him from the inside, made him *want.* But since he'd realized she had left with Cosgrove, Bram could hardly stand to look at her.

"Get dressed," he snapped, lowering his weapon. When she blinked those frightened blue eyes at him, it went all over him. Did she think he was going to hurt her? She'd just spent the past three weeks with a thief and a murderer! "Dammit, put your clothes on."

She nodded, taking a step toward him and the bedroom beyond.

"Uh-uh. Right here, sweetheart."

Her eyes widened. "Not with you watching!"

"Put the dress on," he said softly. "Or I'll do it for you."

"I'm not likely to run out into the storm."

"How do I know you don't have a gun hidden in that room?"

Clearly affronted, she gasped. "Because I don't!"

"I'm not taking my eyes off you. Now, put on the dress."

A spark of temper masked the uncertainty in her eyes. She angled her chin at him, clearly prepared to argue, then she seemed to realize he wasn't bluffing about dressing her himself.

She backed into the corner and stepped into the garment. When she bent to pull the dress over her hips, Bram got a tantalizing view of her breasts, plump and pale and perfect.

He bit his cheek. Hard. Once she was covered and buttoning her bodice, he said, "Now let's try again. What are you doing here?"

Looking uncertain, she said, "There's a storm."

He made an impatient sound. "Don't play with me."

"I—I'm not."

"Why are you here?" Fine grains of dirt floated in the hazy light. "In my cabin?"

"I didn't know it was your cabin. I took shelter so I wouldn't get caught in the storm."

"Don't test me. I've had all of that I want from you."

She froze, her gaze riveting on his face. "You sound as though you know me."

"Of course *I* know you." He bit out his words.

"Well, *I* don't know *you*," she said in a voice thick with tears. Hands clenched tightly at her sides, she was still shaking.

She beat all he'd ever seen. "What are you up to?"

"Nothing. I don't know who you are."

That put a strange heaviness in his chest. "Yeah, I'm sure you'd like to pretend you never did."

"I'm not pretending. I don't know who you are." She swiped at a tear tracking down her ivory cheek. "Or who I am either."

Bram stared at her for a full five seconds, fighting back a roar of anger. The ebony of her hair made the light blue of her eyes even more striking. And her petal-smooth skin had a faint tinge of a blush. There was an innocence about her. Even now, after what she'd done, she looked angelic.

She was so damn beautiful he wanted to touch her, and he hated himself for it.

Trying to come to terms with the fact that he was really seeing her, he repeated scornfully, "You don't know who you are."

She blinked. "You…don't believe me."

"No." Bram took off his hat and smacked it against the wall, knocking off a thick film of dust. He tossed it onto the table.

"Why would I lie?"

"How about because you ran off with a cattle rustler who's also now a murderer? Or because you walked away from your family, your home and me—"

He broke off, pinching the bridge of his nose. The constant buzzing of the wind made his shoulders even more tense. "By claiming you don't remember any of that, you can plead innocence. I wouldn't admit to knowing anything either."

"But I *don't* remember! I don't know anything. Not my name, not where I'm from." Fear and frustration mixed on her face. "You said you know me. What is my name?"

He frowned. She sure was carrying through with this lost memory business.

"Please." Pure desperation shaded her voice. And confusion. *"Please."*

"Deborah." He wondered how far she would go with this. "Your name's Deborah Blue."

"Deborah Blue." Her face fell. "I don't remember being called that. And who are you?"

Could she be telling the truth? She really didn't remember him or herself or Cosgrove? Bram walked slowly over to her and stopped within a foot, studying her eyes.

She lifted her chin and he saw a bruise on her jaw. And a cut on her temple. He went still inside. Had Cosgrove done that to her? The idea shook Bram. He gestured to her face. "What happened to you?"

"I think…someone hit me." She touched the faded streaks of blood on her damp bodice. "There was a big spot of blood beside me. I don't think it was mine."

He might not believe she had memory loss, but someone had roughed her up. A cold fury gripped him. He didn't hold with violence against a woman. Ever. "Are you hurt anywhere else?"

"I don't think so." She curled her hands over the edge of the chair as if she needed support. Though she looked as if she might bolt if he so much as blinked, she didn't move. Her gaze held his. There was no guile in the blue depths and no spark of recognition at all.

"Your name. Please."

His hold tightened on his rifle. Grit seemed to settle in his throat. "I'm Bram Ross."

"Bram Ross," she said softly in the same sweet, almost shy way she had the first time he'd told her to call him by his given name. And just as it had then, the dark velvet of her voice stroked over him like a hand, making his body go tight. Dammit.

"How do we know each other?"

Bram felt as though he'd been kicked in the gut. "We live near the same town, Whirlwind."

"Are we friends?"

"Not exactly." He wanted to grab her and kiss her, ask if she remembered *that*. At the confused look on her face, he said flatly, "I asked you to marry me."

"Oh!" Hope lit her eyes. "So you've been looking for me?"

"No. I'm actually looking for your…beau." Bram could barely force out the word.

"But if you…" She frowned. "I thought *you* were my beau."

"So did I," he muttered under his breath.

"This man you're looking for is my beau?"

"It appears so."

He could see her trying to reconcile what he was saying. Well, hell, he was trying to reconcile seeing her.

Her brow furrowed. "Why would I be with someone who steals cattle, who kills people?"

"I've never been able to figure out why you even talk to that double-crossing polecat, and neither has your brother."

"My brother?"

Bram stared hard at her. Was she pulling his leg? "Jericho's a retired Texas Ranger, married with a baby. He and his wife are in New York City, visiting the nuns who raised her."

"Do I live with them?"

"No, you live with your ma and three sisters on the edge of my property. The Circle R ranch."

She put a hand to her head, her lips bloodless. "This is so much to take in."

"Tell me what you remember."

"Nothing!" The look of irritation on her face was familiar to Bram. It was the same one she'd gotten the night he tried to convince her not to take the teaching job, to stay with him in Whirlwind.

He ground his teeth. "You remember riding here."

"Yes."

"And before that?"

She closed her eyes, pain etching her features. "I woke up outside, behind a building. Two-story. I had no idea where I was, but my head hurt and there was blood on my dress."

"Maybe from that cut on your head." His gaze

dropped to the damp fabric of her bodice where she'd tried to get out the blood. "How did you get Cosgrove's horse?"

"It was behind the building, just as I was." Her brow furrowed. "I heard someone coming. A man. He yelled after me."

Bram's head came up. "Did you see him?"

"No, and I didn't wait to find out who it was. I was terrified—I don't know why—so I took the horse and rode away." She gingerly touched her temple, pain stark on her delicate features.

Bram didn't think she could fake that look of agony, but what did he know? She'd faked her feelings for him for months. "Why did you come here, to my cabin?"

"I didn't intentionally come here. I just rode until I was sure no one was following. When the dust storm came up and I saw the cabin, I took shelter." She briefly closed her eyes, her chin quivering. "My head hurts."

She was pale, her skin waxy in the smoky lamplight. Dust sifted in around the edges of the window frame. "How far did you ride?"

She stared blankly at him.

Reining in his impatience, Bram rubbed the nape of his neck. "How long did you ride before you reached this place?"

"Over an hour. Maybe an hour and a half."

"Was the horse running full-out the whole time?"

"No, about ten minutes." She swayed. "It hurts."

Frowning, Bram steadied her with a hand on her elbow. He wasn't going to get more out of her right now and she really did look spent.

Hooking a foot around a chair leg, he steered her over to the table and sat her down.

She held her head in her hands. "Thank you."

The threadiness of her voice raised Bram's concern. He might be mad as hell at her, but he didn't like seeing her hurt this way. "Is there something I can do?"

"I think I just need to sit for a minute."

He glanced around, his gaze skimming over the silt-layered room. "I don't think there are any headache powders here."

"The pain isn't quite so bad now." She gave him a small forced smile, then closed her eyes.

In the flickering light she looked helpless and fragile. Her pretty mouth was drawn tight with pain. He stiffened as his gaze fell to the bruise on her jaw then moved to the cut on her temple.

He had to fight the urge to hold her and he didn't understand why. She'd left him, run off with a murdering cattle thief. He shouldn't want to be within a hundred yards of her. What was wrong with him?

Cosgrove was the one Bram wanted, the one he'd expected when he had come through the door earlier.

Instead, he'd found the one woman he never wanted to see again, and until this storm blew over, he was stuck with her.

Didn't that just cock his pistol?

Bram Ross didn't much care for her. Right now, Deborah didn't much care for him either.

An hour later, as they sat at the small dining table eating supper, she was as befuddled and uncertain as she had been when she had woken up behind that two-story building. Adding further to her confusion was her strong reaction to the rugged cowboy who had found her.

He was a big man. Beneath his grimy white shirt she could see the play of lean carved muscle in his shoulders and arms. Though his black hair was cut short, the ragged ends suggested it hadn't been trimmed in a while. Whisker stubble shadowed a square unyielding jaw. A raw-looking scar ran up the right side of his face from the middle of his cheek to his temple.

Tall and broad with powerful thighs, the man was daunting, especially when his dark blue eyes turned hard, which they'd done more than once when he looked at her.

His attention sent a shiver through her. She was drawn to him and intimidated at the same time.

Keeping his gun trained on her, he had searched the bedroom for a weapon. He hadn't found one, of course. Then he had gone out and returned with their saddlebags, using the rope to guide him through the storm to the barn and back. Now the whirling dust and nightfall made it completely dark outside.

After dropping the bags in the corner near the back door, he had found a tin of beans and one of peaches, carefully opening them with a knife. He had managed to keep out most of the dust; she had wiped off the tin plate he'd given her. They ate in silence, with her at one end of the table and him at the other. The insistent hum of the wind scraped at her nerves, as did the hovering veil of dust.

She ate slowly, sneaking looks at him. She couldn't seem to stop her attention from wandering to his firm, sometimes-harsh mouth, searching her mind for any memory of him. Touching, kissing, laughing. She'd tried the same for her family and any part of her life.

The harder she tried to remember, the more

her head hurt, but she needed answers. Something to grab on to, to slake the sense of...incompleteness inside her.

Although she believed what Bram Ross had told her, she didn't *feel* any of it.

A million questions, especially about him— *them*—spun through her head. She wasn't sure she was ready to talk about that. From the way his face had turned to stone earlier, she doubted he was either.

He looked up suddenly and she tore her gaze from his mouth.

"You've been staring at me since we sat down," he said baldly.

She flushed at being so obvious. Reaching up, she touched her cheek. "What happened to your face?"

His eyes narrowed and his voice turned hard. "Your beau shot me and his bullet skinned a trail up my face."

She winced. Even though the wound was healing, it had a fresh look to it. "Is that why you hate him?"

"No, that's after the fact. He led a band of rustlers for months, stealing not just my cattle, but my neighbors', too. People who were also *his* neighbors. Due to the drought last year, we had already lost plenty of cattle. His thieving almost cost my family our ranch. Add to that, he murdered someone two days ago during a bank robbery."

This Cosgrove sounded like a horrible person. Deborah didn't want to believe she could be involved with him, but Bram certainly believed it.

The dust tickled her nose and she stifled a sneeze. After a minute, she said, "May I ask you something else?"

"More about Cosgrove?" he sneered.

"No. About me, you, everything."

In the hazy light, his eyes were like dark steel. His gaze trailed from her face to her breasts and back up, making her stomach dip. Hunger flared in his eyes, then was gone. She shivered.

He studied her for a minute, then shrugged.

This man had proposed to her. Shouldn't she recognize something about him deep inside? She had no sense of him other than the fact that he was strong, no-nonsense and gruff. "You said I lived with my mother and sisters?"

"Yes. They're younger than you. Jordan, Michal and Marah."

She searched her mind for an impression or part of a memory. Nothing.

"You have cousins here, too. Riley and Davis Lee Holt."

None of these people sounded familiar. She

tried to calm the panic rising inside her. With a shaking hand, she tucked her hair behind her ear. "You said I lived near Whirlwind. Where is that?"

"North central Texas."

"Do you have kin nearby, too?"

Bram eyed her skeptically. "Yeah. I live at the Circle R ranch with my cousin, Georgia, and Uncle Ike. My brother, Jake, and his wife also live there."

All the names spun in her head. "You're a rancher?"

He arched a brow. "Yes. That's why I live on a ranch."

She flushed. The man irritated the fire out of her, but right now he was the only person who might be able to help her remember.

"What happened to your parents?"

"My pa died years ago and my ma lit out right after," he said with exaggerated patience—as though he were humoring her, not because he believed she needed answers. "Ike raised me and my brother."

She braced herself for the possibility that he might not answer her next question. "When did you ask me to marry you?"

He pushed his plate away, his gaze piercing as

though he was trying to probe her brain. "How long are you going to carry on with this?"

"I'm not carrying on. I need to know." She wanted to smack the disbelieving look off his handsome face. "When did it happen? When did you ask me?"

"A little over three weeks ago." His voice hardened and his eyes went flat. "The day before you took off."

Her head pounded. She had hoped something about her or him would spark a memory, but nothing had. She couldn't even remember something as important as a marriage proposal. "Why did I turn you down?"

A muscle flexed in his jaw as his gaze leveled on hers. Blade-sharp, frigid. "You wanted to take a job as a schoolteacher. I wanted you to stay with me, and you said you'd think about it. Instead, you left the next day."

No wonder he had been so angry when he'd found her in the cabin. Her voice cracked. "I don't remember any of it."

"So you say."

Why wouldn't he believe her? "I'm sorry. I really don't."

Plainly skeptical, Bram pushed his chair away from the table and rose.

Surprised at a quick flare of panic that he

might leave, she asked tentatively, "Where are you going?"

"I've been up since before dawn and I need some shut-eye. You can do whatever you like as long as it's quiet."

She bit her lip. She was tired to the marrow of her bones, but there was only one bed.

He saw her glance toward the bedroom and barked out a sharp laugh. "Don't worry, sweetheart. I'm getting my bedroll. I won't even darken your door. You made your choice real clear."

She swallowed hard. She might not remember him, but she could appreciate what was right in front of her. Stranger or not, jilted beau or not, he affected her. When he looked at her, every nerve tingled and his deep voice sent a tremor to the pit of her stomach.

She didn't like it. "What will we do tomorrow?"

"Depends on the storm. Once it's over, I'm taking you home."

His tone said he couldn't wait to be rid of her. The idea that she had a place to go, that she belonged somewhere, should've reassured her, but it didn't.

Though she had learned a few things about

her family and Bram, they didn't really mean anything.

She had hoped his answers would help her remember, give her some kind of anchor, but they hadn't. Thanks to that big strapping mountain of a man, she felt even more off balance.

She was getting to him just as she always had, and it made Bram madder than hell.

He couldn't get the image of her face out of his head. Undone, disoriented. She had appeared desperate for information and when he had given it to her, a light had gone out of her. Hope.

The way her face had crumpled when he told her about her rejection of his marriage proposal had him wondering if she was telling the truth about losing her memory. Dammit, he didn't want to wonder. He didn't want to care either, but judging by the rush of anger and protectiveness he'd felt upon spying her bruised jaw and the cut on her temple, he did.

Bram swept up the latest layer of dust that had filtered in through the sides of the window and deposited it in an old water pail. After shaking out his bedroll, he spread it and sat down with his back against the wall adjacent to the bedroom. He wanted to focus on Cosgrove, but as usual, Deborah's presence had run everything else out of his mind.

Frustrated, he dragged a hand across his nape. The sooner he got shed of Deborah Blue, the sooner he could continue his search for the murdering rustler who had nearly ruined his family.

It had been almost an hour since she had gone into the bedroom and shut the door. Her look of bafflement had seemed earnest. So had the lack of recognition when she saw him. She had seemed genuinely lost. But he'd trusted those eyes for months, believing she told the truth about her feelings being as strong as his, and look how that had turned out. She claimed not to remember anything. Bram remembered just fine.

He fingered his scar. The wound was still somewhat tender, just like his reaction to her queries about the two of them.

There was no *them*. She'd made sure of that.

He stared at the bedroom door.

Her questions reminded him of what they'd had, how she'd lit out just like his ma. He didn't want to feel anything for her, but he did.

Bram couldn't abide more of her professed memory loss. He wanted her to take responsibility for what she'd done. There had to be some way to get her to admit she was lying about losing her memory. Or at least some way to get her to point him in Cosgrove's direction.

She had the cretin's horse. Maybe she had something else of his.

Bram's gaze went to the saddlebags in the corner. He'd brought his in from the barn along with two that were probably Cosgrove's. Bram rose, picked up the lamp and walked over, going to one knee beside them.

Inside the first pouch was a comb, shaving cup and soap, a straight-edge and hair pomade. His lip curled. Pomade. He reached for the other leather bag, which was considerably heavier.

He flipped up the flap and opened the pouch wide. His pulse thudded hard.

Sweet mercy. He'd been looking for something to tie Deborah to Cosgrove and here it was. His heart sank.

Inside the saddlebag was money. A lot of money. Some loose bills, some in a flour sack. Unless Cosgrove had spent some, it was the forty thousand dollars he'd taken from the Monaco Bank.

In the next instant Bram was overwhelmed by a numbing fury. He surged to his feet, grabbed the saddlebag and stalked to the bedroom.

He threw the door open, lamplight flickering. Standing in the middle of the room, Deborah jumped, one hand at her throat. "You scared the daylights out of me!"

"You keep sayin' you don't know Cosgrove, but this right here proves you do." Speaking to be heard above the storm, he tossed the saddlebag toward her. It landed heavily at her feet.

She eyed it the way she would a snake. "What is that?"

"Money. Stolen money."

Shaking her head, she glanced down, then back at him. Questions were plain on her pretty face.

"You said you were leaving me for a teaching job," Bram snapped, taking a step toward her. "Looks like your real job was being an accomplice to a bank robbery."

Chapter Three

Twin spots of color stained her cheeks. "Accomplice to a robbery? I wouldn't do that."

"How do you know?" he asked archly.

She bit her lip, stooping to look inside the saddlebags. Those innocent blue eyes widened.

Folding his arms, Bram took in the flush on her face, the rapid rise and fall of her chest, the wild trip of her pulse in her neck. He was uncomfortably reminded of how long it had taken him to get the image of her in that chemise out of his mind.

"This is the work of your beau."

She closed the pouch and stood. "How do you know? And how do you know the money is stolen?"

"Because my cousin Georgia and my uncle

Ike were in Monaco's bank when the robbery happened. They both saw Cosgrove's face. Because of that, he shot them."

"Oh, no!" In the dusky amber lamplight, the horror on her face seemed genuine. "Are they—"

"They're alive, although I imagine Cosgrove thinks he killed them. He wouldn't have knowingly left them breathing."

"Why do you think I had anything to do with it?" She skirted the saddlebags. The defiance on her face was mixed with uncertainty. "I told you I don't remember."

"Yeah."

"Did your kin see me in the bank, too?"

"No. You weren't inside."

"Then I wasn't involved," she concluded, looking hopeful.

"Maybe you were waiting outside with horses for a quick getaway." He didn't like that he could detect her fresh scent beneath that of the dirt that hung in the air.

She rubbed her temple, appearing surprised by the possibility. "I can't believe I would do something like that."

"You mean you don't want to believe it."

"Of course I don't want to believe it! Would you?"

Bram recognized the challenging light in her

eyes. "The length of time you rode and the direction from where you came all add up to you making the trip from Monaco. You either left Whirlwind with Cosgrove or met him somewhere. It makes sense to think you'd travel with him."

"Maybe he was helping me get somewhere."

"To Abilene for your job?" Bram could imagine how the bastard would've tried to "help" her. Still, Deborah was cooperating, so he kept that to himself. "If he meant to put you on a train or a stage, he could've done that at a few places before you ended up in Monaco. Maybe you wanted to stay with him."

"You want to believe the worst of me." Lifting a hand to her temple, she winced. "But you don't know."

"You had to be with him or nearby in order to have access to his horse. What I want to know is where did Cosgrove go?"

"And I'm telling you again that I don't know," she said hotly, grimacing.

Was her head hurting? Bram hadn't forgotten how pained she'd looked tonight. For a while he'd thought that had been a ruse to get him to stop questioning her. Now he wasn't sure. "Does it matter to you that people who counted you as a friend were hurt? That a man was killed?"

"Yes, it matters! But I can't tell you what I don't know. Maybe if you gave me more information."

"Like what?"

Still touching her head, she thought for a moment. "How long have you been chasing this man?"

"Three weeks. From your house, I followed him east then south. I lost his trail at Buffalo Gap and returned home for a couple of weeks. Then my uncle sent a wire from Monaco saying that he and my cousin had been shot in a bank robbery. By Cosgrove. Monaco is west of here. My brother and I started tracking him from there. Jake went the opposite direction, but when I found Cosgrove's horse in the barn here, I thought I'd found him."

She lowered her hand. "Instead, it was me."

He nodded.

"I swear I don't know anything about that money, even though it appears I was with him." Her features were drawn tight in the dust-speckled light. "But why do I have the money? Why didn't he take it?"

Bram huffed out a frustrated breath. "The law is looking for Cosgrove. He could've given the money and his horse to you, sending anyone who followed in another direction. That's a good way to throw the posse off his trail."

Paling further, she put her hand to her head again. "Oh."

"The bastard must be expecting to meet up with you somewhere to get the money. I went through his saddlebags looking for a note or anything that might give me a clue as to where he might be, but I found nothing. I need you to give me some information."

"Like what?"

"Where he went or if you're meeting him." Bram ignored his twinge of conscience at continuing to push her when she was plainly hurting. "If you heard him talk about any place."

"How can I do that?"

"Try to recall where you were before you supposedly woke up with no memory." He expected her to refuse him. Sure as hell wouldn't be the first time.

"All right." She closed her eyes, a look of intense concentration on her face. The wind moaned around the cabin and a branch or rock hit the front window.

Bram eased closer to Deborah. "Can you see yourself waking up behind that building?"

"Yes."

"Why were you outside?"

"I don't know."

Bram reined in his impatience, recognizing that she was trying her best. "You said you heard a man yelling after you as you rode away. Did you hear anything else? Music? Wagons? A group of people? Gunshots?"

She opened her eyes. "No, I'm sorry."

"Try harder." When he saw her chin quiver, he softened his tone. "It's important."

Pain darkened her eyes and after a long moment, she said, "I don't recall hearing anything else."

"You say you didn't get a look at the man?"

"That's right."

"Do you recall ever seeing a man about six feet tall, muscular build, with dark hair and dark eyes? He likely would've been wearing fancy clothes. Tailored and expensive."

She looked disappointed and half-spent, with deep lines etching her brow. Her pink-and-white skin had a waxy cast. "I really want to help you, but I just can't remember."

Wondering if he should back off, Bram dragged a hand across his nape, sick to death of the smell of dirt. "Okay, you woke up behind a two-story building. Could it have been a hotel?"

"Yes," she said excitedly, brushing the dust

from the sleeves of her dress. "That's very possible."

It wasn't much, but at least Bram could wire the Monaco sheriff and ask him to find out if Cosgrove had registered at any of the local hotels. Chances were slim Bram would learn anything, but right now this was all he had. It was worth checking.

He realized then that Deborah had closed her eyes again. As long seconds went by, her delicate features grew bleak and a tear rolled down her cheek.

Was she in that much pain? The realization shook him. His insistent questions were taking a toll. Bram couldn't deny that.

"You can stop. I can tell your head hurts when you try and remember."

She looked at him, distraught. Outside, the wind whistled around the cabin. Her voice was thick with tears and she sounded slightly panicked. "There's no memory of anything before I woke up. I'm sorry."

Her obvious discomfort tugged at him. "I believe you."

"You do?"

The relief that spread across her face made him ashamed of how hard he'd prodded her. Hell, he'd bullied her, plain and simple.

The blows she'd suffered had obviously been forceful enough to cause her to lose her memory. He had no idea if it was permanent or not. He'd never even heard of such a thing, but he did believe her.

Which meant she couldn't help him. He would have to find another way to get to Cosgrove.

He believed her. Finally.

Deborah was surprised at the measure of relief that brought. For the first time since regaining consciousness in Monaco, she didn't feel completely alone.

Still, she really needed to remember. Not for Bram, but for herself.

Hours later, instead of sleeping, Deborah wondered how entangled she was with this Cosgrove character.

The wind whined in the background. Had she participated in that bank robbery in any way? Were there other illegal activities she might have been party to? Right now she had no answers.

Though all the excitement and fear of the day had left her exhausted, she had trouble falling asleep. Maybe because of Bram's accusations or maybe just because of the man himself. For someone she couldn't remember, he sure had an effect on her. He made her nervous. And giddy.

When she tried to remember him, an unsettling heat spread through her.

Thinking about it, about *him,* made her head hurt and she'd had enough of that.

The wind buffeted the cabin, hurling dirt and pebbles against the walls like hail. She shook out the sheet before pulling it over her head and closing her eyes. She tried to slow her thoughts so she could get some rest.

After a short time, a dark mist engulfed her and she thought she felt someone touch her. A warm heavy hand, a glimmer of an image and then—

"Deborah!"

She jerked awake to find Bram shaking her. He sat on the side of the bed, concern in his eyes.

Watery daylight flowed into the window-less room through the open bedroom door. A fine layer of dust covered the floor and the bed-clothes. One of Bram's big hands rested on her left shoulder, setting off a flutter of sensation in her belly. Was his the touch she'd felt in her sleep?

"Are you okay?" he asked. "You're crying."

She sat up, her movement stirring the dirt on the sheet. Her mind scrambled through a tangle of emotions—terror, loss, unease. Why was she crying?

"Did you have a bad dream?"

Until now, she hadn't realized. "Yes."

With trembling hands she pushed her hair out of her face. A light sweat had her chemise clinging to her and she gulped in a big draft of dusty air. Oh, dear. She felt as if she were drowning, being pulled down into a seething mass of uncertainty.

A powerful sense of horror pressed in on her. The same horror she had felt when she'd woken behind that building. Swept by a wave of fear and panic, she reached out. One hand gripped Bram's strong forearm. Her head dropped forward, brushing his wide hard chest.

He didn't push her away or pull her close. He didn't move at all. A sob jerked out of her. She wanted to be folded into those big arms. Just the strength in his body, the thud of his heart, calmed the panic tearing loose inside her.

How ridiculous. The man couldn't abide her. Still, Deborah couldn't make herself move away from him.

"Are you sure you're okay?"

"Yes."

He sat stiffly, his voice hoarse. "What was the dream?"

She tried to recall it. A suffocating heaviness

hovered on the edge of her mind, making her shudder.

"Deborah?" he asked quietly.

"I'm not sure. There was nothing, then…I was thrown into some kind of horror." She stared down at her shaking hands. "It was awful, terrifying. I tried to scream, but I couldn't. There was a feeling of violence, something coming closer to me, then it was gone before I could tell what or who it was. I can't make any sense of it."

She shuddered, her voice muffled against his warm muscular torso. One of his big hands closed around her waist, steadying her. With his other hand, he lifted the far corner of the sheet and wiped her eyes.

She realized she was still crying.

"You okay?" The gruff worry in his voice made her want to snuggle into him. He moved his hand up her back, warm, reassuring, and cupped her shoulder.

Pain flared, causing her to flinch.

Bram jerked his hand away. "What is it? Are you hurt?"

She nodded, turning her head to look at her shoulder. "It's sore."

Before she could blink or check for herself, he nudged her hair aside and lifted her chemise strap. He cursed. "There's a bruise here. A big bruise."

She craned her neck to see. The mark was wide and bluish-black.

Bram studied it, too. "This must've happened at the same time as your other injuries."

She looked up, startled to see how cold and hard his eyes were. "Do you think I fell? Or maybe was struck?"

A muscle flexed in his jaw as he shifted his gaze to the cut on her temple. "Hard to know for sure."

His breath drifted warmly against her skin. Just his presence made her feel less shaky. She was overwhelmed with the urge to climb into his lap and huddle into his strength. It unsettled her how much she wanted that. Her grip tightened on the sheet.

The dark stubble along his jaw softened the rough angles of his face. She found herself staring at his mouth, trying to recall how it felt. Despite not remembering, she had no doubt they had kissed.

She became aware then that he was also staring at her mouth.

Before she realized what she was doing, she lifted her hand to his face and lightly touched the raw scar on his cheek.

Their gazes locked and in his she saw heat, hunger, then nothing. A chill crept over his face.

He gently but firmly removed her hand, then surged to his feet and moved to the door.

She tried to dismiss the sudden knifing sense of aloneness. He shouldn't be the only one pulling away. She had rejected the man's marriage proposal, after all.

"Do you think it was Cosgrove who hurt me? Just as he did you?"

"Most likely." Bram's gaze flicked to her face, then to her bruised shoulder. "I came in to let you know we can leave. The storm is over."

The noise outside had stopped, she realized. "So, you're taking me home?"

"Unless you don't want to go."

"Where else would I go?" She prayed her family wasn't as angry at her as he was. "Do you think my family will welcome me back? If I hurt them as badly as I hurt you, they may never want to see me again."

"They'll be glad to see you."

She tangled her fingers in the sheet she still held to her chest. "How far is my house?"

"Less than an hour's ride from here."

She was so close, yet she'd had no idea. She brushed the grit off her hands. "Can you tell me something about my family? So I won't feel as if I'm meeting complete strangers."

He hesitated, plainly reluctant to answer, but finally said, "You, your ma and sisters moved to Whirlwind to be near your brother, Jericho."

Deborah nodded. "Why does my brother live here? Where did we move from?"

"You moved from Uvalde. Your brother came here tracking some outlaws and stayed because he fell in love and married a woman in Whirlwind."

"What else?"

He looked impatient. "I'm not sure what you want to know."

"Anything. Please."

"All of you kids were named after people in the Bible. Jericho is the oldest, seven years ahead of you. Jordan is two years younger than you, Michal a year behind her and Marah's a year behind that."

Deborah had hoped the information might spark some memory, but it didn't. Her mind was still a blank slate. "You said my brother is married."

Bram nodded, keeping his distance by staying at the door. "To a fine woman named Catherine. They have a baby girl, Evie."

His gaze went again to her mouth, putting a tingle in her blood.

Earlier, when they had both studied her bruised shoulder and his face was close to hers, she had thought he was going to kiss her. She had wanted him to.

The admission had her squirming inside. It was disconcerting to have such feelings about a man she didn't remember. Just how well did they know each other? Had they been intimate?

She couldn't bring herself to ask. At least not yet.

She had no idea if her family would welcome her back, but anything would be better than being with Bram and dealing with this edgy anticipation. Wanting him. Because he certainly didn't want her in return.

It was good that they were leaving the cabin. She needed some distance from him.

She flapped the sheet, sending a puff of dirt into the air. "Are you going to return the stolen money before taking me home?"

"No, I'm taking you back first."

"What if Cosgrove comes looking for the money and me? You said you thought he would."

"Oh, he will." Suddenly his gaze turned speculative.

What was he thinking? Not understanding

the flare of apprehension inside her, she studied him. "What should I do if that happens? If Cosgrove finds me?"

"You won't need to worry about it."

"Why not? You just said you thought he'd come looking."

"He'll have to go through me to get to you."

She went still inside. "What do you mean?"

A slow, calculating smile spread across his face, causing a chill to ripple through her.

"When Cosgrove shows up, I'll be waiting." Bram stepped out of the bedroom, looking over his shoulder at her. "I'm going to be your shadow."

Shadow? "For how long?"

"As long as it takes." His gaze shifted back to her, almost as if he'd been talking to himself. "I'll saddle the horses while you get dressed, then we'll go."

She nodded, staying on the bed as he walked out.

He was using her as bait.

Regardless of what they had been to each other in the past, that's all she was to Bram now—a way to get to the man who had stolen from him, tried to kill him and his family.

How much time was she going to have to spend with him? Look how just the past twenty-four hours had gone. Now she was stuck indefinitely with a man she had refused to marry. A man who plainly resented her.

It didn't bode well.

Chapter Four

Bram wanted some distance from Deborah. He needed it. Just a few minutes.

He escaped from the cabin and strode to the barn to saddle their horses. The morning air was still, choked with the smell of dirt. His boots left deep impressions in the drifts stirred up by the wind.

He struggled to dismiss not just the horror he had seen in Deborah's eyes minutes ago after the nightmare, but also the feel of her satiny skin beneath his hand, the sight of yet another bruise on that ivory flesh.

The sheer terror in her face had rattled him, enough that he had been ambushed by a gut-twisting urge to hold her. Kiss her.

But he hadn't. And he wouldn't.

After the incessant shriek of the wind, the lack of sound was stark, disorienting. Like looking into Deborah's eyes and realizing she didn't recognize him. That had sliced right through Bram.

Did she really not remember? Part of him still resisted the notion.

Once they were under way, he wouldn't have to look at her. Or even talk to her if he didn't choose. Itching to get on the trail, he opened the barn door, breathing more easily now that he was away from her.

He was relieved to see Scout looked none the worse for wear aside from the blanket of dust coating his yellow-tan body and black-tipped ears. After saddling the dun gelding and steering him outside, Bram made his way to the back of the barn.

Cosgrove's black mare was covered in dirt. If it hadn't been for the whites of her panicked eyes, she would've blended into the shadows.

The sight of him had her shifting jerkily as if she might bolt. Bram spoke softly to the skittish animal, easing closer. She tossed her head and stepped back, her rump hitting the barn wall. He laid a comforting hand on her neck and stroked until she settled, then he coaxed her into the wedge of light at the front of the barn.

She was limping. With a frown, he stooped to

examine her legs and discovered her right front fetlock was swollen. Likely sprained. She had been fine when he'd left his own mount in here last night.

The mare must have become distressed during the dust storm and tried to rush the door or kick down the wall. At least the injury wasn't more serious. Still, Deborah wouldn't be riding this horse today. Nobody would.

Bram cursed under his breath. Scowling, he tugged off the bandanna he had dampened and used to wipe the most recent layer of grit from his face, then knelt and wrapped the horse's lower joint. He saddled and bridled her, then led both mounts to the porch where Deborah stood with his and Cosgrove's saddlebags.

In her bloodstained dress, she looked small, fragile. The cut at her temple stood out in stark relief against her fair skin.

Her uncertain gaze sought his. That infernal protectiveness rose inside him again. Jaw tight, Bram gestured at the black mare.

"Cosgrove's mare is injured, so you can't ride her."

Alarm flitted across her delicate features. "Did I ride her when I shouldn't have? I was so focused on getting away that I didn't notice she might be hurt."

"If she'd been hurt while carrying you, you would've known. I think she got spooked in the barn during the storm."

Deborah stepped to the side as Bram bent to pick up Cosgrove's saddlebags and drape them over Scout's withers in front of the saddle horn. He settled his own bags on Cosgrove's mare behind her saddle.

Deborah frowned. "If she's hurt, you shouldn't be riding her either, should you?"

"I won't be. I'll be riding Scout."

"Then how—"

"You'll have to ride with me."

"With you?" she squeaked, her spine going rigid.

"Behind me." He sure as hell wasn't having her sit in his lap all the way back to her house.

She licked her lips. "Do you think that's a good idea?"

No, he did not. "I can walk."

"No. I don't want that." She shot a look at the outlaw's saddlebags on Bram's mount. "I guess you don't want to let that money out of your sight?"

"That's part of it. If we run into a threat, the lame horse won't have the burden."

Concern flashed across her face. "Run into a threat? Do you expect trouble?"

"Thanks to the dust storm erasing any tracks, I have no way of knowing Cosgrove's whereabouts."

She paled, her eyes vivid blue in her ashen face. "He could be over the next rise."

"Yes." Bram didn't particularly like scaring her, but she needed to be prepared. "If something happens to me, you ride like hell for help."

She looked stricken.

"Deborah?"

At his sharp tone, she nodded. "Yes, all right."

"Keep the sun in front of you and ride until you come to the Circle R."

"All right."

After checking the cinch on Cosgrove's black mare, Bram mounted Scout and held his hand out to Deborah. "Ready?"

She hesitated.

"What's wrong?" he demanded, impatient to get going.

"I assume I'll have to ride astride."

"Yes."

She bit her lip, looking uncertain. "My skirts…"

He gave a heavy sigh. "Did you ride astride on your way here?"

"Yes, but I was alone. And I tried to make sure no one saw me."

Bram bit off the reminder that last night he'd seen a damn sight more than her stockings or petticoats. The memory of her full breasts and slender thighs revealed by the lamplight shining through the thin cloth of her chemise was seared on his brain.

"You'll be behind me, so I won't see anything. Besides, you wouldn't last two minutes if you tried to ride sitting to the side."

After a moment she stepped to the edge of the porch. He gripped her forearm and swung her up behind him. She didn't weigh anything.

She shifted, tugging her skirts down on one side then the other. Every time she moved, her soft full breasts brushed his back. He couldn't stand much of that.

Jaw tight, he pressed the mare's reins into Deborah's hand. "You lead Cosgrove's horse."

"All right."

From the corner of his eye he caught a flash of a white stocking and the hem of her pale blue floral dress. He glanced over his shoulder, her silky hair tickling his neck.

"Ready?" he asked gruffly.

When she said yes, he urged his horse into motion. Deborah fell full against him, her oomph of breath burning through his shirt.

"Oh!" She jerked away, startling Scout,

who gave a backward hop to keep his balance. Deborah bounced against Bram.

"Be still," he ordered.

"Sorry." She sat stiffly, quietly at his back, holding herself away from him.

Fine with him. All he had to do was get her home and deliver her to her family. He wouldn't let her get to him.

Scout started down a steep hill and Deborah pitched to one side, yelping.

Bram grabbed for her, his hand clamping down on whatever limb he could reach because of her odd angle behind him. He steadied her at his back, registering a froth of skirts over his arm and a thin layer of fabric under his fingers. Fabric like...undergarments. Drawers.

He froze. So did she.

He realized then that his hand was up her skirts, high on her thigh. Beneath his touch, he felt a whisper of muscle. His grip tightened almost imperceptibly, but it was enough to have Deborah making a sound deep in her throat.

A kind of sighing moan that made Bram's body go hard.

He jerked his hand back, batting away the yards of fabric.

"Hang on to...something," he growled, irritated at the low throb in his blood.

She steadied herself behind him, her hands curling over the cantle.

"Where are we?"

"On Circle R land." He looked out over the rippling prairie, a mix of green and gold with patches of orange and red and yellow wildflowers sprinkled throughout. The tall grass made a swishing noise as their horses moved.

"All of this is yours?" Her breath tickled his nape and he caught a faint whiff of her scent.

He nodded.

"Have I ever been here before?" Her voice was small.

"No."

"At least that's one thing I'm not supposed to remember," she muttered.

Bram didn't speak. He focused on the rolling landscape in front of him, the clear sunny day, the lumbering gait of the horse following them. Anything except the feel of Deborah so close to him. So close that he could feel the occasional puff of her breath against his nape.

He clenched his jaw.

Behind him, she slid and slipped around a few times. Not once did she reach for him to steady herself. That shouldn't have irritated him, but it did.

What did she think? That one touch from her

would strip his control, have him shucking her out of her clothes?

Heat surged through him at that tempting thought and he bit his cheek. Hell.

Scout picked his way down the steep bank of a deep gully and Cosgrove's mare gingerly followed behind. The gelding started up the opposite earth wall, lunging forward to gain ground.

Deborah shrieked, canting off to the side.

This time Bram managed to grab her arm. After pulling her up for the second time, he took her hand and curled it around his waist. "Leave it there."

Neither spoke as they continued on.

Bram tried to ignore the feel of her soft curves against him. It didn't help that from the corner of his eye he could see her skirts creep higher on her leg, exposing her drawers to the knee. All that did was stoke the memory of his hand under her skirts.

It was hot. *He* was hot. Because of her.

Feeling as if he were being choked, Bram ran a finger around the loose neck of his shirt. He wanted her until he ached with it. And each minute he spent with her felt as though his skin were being peeled off.

After what seemed like an hour, but was probably only a third of that, they passed the Ross family cemetery, then reached the mouth of the creek that ran across Circle R land and onto Riley Holt's pasture.

The now-dirt-filled creek that held painful memories for Bram.

He stiffened. With her arm around him, she had to feel it.

"Have I been here before?"

It wasn't the warm wash of her breath against his neck that made Bram glance back. It was the wistfulness in her voice.

She was staring hard at the water that had been stirred a sandy-red by the dust storm. Sunlight glittered on the surface, dappled the ground through the leafy branches of an old pecan tree.

"Yes, you've been here. Do you remember?"

"No." Frustration thickened her voice as her gaze met his. "Your reaction made me wonder."

He didn't tell her this was where she had informed him that she was leaving. And ripped out his heart.

Yes, she'd sworn she would return to him, but his ma had said the same and she had never come home. When he had finally tracked down Frannie Ross, she hadn't even recognized him. Just as Deborah didn't now.

That realization made Bram's anger flare to life again.

"Did something bad happen here?" she asked tentatively.

Tightening his grip on the reins, he thought about not answering, but what did it matter? "Guess it depends on your point of view. This is where I proposed."

She was silent for a long moment. So long that he thought maybe she hadn't heard him. "Oh."

"Yeah." The memory still had the power to make him wince.

Bram fought the urge to knee Scout into a run, get away from Deborah as quickly as possible. But the last thing he needed was for her to be plastered to him, holding on for dear life.

Especially after being cooped up with her overnight and feeling her lithe curves against him all during the ride. She was too near, her eyes too soft with a vulnerability that made him want to take care of her.

He ground his teeth so hard his jaw ached, and he urged Scout forward.

The packed trail gave way to hilly grassy pasture. Evergreen trees and brush spotted the rolling landscape. Vibrant patches of wildflowers bloomed across the field.

In the distance, he spotted two of his ranch hands rounding up stray cows. After stopping to speak to them and leave Cosgrove's injured mare, he and Deborah continued on.

When they finally topped the rise near her home, Bram pointed to the log structure at the bottom of the slope. "There's your house."

Her hand tightened on his waist. "I don't recognize it," she said tremulously.

He looked over his shoulder at her, his hat grazing the top of her head. Her pert nose was slightly sunburned, but it was her eyes that held his attention.

The sharp disappointment in the blue depths razored through him. She appeared lost and he saw hope seep out of her, like water from a leaky pail.

When her gaze met his, tears welled in her eyes.

"Oh, hell," he muttered.

"I'm sorry. It's just that I really thought I would remember my own house."

"It's okay."

"I— What if they don't want me?"

Bram stared at her. She had likely been thinking such things during the entire ride. The more distance he had put between them and the cabin, the more heaviness he had sensed from her.

A strange feeling unfurled in his chest. "Of course they'll want you."

"Thank you for bringing me…here. And for helping me." She made as though to slide off.

Bram grabbed her wrist. "What are you doing?"

"You said this was my house."

"Yes, but you don't have to go down there alone." He couldn't just deposit her like a bag of laundry and leave. His voice was gruff. "I'll explain everything."

"You will?"

He nodded.

"Thank you," she said softly, relief plain on her face. "Thank you."

The small whisper of her breath teased his lips and his gaze dropped to her mouth.

He was aware of the rapid flutter of her pulse in the hollow of her throat. The black satin of her hair gathered back in a ponytail that slid over her shoulder. Hair he wanted to free and bury his hands in. Mixed in with that awareness was the infernal protectiveness he couldn't shake.

It frustrated the hell out of him. Pulling his attention from her, he guided Scout into the yard. Bram threw one leg over the gelding's neck and slid to the ground, then turned to help Deborah dismount.

He lifted her down, his hands closing on her taut waist. Her breasts brushed his chest and her hips pressed to his as he slowly set her on her feet. Bram bit his cheek against the urge to pull her full into him. He couldn't let himself get tangled up in their past.

For a long moment their eyes held. A rosy flush stained her cheeks.

She looked away, appearing confused and overwhelmed. And frightened, Bram realized. She had worn the same expression when he had come upon her in the cabin.

His chest ached as he asked quietly, "You okay?"

"I think so."

He lifted his hand to brush a strand of hair away from her face.

"Deborah!"

She started and so did Bram. Together, they turned to face the tall woman rushing toward them.

"That's your mother, Jessamine."

Three younger women burst out of the house, excitement and relief plain on their faces as they moved in Deborah's direction.

"Oh, thank you for bringing her home, Bram!" Mrs. Blue said. "I didn't know you were going after her."

"I didn't." He removed his hat. "I found her at the cabin on the other side of the Circle R."

"The cabin? Why?" Jessamine frowned, her blue gaze shifting to her oldest daughter. "Your note said you were going to Abilene."

"There's an explanation," Bram said. He wondered if her family would have as much trouble with it as he had at first.

"I should hope so." The older woman leveled a look on Deborah. "You've never lied to me before."

Deborah's fingers curled into the loose shirt fabric at Bram's waist. He glanced at her. If she was holding on to him so tightly, she had to be afraid. He noted the paleness of her skin and the alarm on her face. She didn't recognize her mother or sisters.

Without thinking, Bram stepped slightly in front of Deborah, shielding her. "Hold up a minute, Mrs. Blue. We have a problem."

The older woman stilled, as did Deborah's sisters. Jessamine's dark hair was threaded with gray, but the younger women were all raven haired like Deborah. Jordan's eyes were the same sky-blue, but the two younger sisters, Michal and Marah, had silver eyes like their older brother. All of them fixed anxious gazes on him.

"Something's happened," he said.

Jessamine looked around him to her daughter. Her eyes widened. "You're hurt! How badly?"

"She's bruised some." Bram couldn't stop a fresh rush of fury at Cosgrove.

As succinctly as possible, Bram explained how he had been on Cosgrove's trail and tracked the thief's horse from Monaco to the Ross cabin. There Bram had found Deborah instead of the outlaw. He ended with the information that Deborah had no memory.

"No memory?" Confusion clouded the older woman's eyes. "I've never heard of such a thing."

"Neither have I." Bram dragged a hand down his face. "But I think it's true."

Deborah's fist tightened on his shirt.

Jessamine asked quietly, "Is Cosgrove the one who hurt her?"

"Yes, ma'am."

Jordan, closest in age to Deborah, looked at Bram, her gaze steady and troubled. "She doesn't remember anything or anyone?"

He shook his head.

"She'll remember me." The youngest girl stepped forward. "I'm Marah and this is Felix."

The girl reached into the pocket of the apron covering her yellow dress and pulled out a field mouse. Bram knew she had made the animal her pet more than a year ago. Cupping it in her hand, she held the rodent up to Deborah. The mouse blinked.

Deborah's eyes filled with tears and she pressed closer to Bram. "I don't. I apologize."

"But…" Marah's gray eyes flashed with uncertainty as she looked at their mother.

Michal stood quietly, her eyes wide and watchful.

Bram was hit with the need to ease Deborah's way. "She's been through hel—an ordeal. Give her some time, okay?"

"Of course," Jessamine said. "Oh, my dear girl, I'm so sorry."

She came forward slowly and held out a hand to her daughter. After a moment, Deborah released her hold on Bram, stepping up beside him.

"Come inside," Jessamine coaxed. "We'll get you a bath. After that you can sleep or eat, whatever you want."

Deborah glanced up at Bram, her eyes clouded with doubt.

His chest tightened. He shifted, lightly cupping her elbow. "It's okay."

Skirts brushing the tops of his boots, Deborah let herself be drawn into the circle of women.

Michal gave a small smile and squeezed her arm.

"Go with the girls, honey," Mrs. Blue said. "They'll get you a bath."

As the women walked off, Deborah gave

Bram a last pleading look over her shoulder. A look that pierced him right in the heart.

Jessamine turned to him. "She doesn't remember anything?"

"No." His gaze traced the slender, taut line of Deborah's back as she walked away. "And that's not the worst of it. You need to know that Cosgrove will likely show up here."

"What? Why?"

Bram explained about the stolen bank money and his belief that Cosgrove would hunt Deborah down for it.

Alarm pinched the woman's thin features. "If he does that, he could hurt her again!"

"I won't let that happen." Bram might intend to use her as bait—that didn't mean he would let anything happen to her.

He shared his plan to provide protection for Deborah. "I'm headed into Whirlwind to tell Davis Lee everything."

Hearing hoofbeats, he looked across the prairie, recognizing the roan gelding loping toward them. "That's Duffy Ingram, one of my hands. I told him to follow me over here. He'll stand watch until I return tonight."

"Do you really think that's necessary?"

"Yes, ma'am. In fact, I've arranged for someone to be here around the clock."

Her eyes widened.

"Duffy will share daytime duties with Amos Fuller, another of my ranch hands. They'll each take an eight-hour shift and I'll be here at night."

"I'll let the girls know we need to be aware. And armed."

Bram nodded. One advantage of having a Texas Ranger son was that Jericho had taught all of the Blue women to shoot. And to hit what they aimed for.

Once he had introduced Duffy to Mrs. Blue and left instructions that the ranch hand not let Deborah out of his sight, Bram mounted up. His gaze went to the house, and he hoped she would soon feel at ease.

Now that it was time to go, he didn't feel right about leaving her. He snorted. What a half-wit. Hadn't she planned to do that very thing to him?

He had to remember that. Had to remember she was his way to Cosgrove and that's all she was.

Deborah watched Bram ride away. He didn't go in the direction they'd come, but instead guided his mount past the house.

She *had* remembered the place where Bram had proposed. Not the way he had remembered, with details, but when they had paused at the water, she had been overcome by anger followed by a heavy sadness. Then an image, a flash of... something. And a pounding in her head.

His explanation of what had happened there accounted for the suffocating sadness that had rolled over her. That piece of memory had left her half expecting to remember her family. But she didn't.

As she had stared at them, the realization had hit her like a blow. For a moment she hadn't been able to breathe. Panic and crushing disappointment slammed her hard enough that she had wanted to lean into his wide chest, let him shelter her from a dark bitter crush of emotion. But she hadn't.

"Bram's going into Whirlwind." Mrs. Blue— her mother—joined the others on the porch and looked at Deborah. "Oh, that's a nearby town."

She appreciated the information even though this was something she actually knew. "He told me about Whirlwind."

"Good." The other woman smiled softly.

As Bram kneed his horse into a lope, Deborah tore her gaze from his broad shoulders and turned to her family.

Mrs. Blue continued, "He plans to talk to the sheriff and explain what's going on."

"Did he tell you about the money?" she asked. "And Cosgrove?"

"Yes."

"Cosgrove!" Jordan frowned. "What does he have to do with anything?"

"I don't like him, Deborah," said the girl with the mouse.

Deborah recalled her name was Marah.

"What money?" Michal asked, pulling her long black hair over her shoulder.

Jordan watched Deborah somberly. Almost warily. "Do you really not remember Bram?"

"No."

"You're completely smitten with him."

Mrs. Blue herded them toward the door. "Let's go inside. Your sister might like to eat or bathe. And we can talk."

Sister. Deborah looked at the women around her. All raven haired, all pretty, all showing the same puzzlement that she felt. And she didn't recognize a single one of them.

Any more than she recognized the man who had asked her to marry him. The man she was supposedly in love with.

Chapter Five

"What do you mean, you found Deborah Blue and forty thousand dollars?" Whirlwind's sheriff, Davis Lee Holt, shoved a hand through his dark hair, his blue eyes narrowed on Bram.

Bram pointed to the saddlebags he'd brought inside the jailhouse and dumped beside the other man's scratched oak desk. "Take a look in there."

Sunlight glittering off his badge, Davis Lee knelt and flipped open one pouch, then the other. He let out a slow whistle. "Forty thousand dollars. This is from the Monaco robbery."

"Yeah."

His friend rose. "What's this about Deborah? I didn't know she was missing and needed to be found. When you left Whirlwind and headed to Monaco, I thought you were going after Cosgrove."

"And that's what I did," Bram said. "But he isn't who I found."

Staring out the window toward the smithy next door, he explained how he had come upon the woman he'd hoped to marry. The woman who didn't even know who he was!

Davis Lee eased down on the corner of his desk. "Deborah's note said she was going to Abilene to meet with the school board about her teaching position. How did she end up with Cosgrove?"

"She says she doesn't know."

The lawman barked out a laugh. "Then who would?"

"She can't remember anything or anyone."

"Not even her family?"

Bram shook his head, lifting a hand to greet Ef Gerard, the black man who owned the smithy. Ef gave a broad smile and returned the greeting.

"Or you either?" Sobering, Davis Lee eyed Bram consideringly.

"That's right."

"How can that be?"

"Evidently I'm not all that memorable," Bram muttered. Which blistered him up good.

"How does someone lose their memory?"

"I have no notion."

"Have you talked to Annalise?"

"Not yet." Bram planned to visit the doctor before he left town. Annalise Fine was a life-long friend who had recently returned from back East. She and Matt Baldwin had reunited after seven years apart.

Bram bet Annalise would never forget the man she claimed to love.

He turned back to the sheriff, bracing one shoulder against the wall beside the window. "Deborah's hurt, too. She has a cut on her temple, and her face and back are bruised."

Davis Lee's jaw firmed. "Did Cosgrove rough her up?"

"Could be. She *was* with him."

"Doesn't sound like it was willingly."

Bram wanted to believe it wasn't. He shrugged. "Who knows?"

The lawman arched a brow. "I'd think *you* might know, seeing as how close you two are."

"Were." He didn't know anything. "How close we *were*."

"I thought the pair of you—"

"No." Bram cut him off.

His friend studied him for a moment. "Cosgrove could've made her write the note to her family to keep anyone from knowing she was with him. And to keep anyone from coming after them."

Three weeks ago Bram had been so furious upon reading her words that it hadn't even entered his mind to wonder if things weren't the way they seemed. Had he missed a clue because he was angry that she'd left? He didn't think so, but he wanted to see the note again.

He glanced at Davis Lee. "Deborah also could've written the note of her own free will, too. For the same reasons."

"True, but I don't think she would go anywhere with Cosgrove willingly. Do you? I mean, do you really think so?"

Yes. But Bram didn't want to get into an argument over this with the sheriff. "I'm keeping my mind open to the possibility until I get some proof one way or another."

"She's sweet on you. Why would she run off with that bastard?"

She'd been so sweet on him that she'd refused to marry him.

"She's not all that sweet on me." Done with talking about Deborah, he said, "I assume Jericho isn't back from New York City or Mrs. Blue would've told me."

"That's right."

Deborah's sisters had overwhelmed her

enough. Bram had no idea how she would've reacted to her older brother. Though quiet, the former Ranger was big and had an intimidating presence until you got to know him.

Davis Lee stroked his chin. "Do you think we should send a wire letting him know what's happened?"

He thought a moment. "There's no point in it. Mrs. Blue said she wrote him that Deborah had gone to Abilene to see the board about her teaching position. Jericho never knew his sister might have been in danger. All we could tell him is that she was possibly abducted and now she's home safe. There's nothing he can do about it."

"You're right. You can just tell him when he returns from New York."

Bram nodded.

The other man's gaze went to the saddlebags on the floor. "You planning to turn in this money? Want me to wire the Monaco Bank and let them know it's been recovered?"

"No."

Davis Lee studied him. "Cosgrove will come for that money."

"I'm counting on it." Bram's voice hardened.

The lawman stood. "That will put Deborah in danger."

"That's why I'm sticking to her like a burr to a saddle blanket."

"And when Cosgrove shows up, you'll trap him."

"Right." Hate for the man bubbled up inside him.

"I wouldn't mind getting my hands on the man," Davis Lee said.

"First come, first served."

"I don't like the idea of the bank not knowing their cash has been recovered."

"If I return the money, Cosgrove might not show unless he has another reason to."

"You mean, if Deborah has or knows something he doesn't want her to," the other man finished.

"And until or unless she remembers what happened, we won't know if that's the case. The only way to make sure Cosgrove comes back to Whirlwind is to keep the money. Or let him think we have."

Davis Lee's eye glinted. "What if I return the cash, but the bank doesn't announce it? Cosgrove would still believe the cash is with Deborah."

"Do you think the bank would go along with it?"

"You're offering them their money as well as the murdering son of a bitch who stole it and killed one of their people. I think the banker could be convinced, but he isn't the only one you'd have to persuade."

"The law, too." Bram realized what he meant.

Davis Lee nodded. "I know the sheriff in Monaco. He's a good man. I bet he'd be happy to get their bank robber just dropped in his lap. I could go with you. Might be good for Deborah to go, too, and see if she remembers anything."

It was a good idea, but Bram shook his head.

"Why not?" Davis Lee asked.

"That trip, right now, would be too hard on her." Bram could still feel her tight grip on his shirt when she had seen her family for the first time. She had been overwhelmed. "And not just physically."

"She's pretty beat up, huh?"

Bram nodded. Davis Lee hadn't seen the stark terror in her eyes, the marks on her. How overcome she'd been just seeing her mother and sisters. She wasn't ready.

"Well," Davis Lee said, "you and I can go."

Bram would have preferred to take the money and talk to the banker himself, but it was more important that he stay close to Deborah. "What would you think about taking the money and talking to the banker yourself?"

"You don't want to leave Deborah?"

Not liking his friend's phrasing, Bram said tightly, "More like I don't want to chance Cosgrove showing up while I'm gone."

"All right. I'll leave early tomorrow morning and let you know as soon as I can if Monaco's sheriff and banker are agreeable to the plan."

"Thank you."

"Will you tell Deborah or Aunt Jess?"

"No reason to. It doesn't change anything. And the fewer people who know about this, the better chance the plan will work."

"True."

The two men shook hands and Bram left, headed for Annalise's clinic. As he angled across Main Street toward her clinic at the other end of town, he recalled how lost Deborah had looked, how alone the last time he'd been with her.

How was she doing? Was she settling in?

He'd know soon enough when he showed up tonight for his turn at watch. Why couldn't he stop thinking about her? There were plenty of other things and people who needed his attention.

Maybe Jake would have Ike and Georgia back at the Circle R by the time Bram arrived. He hoped so. He wanted to see with his own eyes that his uncle and cousin were all right. And he wanted to talk to his brother about this craziness with Deborah.

The woman didn't even remember him and she had him turned inside out, but he had no intention of letting her know.

For once, since the shoot-out at the Eight of Hearts ranch, Bram had the upper hand. He intended to keep it. And when this was over, he would walk away from Deborah. Just as she had walked away from him.

The relief Deborah had expected to feel at being away from Bram hadn't come. Instead, she had wanted him to stay.

Several hours after he had gone, she had learned a few things about her life. Not because she had remembered, but because her family had told her.

They had shown her the note she had written. Despite having no recollection of doing it, she knew the handwriting was hers.

She also knew now why she had insisted on taking the teaching position before she would marry Bram. What she didn't know was why that had caused him to force her to choose between him and the job.

Something he had said in the cabin nagged at her, something relevant, but she couldn't recall it.

Though she kept busy, a restless energy moved through her and she seemed unable to keep from listening for Bram's return.

After supper, her mother and Michal had settled in the front room to work on Michal's new dress for the Fourth of July celebration.

She glanced at Jordan, who stood beside her in the kitchen washing dishes while Deborah dried and Marah put things in their place.

"The night Bram and I fought, did I explain that I wanted the job so desperately because I had given one up before for another man?"

Her sisters had informed her that she had been engaged before their family moved to Whirlwind. "Did I tell Bram that my former fiancé said he wanted to start a family right after we married so he didn't want me to teach?"

"I'm not sure," Jordan said. "Or even if you told him that when you and Sean fought about your taking the job, he called off the engagement."

Was she a demanding and unreasonable person? "Do I fight with every man who shows interest in me?"

"No. You aren't like that," Marah insisted.

Jordan nodded. "You had been offered a teaching job and gave it up for Sean. You said you wouldn't do that again."

Had she explained her reasons for turning down Bram's proposal? Deborah wondered. If so, why hadn't he understood? She intended to ask him.

Jordan poked her head around the kitchen door, then asked in a low voice, "How were things between you and Bram during the storm?"

"They were…tense."

"I bet there was only one bed," she said matter-of-factly.

Deborah understood now why her sister hadn't wanted their mother to overhear.

Marah's eyes widened. "Did y'all sleep in the same room?"

"No." Although he had seen her half-naked. Her face heated. "There was only one bed, but he let me have it."

"He's a gentleman," Marah said dreamily.

The way he had looked at Deborah, right through her undergarments, hadn't been gentlemanly in the least, but she would keep that to herself.

"He gave me the bed so he could keep an eye on me. At the time, he believed I'd been with Cosgrove of my own free will."

"He thought you were lying about losing your memory?" Jordan looked at Deborah in surprise. "I can't believe he doubted you."

"Neither can I," Marah agreed.

"He was still very angry about the proposal and about my leaving." She glanced at both of her sisters. "Thank you for being so understanding and believing me. I appreciate y'all trying to help me recollect things."

Marah gestured toward the cool dimity dress Deborah had changed into after bathing and washing her hair. "Did you remember that's one of Bram's favorite dresses?"

"No."

Her sister's face fell.

Deborah looked down at the white fabric sprinkled with tiny purple flowers. From the wardrobe she shared with her sister, she had automatically reached for the dress with the square neck edged in lace. Would Bram notice, think she had done it on purpose? If she had known it was one of his favorites, she wasn't sure she would've chosen it.

Michal had helped her sweep her hair up to keep it off her neck. Though the screen door allowed in the occasional breeze, heat from the cookstove still lingered in the room, curling little wisps of her hair around her face.

As she watched Jordan put away the clean dishes, Marah asked Deborah more questions. Did she remember how old she'd been when she taught her first school? Did she recall helping Marah nurse Felix back to health after the mouse had nearly been killed by a cat? Did she recall sharing a bedroom with Jordan?

No, no and no. Every question made Deborah feel as if she were letting down her family. She hated it.

She caught Jordan shaking her head at their sister and was relieved when the younger woman began to tell her things rather than ask about them.

"You'll be so proud of me," Marah said. "I finally know all of the Great Lakes states."

"You had trouble with that?"

"An awful lot." Marah rinsed the skillet and passed it to Deborah. "Minnesota, Wisconsin, Illinois, Pennsylvania, New York, Indiana and Michigan."

"And?" Deborah prodded.

"There's one more?" her sister asked dejectedly.

Deborah nodded.

"I always forget— Oh! It's Ohio."

"Very good."

"Hey, you knew I'd left out one of the states. You remembered something!"

She didn't want to dampen her sister's enthusiasm, but she hadn't remembered. "It's just something I knew."

"Because you're a teacher." Marah nodded.

Jordan smiled. "It seems you haven't forgotten everything."

"Do you think I'll remember other things, like what happened to me in Monaco?"

"I don't know why not," Jordan said. "You didn't expect to remember what you just did."

"I hope you're right. I especially want to recall everything that happened with Bram."

"We only know what you told us the night the two of you fought. You were so mad you didn't want to talk much."

"And you said he was angry, too," Marah added, hoisting herself up to sit on the cupboard beside the sink.

"You'd better get down from there. You know Mother doesn't like it," Deborah said.

Marah and Jordan both grinned. After a second, Deborah did, too. "I remembered something else."

As dusk settled outside, Jordan lit the fat-bellied lamp. Smoky amber light filled the kitchen.

Marah crossed her ankles, leaning toward Deborah. "Bram must not still be mad at you or he wouldn't be so bent on protecting you."

"He's only staying close because he thinks this Cosgrove fellow will show up for that money. Bram plans to capture him for stealing it."

"And for shooting his uncle and cousin," Jordan said.

"And for what that polecat did to you," Marah added. "I bet that made Bram really mad."

Deborah wasn't so sure about that.

"What did?" Bram's deep voice coming from just outside the screen door startled all three females and they jumped.

"Nothing," Deborah said at the same time Jordan answered, "That Cosgrove hurt Deborah."

The door squeaked as he stepped inside and swept off his hat. His shadow fell across the room. "Ladies."

Jordan and Marah both greeted him with big smiles. His smile faded as he met Deborah's gaze. At the banked heat in his eyes, her stomach dipped and she couldn't find her voice for a moment.

He had cleaned up, too, and my, my, he looked fine. His black hair was damp, curling against his strong nape. She couldn't stop her gaze from tracking over the wide shoulders molded by a clean white shirt, the tuft of dark hair at the top of his unbuttoned shirt placket, over his flat belly and down long legs to dusty black boots.

A shiver worked through her.

Marah hopped down from the cupboard and gave her a quick hug. "Deborah remembered something!"

"That right?" Bram's eyes narrowed on her.

"Not really. Not what you're hoping for anyway." Now that she had gotten past the surprise of her reaction to him, the seething energy inside her calmed. As if she'd been waiting for him.

She told herself it was because he was currently the one familiar face in her world. "It's not really a memory."

"You knew to correct me when I messed up my geography," her sister pointed out. "You used to do that all the time."

"And you recalled that Mother doesn't like Marah on top of the cupboard," Jordan said.

Deborah gave an apologetic smile. "But it doesn't tell me anything new."

"Any little bit has to help," Jordan put in.

"I agree." Bram studied Deborah, his gaze piercing in the flickering lamplight.

Jordan glanced at Marah, then nudged her toward the door. "We have some sewing to do."

"We do?" Frowning, Deborah's youngest sister looked from Jordan to Deborah, then realization dawned on her elfin face. "Oh! Yes, we do."

"That reminds me," Bram said. "None of you should go anywhere without me or one of my men."

"All right." Jordan hurried Marah out of the room.

Deborah inwardly rolled her eyes at their obvious ploy to leave her alone with Bram. They would be disappointed when he left right behind them.

But when she turned back, he stepped closer. She caught a glimpse of unguarded hunger in his eyes that burned right through her. Then he shuttered his gaze. It didn't matter. She was keenly aware of herself—the rub of her chemise against her breasts, the tickle of her hair against her neck.

Deborah was topsy-turvy and it had nothing to do with her memory loss. It had to do with the big man standing close enough for her to feel his body heat, to draw in the clean outdoorsy scent of him. It made her go soft inside.

"Um, have you seen your uncle and cousin? How are they?"

He gave her a curious look.

She glanced down to see if she had something

on her dress. She didn't. "What? Why are you looking at me like that?"

"You don't even remember Ike and Georgia."

"I'd still like to know if they're all right. Besides, I thought you might be tired of talking about me."

Emotion flashed through his eyes. He cleared his throat. "It will take them a while to heal, but they'll be okay. It's kind of you to ask."

The intent way he studied her had her steadying herself with a hand on the counter beside her. "Did you eat supper? We have plenty of ham and potatoes left."

"I ate. Thanks. I wanted to talk to you."

"I haven't remembered anything. Well, except for geography," she said with a half laugh, fingering the lace edging her neckline.

Bram's gaze shifted to her hand, where it rested near the swell of her breasts. Her skin tingled as if he'd touched her there.

Dropping her hand, she tangled her fingers in her skirt. Having him so close played havoc with her pulse. "My mother showed me the note I wrote saying I'd left for Abilene. She and my sisters think Cosgrove forced me to do it."

Bram scrutinized her face, his bronzed features hardening. "I'm inclined to believe that."

"But you don't think— Do you think that's

what happened?" She really wanted him to say yes.

"I don't know." His voice was even, hard to read.

He ran his hat through his fingers, easing closer. "I spoke to Annalise when I was in town earlier."

At Deborah's blank look, he explained, "Annalise Fine, Whirlwind's doctor. She's engaged to Matt Baldwin. She's the woman who was held hostage during the shoot-out with Cosgrove I told you about."

"Oh," she said softly, her attention going to the scar on the right side of his face.

His mouth tightened. "You've helped Annalise before in her clinic."

"I'm sorry. I don't—"

"Remember," he finished. "It doesn't matter. What I wanted to tell you was that she's never treated anyone for losing their memory."

A sharp ache pierced her chest. "So you're back to thinking I'm a liar," she said coolly, turning away.

"No." His large hand closed gently around her wrist to stay her. "She's never treated it, but she's heard of it."

"What did she say? Will my memory come back?"

"She doesn't know."

"I don't understand how everything can just be gone." Her voice thickened. "How I can have nothing in my memory."

"The way she explained it to me was to compare it to sleepwalking," he said quietly. "Annalise said that sleepwalkers often act in ways that are different from their normal behavior and when they wake up, they have no recollection of what they did."

"Sleepwalking? But I've never done that."

He gave her a look.

She sighed. He was right. How did she know what she'd done? That was something she would ask her family. Her next thought brought mild panic.

"What if I can't remember anything because…it didn't really happen?"

"Something happened," Bram said tightly, grazing a thumb carefully against her jaw, careful not to touch her bruise. "You didn't do this to yourself."

She looked up into his eyes, her pulse scrambling at his touch. She was struck by an urge to curl her body into his, to feel those big arms around her. But she didn't.

"Do you think my injuries have anything to do with my memory loss?"

"It's possible." His gaze searched her face. "How are you feeling?"

"Much better. There's still a twinge or two, but I'm fine."

"Annalise said she would find out as much as she could about this and let me know. She'd also like to see you."

"As a doctor?"

For some reason, that made him smile. "Yes, as a doctor. It won't hurt to let her check you over."

"All right."

His thumb brushed her chin. "I see you were able to clean up."

"You, too." She smiled, quite aware that he was still touching her. She stood motionless so as not to break the connection.

"You're awful pretty." His gaze moved from the flat plane of her chest bared by her neckline to her mouth. His eyes darkened.

She remembered that look! And the answering flutter in her stomach. Before she realized it, she had taken a step toward him.

"Damn." He shifted closer, too, muttering, "Ought to kiss you and see if you remember that."

His voice was so low she barely caught his words, but when she did a wave of heat flushed her body. Nervous now, she moistened her lips with her tongue, and a nearly pained look came over his face.

For a split second she thought he might kiss her. She wanted him to, because she suddenly, shockingly also recalled the feel of his mouth on hers. She wanted to feel it again.

His eyes shuttered against her. He dropped his hand and stepped back.

Telling herself it was silly to be hurt by his withdrawal, Deborah laced her fingers together. In a flash, she recalled what he'd said to her at the cabin that had bothered her earlier. "May I ask you something?"

"Yes," he said warily.

Deborah licked her lips again. "Did your opposition to my going off to teach have anything to do with your ma leaving you?"

He stiffened. "I thought you didn't remember anything about me."

"You mentioned her at the cabin and it made me wonder."

"Why are you asking?" His voice was brusque.

She frowned. "I was just trying to figure out why you were so against me teaching school."

"Not teaching school. *Leaving* to teach school," he clarified.

"My sisters said it was only for two terms."

"In Abilene." His jaw went anvil-hard. "A four-hour ride from my ranch."

"So it did have something to do with your mother abandoning you?"

Features growing dark, he stared at her a long time, then turned to leave. "I'll be outside. If any of you need to come out, don't startle me. My gun's loaded."

The door banged shut and soon she heard the thud of his boots on the front porch.

From the way he'd skedaddled, she knew she was right, but it didn't really help her. She had learned a bit about herself, but the only thing she had learned about Bram was that the man affected her much more than she liked. Just a look from him could heat her up like a Texas summer.

Her mind might not remember, but her body did.

Chapter Six

He didn't have the sense God gave a saddle horn. How else to explain the fact that Bram had come *this* close to kissing Deborah last night?

The rest of the night had been uneventful, which was a damn good thing. Early this morning Bram had left Amos at the Blue homeplace, then gone to the ranch to sleep and wash up, although he hadn't done as much sleeping as he'd needed. Thinking about Deborah in the dress she'd worn last night had made him restless.

Had she worn it because she recalled how he liked the way those little purple flowers made her eyes even more blue? Or because the bodice bared a little more of her velvety skin than usual? He sorely doubted it, because so far she hadn't remembered a blasted thing about *him* or what *he* liked.

She had remembered geography. Flashes of words from her mother. Bram wasn't even surprised that her schooling was one of the first things to pop up in her mind. Her vocation had taken priority over him even before she had lost her memory.

That afternoon, he waited in the front room of Annalise's clinic with Mrs. Blue while the doctor examined Deborah.

Her mother sat quietly in a nearby chair and he stared out the window toward the jail, threading his hat through his fingers. With Deborah's note in the pocket of his denims, he had thought to show it to Davis Lee while she was with the doctor, but upon ushering her into the clinic, Bram decided he should stay.

All he could hear from behind the curtain separating the clinic's examination room and the front room were murmurs, some from Annalise, a few from Deborah.

"Thank you again, Bram," Jessamine said.

He turned to find her smiling at him. "For what?"

"For getting my daughter home and making sure she'll stay safe."

He shifted uneasily. He deserved no thanks

for that, not when his real aim was to set a trap for Cosgrove.

Her mother continued, "She looked so dazed as we drove into town that I'm glad I insisted the girls stay home. She's not used to them yet. I think bringing them into town where she also doesn't remember anyone would've just made things more confusing for her."

He tended to agree. He was also glad the older woman had accompanied them, because her presence kept him from being completely focused on Deborah. And her sweet scent. Helped him keep up his guard against the woman who had planned to leave him.

The tap of heels had him looking up to see Annalise pushing back the curtain. He straightened. Had she found other injuries? Had Deborah been violated?

Bram could hardly make himself think about it. If it turned out Cosgrove had forced himself on her, Bram would do murder. After making the bastard suffer.

Annalise smiled at him and Mrs. Blue. "Why don't both of you come in and have a seat? Deborah said she doesn't mind if I speak in front of y'all."

Bram let the older woman precede him. As she stopped to put a hand on her daughter's shoulder,

Bram pulled Annalise aside and asked in a low voice, "Is she okay? You know, everywhere?"

Annalise touched his arm. "I think so. Let's go on in so I can tell her mother, too."

Nodding, he followed her into the room with two long narrow cots, a small table holding a lamp, and a glass-front cabinet filled with medicine, bandages and other things he couldn't identify from here.

Deborah sat on the edge of the nearest cot looking so fragile that his throat tightened. Ever since he'd found her, the possibility of her being raped had slowly worked through his mind like poison, eating away at him.

Annalise's green gaze took in all three people in the examination room. "Aside from the bruises on her face and back, Deborah has wounds that could only have come from her defending herself. She fought against whatever happened to her and she would've fought if someone had tried to force themselves on her."

Deborah winced, looking down at the floor. A flush spread up her neck to her face.

"If she had been hurt in that way, I would have found signs of that and there were none."

The relief was so strong that Bram felt almost dizzy. As Jessamine patted her daughter's leg, Bram slid a look at Deborah. She barely held his gaze, telling him she was embarrassed that they were discussing this, but he saw relief in her eyes, too.

Still, the possibility prompted him to ask the doctor something else. "What are the chances that Deborah can't remember what happened because she saw something awful or because something horrible happened to her?"

"It's possible," his friend said, "but I tend to think if that were the case then she would have only blocked out that event, not her entire life. Still, I just don't know."

There was always the chance Deborah had been willingly intimate with Cosgrove, but Bram didn't think so. She hadn't been loose before.

Even so, he asked, "Would this memory loss make her do things she normally wouldn't?"

Deborah looked alarmed, as if the thought hadn't occurred to her.

"I don't believe so, but there's no way to know for sure. After you left yesterday, I wired my friend in Philadelphia, Dr. Hartford, to ask if he'd treated anyone with memory loss. He's had a few cases and is sending me the details by post. Maybe I'll have a better idea after I hear from him."

"So we aren't going to know anything else

until the letter arrives?" Bram couldn't keep the aggravation out of his voice.

"I'm afraid not." The doctor gestured toward the glass-front cabinet and the three thick books on top. "I looked in my medical texts and couldn't find anything other than what I told you."

"About the sleepwalking?" Deborah asked quietly.

"Yes. There's a doctor in France who is researching problems of the mind, but his work isn't available here. In any case, it's still preliminary so I don't know if it would provide any answers."

"So there's no way to know if Deborah will regain her memory?" her mother asked.

Annalise answered cautiously, "It's a good sign that she recalled some of her education and had a memory about you."

Though Bram didn't blame his friend for not giving a solid answer, it was frustrating.

Deborah tilted her head. "So, something or someplace familiar could help me to remember?"

"It could."

Bram tapped his hat against his thigh. He really wanted her to recall the past, but... "She gets headaches when she tries that, Annalise."

The doctor nodded, saying to the young

woman, "I can give you some powders for relief, although I'm afraid I don't know how to prevent it from happening."

"Would the headaches stop if she didn't try to remember anything?" Bram asked.

"Not necessarily." She looked at Deborah. "It sounds as though you have remembered a few things without trying, just by being at home."

"Maybe that would happen somewhere else," the patient said. "Are there places in town where I go often?"

"Haskell's," Bram said. At her confused look, he explained, "The general store."

"And your brother's house," Mrs. Blue added.

Noting the concern in Annalise's green eyes, Bram frowned. "What is it?"

"Like I said, there just isn't much information about this—"

"But?" He wished she would just spit it out.

She gave him a look before saying to Deborah, "There's a chance that *trying* to remember could make you more confused. I just don't know. It's very frustrating that I don't know yet how to help you."

Deborah's gaze went to Bram. "I want to try to recall whatever I can."

Why was she looking at him? It wasn't as if he could stop her. Still, he wasn't sure it was a good idea. Annalise's hesitation made him reluctant for Deborah to attempt something that might do more harm than good.

The patient slid her feet to the floor and stood. "Let's go to the store and see if it helps."

Mrs. Blue and Bram both looked at Annalise. The doctor considered for a moment. "If it becomes overwhelming or you start to panic or hurt, don't force it."

Deborah nodded.

The doctor's eyes were still troubled. "Maybe…only one of you should go with her. You never know how many people will be in Haskell's at a given time and it could be too much."

"I can't believe I have to be careful about going into a store," Deborah muttered.

She sounded so much like her old self that Bram hid a smile.

"I know it seems a bit much," Annalise said. "But until I know more, I want to be cautious."

As impatient as Bram was for Deborah to recall everything, he saw the wisdom of his friend's suggestion.

Mrs. Blue seemed to, as well. "Bram, why don't you and Deborah go to Haskell's? I need to check Catherine and Jericho's garden to make sure nothing needs to be picked."

"All right." He slid a look at Deborah, who nodded. He wasn't sure if going to the store was a good idea or not, but she seemed determined. Resigned, he glanced at Mrs. Blue. "We can get the supplies you need if you tell me what they are."

"I made a list." The older woman pulled a piece of paper from her reticule and passed it to him. "Why don't the two of you come to Jericho's after you've finished at the store?"

"Maybe I'll remember something there, too." Hope brightened Deborah's face.

Annalise walked with them to the door. "I'll get in touch as soon as I learn anything else."

Bram nodded.

"Thank you," Deborah said.

Mrs. Blue patted the doctor's hand. "We appreciate everything."

"It wasn't much," Annalise said apologetically.

"It gave me some peace of mind," Jessamine said.

Bram, too.

After bidding them goodbye, Deborah's mother started across the street toward the Whirlwind Hotel and Catherine's house up the hill beyond.

Bram steered Deborah to the right, past Cal

Doyle's law office and to Haskell's next door. The owner, Charlie, stood outside the store propping the door open.

With Deborah beside him, Bram stepped up onto the planked boardwalk and under the awning that provided shade from the midday sun. "Afternoon, Charlie."

The thin, dark-haired man smiled. "Hello, Bram. Miss Deborah."

"Hello," she said quietly.

"Nice to see you looking so well." The store owner, just under six feet tall, smiled.

"Thank you."

She eased closer to Bram, although he didn't know if she was aware of it. He squashed the urge to take her arm, to touch her at all. He motioned her inside as he said to Charlie, "We came to get some things for Deborah's ma."

"Very good." The older man followed them inside, then went around the long counter that greeted customers when they first entered.

Behind the counter a faded blue curtain separated the store from the back office. On the far side stood a table filled with bolts of fabric in every color.

Bram glanced around the store, scanning a stack of wooden tubs between a barrel of nails and a crate of brooms. He was glad to see they were the only customers.

Charlie hooked a thumb toward the curtained doorway. "May's in the back with a customer looking at rug swatches."

Bram nodded, stepping closer to Deborah to say in a low voice, "May is Charlie's wife."

She threw him a grateful look and he watched as she slowly took in everything around her. Her gaze lingered on a box of fancy soaps and for a moment he thought she might examine a few as she always did, but her gaze continued on to a shelf of shoes, a bin of wool socks.

Charlie stepped behind the scratched counter. "What can I get you?"

Bram glanced at Jessamine's list. "Need five pounds of Arbuckles'."

As the other man set five of the one-pound bags on the counter, the scent of coffee beans filled the store. "And a bag of flour. I can get the soda crackers from the shelf."

Deborah looked over to read the paper in Bram's hand. "I'll get the apples."

Walking back toward the door, she chose several apples from a wooden crate, then made her way to the counter to set them down before rejoining Bram.

"How's your family, Miss Deborah?" Charlie asked.

She stared blankly at the man, then recovered quickly. "Everyone's fine. Thank you."

"When's that brother of yours coming home?"

"I—I'm not sure." She looked at Bram uncertainly.

Oh, hell. It hadn't occurred to him that people might ask her questions. Why hadn't he thought of that? Well, it was too late now.

A young blond man wearing dark trousers and a white shirt with suspenders walked through the front door carrying a wooden box full of work boots. "Hey, Bram. Hey, Deborah."

"Hi, Mitchell." Bram returned the greeting.

Flushing, she murmured, "Hello."

The helplessness on her face told Bram she was self-conscious about not knowing anyone. He eased over next to her and leaned close as though looking at a pair of socks. "That's Charlie's nephew."

"Thank you," she whispered.

The gratefulness in her voice made him want to take her in his arms, but he didn't.

He moved away to bag up some nails as Deborah walked over to the fabric table. She ran her hand over a pale pink-and-green stripe.

The rushing tap of heels made him turn toward the door.

Josie Holt, green eyes shining, gave him a broad smile. Seeing Deborah, the petite brunette headed straight for her and enveloped her in a hug.

Damn. The confusion on Deborah's face made Bram realize that she had no idea the seamstress was a good friend of hers, and he couldn't very well yell it out to her.

He made his way over to the women. "Well, hello, Josie Holt."

She released Deborah and turned, giving him a funny look. "Hello, Bram Ross."

Deborah smiled her thanks at him and Bram's heart kicked hard.

Josie's gaze shifted back to the other woman. "How are you?"

"Hi, Josie." Deborah smiled a real smile. Bram knew it was because the vivacious woman had that effect on people and not because Deborah had remembered her friend.

He leaned a hip against the fabric table. "What are you up to?"

"I needed to run in real quick and see if Mitchell was able to pick up my lace when he went to Abilene."

The young man poked his head out of the back room. "It's here. I'll bring it out shortly."

"No hurry." Josie smoothed back her hair.

Next to her rich brown locks, Deborah's hair looked like silky midnight. Bram shifted his gaze to the seamstress. "Where's Tannis?"

"She's with her father at the jail." Josie beamed. After suffering at least two miscarriages, she and her husband had finally been blessed with a little girl.

Bram grinned. "Don't know many two-month-old babies in the hoosegow."

Deborah's eyes widened.

Josie chuckled. "I told Davis Lee I'm not sure I want her to be so acquainted with a jail cell."

So Davis Lee was back from Monaco. Bram wanted to talk to the lawman and find out what had happened there, but he didn't like to leave Deborah. He would see the sheriff on his way out of town.

Mitchell came out of the back to give Josie a folded length of lace.

"Thank you, Mitchell." She turned to Deborah, studying her for a moment. "You look well."

"Thank you," Deborah said quietly.

Just as Josie started to ask a question, a tiny dark-haired woman rushed from the back room and hurried over to Deborah.

Millie Jacobson.

Bram tensed.

The town's worst gossip took the younger woman's hands in hers. "Oh, my dear, I heard you were caught in the dust storm. How awful for you!"

Oh, no. Hell, no. How had Millie heard about that? Bram straightened, moving to Deborah's other side, ready to herd her out of the mercantile.

Josie edged closer to Deborah, as well.

Millie's brown eyes gleamed. "You are so lucky that Bram was there. I would've been frightened out of my wits!"

Wouldn't have taken long, he thought darkly even as he smiled at her. "Not to run off, Millie, but we're supposed to meet Mrs. Blue."

"I need to go, too." Josie positioned herself so that Deborah was between her and Bram. "Goodbye, Millie. Bye, Charlie!"

"Bye, Josie," the store owner said.

"Hmmph." That was from Millie.

Once in the street and a few feet from the mercantile, Josie looked from Bram to Deborah. "What was she talking about? You were both caught in the dust storm?"

He glanced over his shoulder to see the older woman had followed them as far as the doorway and now stood there staring. He gave Josie a meaningful look. "Can we talk about it later?"

She nodded in understanding. "Of course. Good to see both of you."

"You, too," Deborah said.

As the petite beauty started across the street toward the jail, Bram touched Deborah's elbow and guided her in the opposite direction.

"Sometimes it's good not to remember," he muttered.

She looked up, her smile fading when she saw the scowl on Bram's rugged features. "Who was that woman?"

"Millie Jacobson, the worst gossip in Whirlwind."

"How did she know we were together during the dust storm?"

A muscle worked in his jaw. "The only ones who know besides us, our families and Davis Lee are Duffy and Amos. I'll speak to both of them. They know they aren't supposed to talk about it."

"You told your family?" Deborah asked.

"Had to," he said sharply. They angled between the church and the Whirlwind Hotel and started up the hill.

She hurried beside Bram, trying to keep up with his long strides. He'd been careful all day not to touch her. The one time he had, outside the store a moment ago, had been so brief that she thought she might have imagined it.

She glanced back toward the mercantile. "Do you think that lady will cause trouble?"

"She sure likes to." He slowed, allowing Deborah to catch up to him.

After a moment, she said, "Thank you for helping me with people's names."

"You're welcome. I should've realized people would expect you to know them, answer questions."

"I didn't consider that either. I was so concerned about trying to recall something in there."

"Did you?"

"No." She tried not to feel discouraged. "Maybe I'll remember something at my brother's house."

"I bet you will."

She appreciated his encouragement. Since their visit to the doctor, he seemed less aloof.

After he had walked out on their conversation last night, she hadn't seen him again until he arrived after lunch to bring her to town. He'd been quiet during the entire trip, seemingly unaware of her. His decision to stay with her at the clinic had surprised her until she realized he likely wanted to hear about her condition straight from the doctor and not her.

Still, he'd been as relieved as she had at Dr. Fine's news that she hadn't been violated.

She looked up to find his attention fixed on her. Her stomach fluttered.

"Just so you'll know, Josie's married to Davis Lee, the sheriff. He's your cousin."

"Ah, okay. I imagine I'll meet him at some point."

"Yes." As they reached the top of the hill, Bram pointed to something ahead.

Deborah's gaze followed the direction of his finger to a pale yellow frame house. "Is that where my brother lives?"

"Yes."

She recalled nothing. Yet. She would remember something here. She had to.

They passed the front porch and stopped at the corner of the house. Deborah peered around Bram to see Mrs. Blue—*her mother*—kneeling in a patch of vegetables.

There was a root cellar on this side of the house and a spring house. Both unfamiliar. Maybe going inside would jolt something in her mind.

Mrs. Blue turned, placing a sweet potato on

the small mound of vegetables beside her, which also included freshly dug carrots.

"How did it go at the store?"

"I didn't recall anything." Though Deborah feared seeing disappointment on the other woman's face, all she saw was patience and understanding. "Bram had to tell me who everyone was."

"I'm sorry, honey. Are you all right?"

"Yes." Though she was warmed by the woman's genuine caring, her smile was wobbly. "Just a little frustrated."

"I can only imagine. Would it help if I came inside the house with you?"

"I don't know." She searched Bram's blue eyes.

"Maybe you should try it alone at first," he said.

"Very well."

Jessamine nodded. "Let me know if there's anything I can do or if you change your mind."

Deborah nodded, stepping up on the porch with Bram. He opened the front door, the fresh air displacing the musty smell of the closed-up house. A white curtain fluttered at the front window.

She moved inside.

"I'll wait out here, too."

The thought of doing this without him left her feeling adrift for a moment. "I—I'd rather you come inside. If you don't mind."

"All right." As he stooped to avoid hitting the top of the door frame, an image flickered in her mind.

A tall man. Very tall. He was black haired and also stooping to come inside. Then the picture was gone.

For the first time since coming into town, she'd had a flash of...something. That was a good sign, wasn't it?

Encouraged, she took in the large front room that also accommodated a kitchen. To her left was a fireplace. A bathing tub was propped against the adjacent wall. A dark dining table and chairs stood in front of her, with a cupboard along the wall behind. A framed sampler hung above the cupboard.

The name "Blue" was embroidered in the center with Catherine's and Jericho's names on either side of it. Below their names was a date.

Bram moved up beside her. "You made that for their wedding day."

She skirted the table, studying needlework that was neat and precise. The fact that she felt no connection to it at all had her searching her mind hard and coming up empty.

Bram pointed to an open doorway straight across from the table. "That's Catherine and Jericho's bedroom. When you stay here, you sleep in Andrew's bedroom."

He walked a few feet down a short hall to another open doorway. "Andrew is Catherine's younger brother. He gives up his bed anytime you or your sisters visit."

Deborah walked toward Bram and eased past him into the room. She managed to ignore his dark male scent and the distracting brush of his hard thighs against her skirts. The space was small, with a narrow bed and nice-sized window. She didn't recognize it or the small bedside table that held a lamp and a carved wooden quail.

She squashed a flare of panic. "Have I spent a lot of time here?"

"Quite a bit." Bram's deep voice was soothing, yet she wasn't soothed.

After another thorough look around, she stepped back out with him and studied the front room again. The sink, the fireplace, the now-open front window. Nothing.

"We can go outside and walk around, check out the barn if you want."

She nodded, still hopeful despite the fact that her spirits were falling fast as they walked to the other side of the house and down the narrow hallway toward the back.

Though he opened the door for her, she paused, studying the barn about fifty yards away, the prairie beyond the weathered gray building.

She moved out to the stoop, closing her eyes as she listened to the muted sounds from town—the rattle of a wagon, the low buzz of voices, a child's laughter. She waited for something to come into her mind. Anything.

Unlike when Bram had stopped at the creek where he had proposed, she felt nothing, good or bad. She'd really thought she would find something familiar here.

Tears tightened her throat. Trying to steady her voice, she said over her shoulder, "You can go back inside. I'll be right there."

"Nothing, huh?"

She shook her head, afraid if she said more she would cry. Bram didn't move, just waited behind her. Why couldn't he go away?

"It's understandable to be disappointed. And mad, too, I reckon. I figure I would be."

She didn't answer.

"Sorry," he said softly. "I thought this place might help you."

She curled her hands into fists until her nails bit into her palms. She wanted to scream.

His big hot hand closed gently over her shoulder and squeezed. Bram felt her tremble.

She looked back at him, tears welling in her eyes. "I thought I'd remember something. Just one thing."

She turned away, but not before he saw a tear fall. Hell. A sharp ache pierced his chest. When her shoulders sagged, he couldn't stand it.

Even as he told himself he would be sorry, he pulled her into him and wrapped his arms around her. She buried her face in his chest. He didn't know what to say, so he said nothing.

They stood like that for a long moment. He grew painfully aware of her teasing scent, the full press of her breasts against his chest, the cradle of her hips.

Unable to step away, he smoothed her hair back and tilted her face up to his. Her eyes were liquid blue, her cheeks wet with tears. The vulnerability on her delicate features clutched at something deep inside him. Bram knew the smart thing would be to release her and fetch her ma, but he couldn't muster up one ounce of smart. He couldn't imagine how it would be to remember nothing, to have no roots, no history. To feel so alone.

Cupping her face in his hands, he thumbed away her tears.

Before he realized what he was about to do, he bent his head, intent on her mouth. Then he stopped.

What the hell? Kissing her was the stupidest thing he could do.

He started to straighten, taken aback when she gripped the front of his shirt with both hands.

A flush tinting her cheeks, she said shakily, "I want you to do it."

"What?" He couldn't have heard her correctly. "No."

She licked her lips, her gaze pleading as she whispered, "I think I…remember that."

His heart started hammering hard. This was a bad idea—he knew it—but when she pulled him closer, he went. His mouth covered hers.

At first she tensed, and disappointment speared him. Just when he would've pulled away, she melted against him, her arms going around his neck as she kissed him back.

Sweet mercy. Filled with the fresh scent of her, the feel of her, he curled her tight into him.

That should've been enough for her to recall if she was going to, but he couldn't stop. He cradled her jaw with one hand, his other one sliding to her waist and angling her to him for a better fit.

She opened her mouth, inviting him in. She had the same sweet hot taste he remembered.

The same soft sound in her throat that triggered a savage swirl of need. She held him tight, her breasts flattened against his chest. She pressed into his arousal.

Sharp, searing need blazed through him, nearly pulled him under. He wanted to get his hands, his mouth, all over her.

Finally he managed to lift his head, his breathing ragged. Her mouth was wet from his. She opened her eyes and when he saw the desire there, the surrender, he nearly kissed her again.

He struggled to level out his breathing, to think. "Shouldn't have done that."

He had no idea where the words came from, because he didn't believe them.

"Oh, yes," she breathed, excitement in her voice. "You should have."

His gaze searched hers. "Did you remember?"

"Yes. Yes." She flushed.

He knew she was turning that delicate pink all over. Oh, yeah, he remembered that.

She went to her tiptoes, reaching for him again. His hand flexed on her lithe waist. He wanted more and was about to take it when her ma's voice sounded in the house.

"Deborah? Bram?"

They both froze. Deborah's alarmed gaze

flew to his. She opened her mouth, but nothing came out.

Bram could barely speak himself. "Out here," he said hoarsely.

"Any luck?" Mrs. Blue asked.

What was he supposed to say? *Your daughter and I were just working on getting intimately reacquainted?*

The violent pounding of his blood finally began to quiet. "Nothing in the house sparked a memory," he managed.

"That's too bad," Mrs. Blue said, her voice growing closer.

The dazed look left Deborah's face and Bram released her, forcing himself to step away.

Before her mother could come out and see what they had plainly been doing, Bram opened the door. After a slight hesitation, Deborah preceded him inside. She looked poleaxed. He sure was.

Damn.

She'd finally remembered something. Why did it have to be that? Why did it have to be *them?*

The feel of her mouth against his had blasted every bit of common sense out of his head. Keep his guard up? Hell, she'd plowed right over it.

Chapter Seven

What had happened at Jericho's house a few hours ago set Bram back on his heels. Ever since kissing Deborah, he'd wanted more and his common sense had been pistol-whipping him for it.

He wasn't getting involved with her again, memory or no memory.

After supper he sat in the large front room of the ranch house, visiting with his family before he had to leave for her place.

Sprawled in one of the wide leather chairs at the end of the deer-hide sofa, he patted his stomach. "Good supper, Emma."

"Thank you." His slight, blonde sister-in-law smiled warmly.

Bram was finally used to her fair hair. The mix of gold and silvery-blond strands was her natural color. When he first met her, her dark brown hair had been the result of dye, though he hadn't known it at the time.

His brother, Jake, stood in front of the rock fireplace, watching Molly as she played with a doll on the bearskin rug in front of him. When the little girl had been left on their doorstep last year, Jake had kept his distance. Now he was as wrapped around her finger as the rest of the family, and had adopted her.

The blonde toddler, who was Emma's half sister, pulled herself up by grabbing Jake's leg. Releasing him, she took a halting step toward Bram and stumbled. He and Jake both lunged for her, but she didn't fall. She steadied herself and tottered over to him, throwing herself into his lap with a squeal.

He scooped her up, tossing her into the air until she shrieked with laughter. He glanced at his uncle and his cousin who had been shot by Cosgrove during the Monaco bank robbery. Jake had told Bram that Ike and Georgia still tired easily, and that Emma helped with everything she could.

"Uncle Ike, Georgia, how are you both feeling?"

"We're coming along, son." The older man, lanky and not quite as tall as Bram, gave a weak smile from the other leather chair at the opposite end of the sofa. The thick bandage on his wounded shoulder bulged beneath his tan shirt.

Sitting beside Emma, Georgia smiled, touching her left arm, currently in a sling. That hand had been withered since she was a young girl. "At least Cosgrove shot me in the arm that's already crippled. Since I can still use my good hand, I'm getting by just fine."

Bram knew his family members were lucky that animal hadn't stayed around to make sure they were dead.

"Speaking of Cosgrove," Bram said, "Davis Lee was able to convince the Monaco sheriff and bank manager to keep quiet about the return of the stolen money."

"That's good." Jake grinned as Molly crawled up Bram's chest. "Now all you have to do is hope Cosgrove walks into the trap."

"Oh, he will. He'll come for that money."

The toddler bounced in his lap. "More, Unca Bwam!"

Grinning, he stood and settled her on his shoulders, moving her little hands away from his eyes to his head. When Emma started to rise, he shook his head. "It's okay. I've got her."

As the little girl waved at everyone from her tall perch, Emma settled back on the sofa. She had shown up at the Circle R and was hired on as a housekeeper and baby nurse soon after Molly had appeared in a washtub at the front door. After she and Jake had married, they had told the family that Molly was Emma's half sister. She had fled an abusive stepfather in an attempt to protect the infant from the man.

Georgia's brown gaze sought Bram's. "I guess you'll be going to Deborah's again tonight?"

He nodded, trying to keep thoughts of that kiss out of his head. Wondering if it had stuck with her the way it had with him. Thinking about how she'd looked at him, how she'd felt beneath his hands put a hard throb in his blood.

Emma smiled. "How is she doing?"

"Physically she's healing, but she hasn't remembered much." Adding to his frustration, their visit to Annalise had provided no ideas about how to change that.

As relieved as Bram was that Deborah had recollected something, he was aggravated that he couldn't stop thinking about getting another taste of her.

He lifted the baby from his shoulders and bussed her on the cheek. She gave him a loud, wet smack in return.

"Guess I'd better get going. Duffy's probably

chomping at the bit to get back here and grab some sleep."

Emma rose, taking the child from him. After saying good-night to everyone, he headed to the barn and lit the lantern hanging just inside the door. He saddled Scout, then checked Cosgrove's injured mare.

The swelling in her fetlock had gone down, but the joint still needed to be wrapped. After doing that, he broke down a bale of hay, grabbed the pitchfork and tossed the new straw into her stall.

Thinking about Cosgrove made him think about Deborah. Why couldn't he get the woman out of his head? he fumed. He'd let his guard down for those bittersweet moments when his mouth was on hers, but he couldn't do it again. Wouldn't do it.

He headed out of the barn with two buckets, filled them at the pump then returned to leave one in the mare's stall and the other in his gelding's. His feet were dragging about going to Deborah's. His reluctance wasn't due to fatigue, although he wasn't sleeping well. It was because that kiss had unleashed all manner of memories he didn't welcome.

The slide of her creamy skin beneath his

tongue, the weight of her breasts in his hands, the warm fragrance of her bare flesh.

The revelation that she remembered kissing him sawed at Bram. On one hand, he was glad and relieved. On the other, it tempted him to kiss her again, see if that caused her to remember anything else. That thought had teased him all afternoon.

He braced a shoulder against the stall frame, watching shadows shift as Scout scratched his nose on a wooden slat.

"Need any help at Deborah's? I could stay there tonight, if you want."

He glanced over his shoulder as Jake strode into the barn. He should probably let his brother relieve him so he could get some distance from her, but Bram couldn't bring himself to do it.

"I appreciate the offer, but I'm fine so far."

"Still want me to take a look at that cheek billet?"

"I'd appreciate it." His brother made saddles and tack on the side. People came from all over to commission his work.

Jake moved into the stall where Scout stood. "How's the mare doing?"

"She's coming along. She'll probably be healed up by the time Cosgrove shows."

"Too bad that bastard won't be riding out of here unless he's slung over her back."

"That's right." Bram watched as his brother examined the harness strap that passed through a buckle.

"The billet's fine." Jake slid him a look. "You still set against trying to work things out with Deborah?"

"What's the point?"

The other man moved to lean against the stall wall across from Bram. "Deborah said she would come back after two school terms. I never understood why you finished things between the two of you."

Bram's jaw tightened. "When Ma left, she said she was coming back, too."

Jake frowned. "Why would you think she'd be like Ma?"

"Because she made it clear she was leaving Whirlwind, no matter what."

"You didn't have a chance to try to change Ma's mind, but you can talk to Deborah again and maybe change her mind."

He'd tried that and had had as much luck with Deborah as he'd had with Frannie Ross. Bram propped a booted foot on the stall wall at his back. It wouldn't hurt his brother to know now what he had done. And it would stop Jake from talking about the woman Bram didn't want to discuss.

"I did try to change Ma's mind."

"What! When?"

"That first cattle drive I went on?"

"To Denver. You were fifteen."

"I went on that particular drive because I found out she was there."

Confusion plain on his face, Jake shook his head. "Why didn't you ever tell me?"

"No sense in you having to hear just how much she didn't want us." Even he had been surprised at their mother's utter lack of interest in her own sons.

"Why did you go after her?"

"I wanted to know if I was the reason she left."

"I never knew you thought it might be your fault," his brother said quietly. "Why would you think that?"

"She said goodbye to you, told you she'd be back shortly." Bram plucked a piece of hay from his shirtsleeve. "She never said anything to me."

Jake's mouth tightened. "I didn't know that."

Bram shrugged. "No reason you should. When I found her, she didn't even recognize me."

"What?" Anger burned in his brother's dark eyes. "How could she not know who you were?"

"Evidently she put us out of her mind. I told

her who I was and she said I'd wasted a trip, that she wasn't ever coming back here."

"And you're afraid Deborah will do the same? Leave and forget all about you?"

Bram gave a harsh laugh. "She's already done that."

Jake grimaced. "That was a bad choice of words."

"No, it's right. If her feelings had been as strong as mine, don't you think she would've remembered me by now?"

She remembered you kissing her, a little voice whispered.

"I don't know," Jake answered slowly. "Sounds like *nobody* knows anything about memory loss, including Annalise. Couldn't you try to help Deborah remember?"

He dragged a hand down his face. "Annalise doesn't know if that's a good idea. Besides, she remembered something when we…"

"When you what?"

"Kissed," he mumbled, looking away. "Earlier in town. At Jericho's."

"What exactly did she recall?" A smile sounded in the other man's voice.

Bram shifted uneasily, ready to get going. "Kissing me. Before, I mean."

His brother grinned. "Maybe you should build on that."

"Meaning what?"

"Well, kiss her again."

"No." He'd done that against his better judgment. And as much as it riled him to admit it, Bram wouldn't be able to stop at kissing. "No."

"Why not?"

"I'm not startin' back up with her." He moved into the stall and led his horse out. "It won't go anywhere."

"It might help her remember."

"And if she does remember, she'll leave, just like she planned." Before his brother could say more, he continued, "And if she doesn't recollect and I get tangled up with her, I'll always be waiting for her memory to return."

Understanding spread across Jake's features and he sobered. "There's no good outcome, is there?"

"Not that I can see."

Hours later, Deborah could still feel Bram's mouth on hers. She stood at the half-open window of the bedroom she shared with Jordan, listening for his return. What she and Bram had shared had been more than a kiss. It had been a real memory. One she had recalled consciously.

Though he'd been reluctant at first, he had relented and given her what she had asked for. He was softening toward her. Which was good, because she felt more and more drawn to him.

She looked out over the buffalo grass rippling in the breeze and across the prairie toward Whirlwind. The fading golden-pink of late day gave way to darkness. Now that the sun had set, the June temperature was more bearable.

Bram had arrived before nightfall last night. Anticipation swirled inside her. Where was he? Had he thought about that kiss as much as she had?

From the corner of her eye she caught a flash of lantern light, a movement, and turned to see Duffy Ingram come from the back of the house. She smiled at the wiry ranch hand who had eaten supper with them.

Once an hour, the older man stretched his legs by walking around the house and the barn and chicken coop. His boots made a soft noise in the grass as he neared. Stopping at the window, he touched a finger to the brim of his hat and smiled, his hazel eyes crinkling.

"Is everything all right?" she asked.

"Yes, ma'am." He peered around her, acknowledging her sisters. Jordan lay on the bed behind her and Michal sat in a chair next to the table holding the lamp. "Evenin', Miss Jordan, Miss Michal."

"Good evening, Duffy." From where she lay reading on the bed, Jordan waved.

"H-hello." Michal kept her gaze on the bodice she was stitching.

Duffy walked on as Deborah glanced at her stuttering sister. Though the third Blue daughter was an excellent seamstress, she had problems speaking smoothly to anyone outside the family.

Deborah wondered if she had ever known how to help Michal. If so, she wished she would remember that. Thinking about recalling things had her thoughts circling back to Bram. Not that he'd been out of them for long.

Kissing him was the clearest memory she'd had while at her brother's, the only one she could fully identify, the one she couldn't leave alone. But it wasn't her only recollection there.

Instead of reliving that kiss, she should be more concerned with trying to figure out who the man was in the image she'd seen earlier.

She looked around the bedroom. The bed was slightly bigger than the one shared by the two youngest siblings. A wardrobe of dark walnut was backed against the far wall and held their clothing and shoes. In the adjacent corner was a polished vanity of the same walnut with a standing mirror beside it. The small table holding a pitcher and washbasin sat opposite the foot of the bed.

Marah and Michal slept in the next room, and on the other side of the house their mother had a room that had been built last year.

"You're being awful quiet." Jordan looked up from the book she was reading.

Michal nodded, biting off a length of thread. "You didn't say much about your visit to town. How was it?"

"It was all right." She had told them earlier what Dr. Fine—Annalise—had said about her condition, but not much else. "Bram took me to the general store. I met Charlie Haskell and his nephew."

Michal spread the fabric on her lap, eyeing the pink bodice front critically in the amber lamplight. "Did you meet May, Charlie's wife?"

"No." Deborah stayed at the window. "She was helping someone in the back, a lady named Millie Jacobson. I did meet her."

"Ugh," Jordan said.

Michal and Jordan grimaced, just as Bram had.

Deborah laughed, feeling increasingly comfortable with her family. "I also met Josie Holt. She seems nice."

"You like her very much. I mean, you did. When you knew her. Or…remembered her." Jordan frowned. "How do I say that?"

Deborah understood what she meant.

"Josie is a wonderful seamstress," Michal said.

"Better than you?" She found that hard to believe.

"If you ask Michal," Jordan said with an affectionate look at their sister. "I think she's every bit as good as Josie, though. So does Josie."

"I'm not. I try to learn from her whenever I can."

Jordan glanced over at Deborah. "You haven't said if you remembered anything in town."

She didn't want to share what she *had* remembered and she wasn't sure she could describe the too-brief image she'd had of the tall man.

What could it hurt, though? At worst, Deborah would know exactly what she knew now. At best, she might learn something new.

"Deborah?"

She pulled her attention back to Jordan, whose frown indicated she had asked a question, maybe more than once.

"Did anything happen in town at all?"

"Maybe at Jericho and Catherine's?" Michal asked. "Mother said you went there."

Deborah wasn't telling her sisters about kissing Bram. Or that since then she had been stunned by phantom sensations of his mouth on her in other places. Her neck, her shoulder. Her breasts. Heat shot through her and her stomach dipped. She had no idea if they were real memories.

"There was one thing," she said. "But it was just an image of a man. No detail."

"That's something." Michal tilted her head. "Isn't it?"

"There wasn't much to the picture in my mind."

"Can you describe what you did see?"

She was quiet for a moment. "I saw a man stooping to come into the house. A very tall, dark-haired man."

"What did Bram say?" Jordan asked.

"I didn't tell him." Her mind had been too taken up with kissing him. "I wasn't sure what to say. What I saw was so hazy."

"Maybe Jordan can draw him from your description," Michal suggested.

Deborah's eyes widened. "Do you draw?"

Jordan nodded.

"She's very good." Michal flipped the bodice to stitch something on the inside.

"It's worth a try," Deborah said. Plus maybe

it would help distract her from wondering what other places Bram might have kissed her.

Jordan rose and moved to the foot of the bed. Opening the hope chest there, she took out a pad of paper and a charcoal pencil. "Tell me what you can."

"It was so fast. And vague." She huffed out a breath in frustration.

"Try closing your eyes," Michal suggested.

Deborah did. "All right."

"How tall is he?" Jordan asked.

"Taller than Bram, I think."

"Was he wearing or holding a hat?"

Deborah thought hard. "No."

"You said he had dark hair," Michal prompted. "Could you tell if it was black or dark brown?"

"Black, I think. I'm not sure. That was just the first thing that came to mind when you asked me."

She heard the rattle of paper and opened her eyes.

Jordan made a few strokes on the paper. "Hair short or long?"

"Nicely trimmed and reaching the top of his shirt collar." She searched her mind. "No sideburns."

This might work. There was more to the impression than she had realized.

"That's good," Jordan said. "What else?"

"His eyes were light, I think. Black shirt, black trousers. Wearing a gun belt."

"That could be any number of men around here," Michal said.

"True." Her shoulders sagged.

"Still, you're doing great." Jordan gestured to the sketch. "Anything else you can tell me?"

She frowned, closing her eyes again. "There's something…a scar or some kind of mark on the left side of his face."

"Oh!" Michal exclaimed.

Deborah's eyes flew open. "What?"

"I might know who it is," Michal said.

Jordan continued to draw. "Where's the scar? Cheek? Jaw? Eye?"

"High on his left cheekbone."

A smile stretched across Michal's face and she fairly vibrated with excitement.

Jordan quickly moved the pencil across the paper, then turned the sketch toward Deborah. "Does this look anything like who you saw?"

She studied the man's stern chiseled features softened by the lightness of his eyes and a half smile. "Yes, that's him!"

"It's our brother, Jericho."

"Our brother?" She stared at the drawing.

Now that his face was defined, he looked familiar. Hope rose inside her.

Jordan set the pencil aside. "It makes sense that you would get an image of him, since you've spent a lot of time in that house."

Michal rose and hugged her. "You remembered something!"

Now she had another memory! She couldn't wait to tell Bram. Excited, she squeezed Jordan's hand. "Thank you."

"You're welcome. Maybe it won't be long now before you get your whole memory back."

"I hope you're right." Then she would know why she had gone with Cosgrove. If she'd taken his horse in an attempt to escape him or someone else. If he was the man she'd heard yelling after her when she had ridden out of Monaco.

Michal hurried out of the room. "I'm going to tell Mother."

Deborah again looked at the sketch. "You really are very good, Jordan."

Her sister shrugged. "I like doing it."

"Thank goodness you can. It's because of you that I figured out Jericho was a real memory. Have you sketched other things?"

"Quite a few."

"I'd like to see them, if you don't mind."

"All right." Her sister looked pleased.

The sound of hooves interrupted them and Deborah's gaze eagerly went to the window.

Jordan laughed. "Maybe you'd rather see Bram first."

She flushed. "No, that's okay."

Her sister grinned. "Go ahead. It's fine."

"All right. Thank you." As she left the bedroom with her sister, her heartbeat sped up when she heard the low timbre of his voice.

"Ladies."

"Good evening, Bram," Jessamine said.

"H-hello." That was Michal. "D-did you eat supper?"

"That depends. Did you make those molasses cookies I like?"

"I can make some."

"Not on my account, though I appreciate it," he said kindly. "I'm still full from supper."

"All right."

Jordan stepped out as Deborah paused in the doorway, something inside her shifting at the sight of him. Holding his mount's reins, he stood with his back to her as Marah stroked his gelding's nose. A white shirt and denims molded his powerful body. He'd removed his hat, revealing his strong tanned nape and the slight wave in his black hair.

Had she felt like this around him before she

had lost her memory? As if she couldn't get a full breath. As if she had a constant flutter in her stomach.

Marah looked away from the dun to Bram. "Duffy found a covey of quail out behind the barn and I saw them!"

"Good thing I brought my rifle," Bram drawled. "I've been hankerin' for some quail."

"You are not shooting them!"

"You didn't tell me about them because you wanted some for supper?" he teased.

"Hmmph, you know what I think about killing those birds."

He chuckled. "I reckon I do and so does the whole of Whirlwind."

Marah made a face at him, then her gaze shifted to Deborah, her eyes lighting up. "Deborah has something to tell you."

"That right?" He turned, his broad shoulders blocking most of the view of his horse. His smile faded, his gaze sliding over her.

She was startled by the prickling sensation of his mouth on her shoulders, her neck. Feeling her face heat, she said softly, "Hi."

"Hey."

Jessamine herded the other girls inside. "Let Deborah tell him."

"But—" Marah began.

"C'mon, Marah." Jordan hooked an arm through her sister's and tugged her inside.

Deborah smiled as Michal followed their mother.

Bram hung his hat on his saddle horn and shoved a hand through his hair, leaving furrows in the dark thickness. "Your sister seems excited about something."

"Yes. I am, too."

"You can talk while I brush Scout down."

"All right." Disheartened that he didn't immediately ask about her news, she followed him around the house to the barn.

"After our trip to Whirlwind today, I wrote down everything I learned."

"That's good. I talked to both Duffy and Amos Fuller. Fuller's the one who flapped his gums to Millie. If he says anything else out of turn, he's gone from the Circle R."

She nodded, wondering if Bram's only reason for warning the ranch hand was that he didn't want gossip spreading. Or if he didn't want anyone to think he and Deborah might still be courting.

She couldn't keep her gaze from trailing down his strong back or admiring the muscular thighs gloved by his jeans. He led the gelding to the barn and lit the lantern hanging outside the door before unsaddling his mount.

Beneath his white shirt, the muscles in his shoulders and arms bunched. Her gaze went to his hands, bronzed and big. Hands that had locked her to him earlier, held her as if he would never let her go.

Heat moved under her skin. Just looking at him made her go soft inside.

He walked into the barn, settling the saddle over a sawhorse. "What was it you wanted to tell me?"

His tone gave her pause. She wasn't imagining the hint of coolness in his words. "Did something happen at your ranch? Something bad?"

"No." He returned and removed the horse blanket. The black stripe down his dun's back was dark with sweat.

Something was wrong. Something Bram obviously didn't want to discuss with her. Still, she wouldn't let it dim her enthusiasm over what she had remembered.

"When we were at my brother's—"

"Listen." He slipped the bridle off with one hand, his gaze leveling on hers. "If you want to talk about that kiss, it never should've happened."

Even as her heart sank, anger flashed through

her. Along with hurt. "Yes, that's all I've thought about since it happened," she snapped, because it was true. "My goodness, I don't know how I managed not to swoon when you got here."

"All right, I get your point," he growled, taking a brush out of a nearby bucket and beginning to sweep the horse with it. "What do you want to tell me?"

"When we were at Jericho's, an image flickered in my mind. It was brief, though it was enough of a picture that I could tell it was a man coming into the house."

Bram straightened, interest flaring in his eyes. He rested an arm on his gelding's back.

Ah, now he was listening to her.

"Why didn't you mention this?"

"I wasn't sure if what I saw meant anything, but I couldn't stop thinking about it." Thank goodness he didn't know she also hadn't been able to stop thinking about kissing him.

"I told Jordan and she suggested I try to describe what I could. When I did, she was able to sketch him. Here it is."

She held out the paper, now curled into a roll.

He took it, his fingers brushing hers as he pulled away quickly and straightened the drawing. His gaze dropped to the paper. "I'll be," he muttered. "It's your brother."

She nodded. "And there are other things I may remember."

"Like what?" He returned the sketch.

Should she tell him? He'd all but said he didn't want to talk about that kiss. Well, she didn't really want to talk about it either, but there were things she needed to know. "Things like other times, um, places, you kissed me."

He turned away, tossing the brush into a bucket holding other brushes, a hoof pick, hoof knife and a rasp. Uncertain now, she wrapped her arms around herself. Was she really going to ask him? She certainly couldn't ask her family.

He smacked the gelding's rump and sent it loping into the corral. He faced her, impatience crackling in his eyes.

She swallowed hard. She couldn't just come out and ask him if they knew each other in the biblical sense. "I think I remember you kissing me in other places."

Hunger darkened his eyes and his gaze did a slow slide to her breasts.

Oh, my.

When he looked back up, his face was shuttered against her. "I assume you don't mean kissing you in different locations, like in town or behind the church."

Embarrassed, hardly able to speak, she nodded. "Yes. I mean, no."

He arched a brow.

He wasn't going to make it easy on her, and for a moment she thought about dropping the subject. He obviously wanted her to. And that was why she wasn't going to.

"Well?" he demanded.

Hand trembling, she pointed to a spot on the side of her neck. "Did you kiss me here?"

He nodded, his eyes glittering in the shadows. She could clearly see the desire on his face, the scar that looked harsher in this light. Which meant he could probably tell that she was blushing.

She lifted her braid and touched her nape. "And...here?"

"Yeah." His voice was rough.

A phrase skipped through her mind. *Here, there or anywhere.*

It tugged at her memory, then vanished. She had no idea what the words meant, if anything.

"Deborah?"

She shifted her attention back to him. Her hand flattened on the plane of her chest and his gaze followed. The heat in those blue eyes made her knees weak. She couldn't ask if he had kissed her there, but when she met his gaze, she knew his mouth had been there and lower.

Where *hadn't* he kissed her? "Just how intimate were we?"

"Your virtue is intact." He bit out the words.

Any acceptance she'd seen in him earlier was gone. He was angry. Why? What did he have to be angry about?

She was afraid she knew. "You regret kissing me."

"In point of fact, *you* kissed *me.*"

She froze, her mind calling up what had happened. At the time, she had felt he was kissing her because he wanted to. Almost *needed* to. Horrified, she could barely push out the words. "Did you only do it because I asked you?"

"Yes."

Temper flaring, she said, "You didn't seem to mind while we were doing it."

"You may have forgotten what happened between us, but I haven't."

The bitterness in his voice sent a sharp pain through her. She couldn't stay out here with him any longer. Somehow she managed to choke out, "I see. I'm glad to have that sorted out. And thank you so much for your help today. Sorry to have troubled you. Good night."

Tears blurring her vision, she turned and walked back toward the house.

Behind her, she heard him curse, but she kept walking. Her chest felt hollow and tight. She had thought he was softening toward her. She'd been wrong.

Chapter Eight

Bram had just lied through his teeth. He watched Deborah turn in a whirl of skirts and walk away, her shoulders as rigid as a wagon brace.

The hurt that had flared in her eyes made him want to kick himself. He should apologize, but he didn't. Already he was more involved than was smart. He had to leave things be.

He didn't see her again until supper the next evening. Mrs. Blue had invited him, and though he had started to decline, his parting conversation with Duffy changed his mind.

The Circle R ranch hand had reported that Mitchell Orr, the store clerk, had driven out today and stayed a good long while. Though Orr was friendly with the entire family, the man had spent most of his time with Deborah.

Bram had been on edge since last night, the news about her visitor setting his jaw—and not because he feared Orr might be a threat to Deborah's safety.

The last glaring rays of the sun had softened and now Bram sat opposite Mrs. Blue at one end of her walnut dining table. Jordan and Marah sat to his left, while Deborah and Michal had taken the places to his right. Deborah had barely spared him a glance. Bram had spared her more than his share.

Tonight she looked cool and fresh in a pale blue dress that set off her ivory skin and raven hair. Tendrils escaped from her upswept hair, curling at her nape and around her face. He tore his gaze from the elegant line of her neck.

More than once, his gaze wandered to her soft pink mouth and he would find himself thinking about their kiss yesterday. Then he wondered if Orr had tried to kiss her.

By the time dessert was served, Bram's muscles were as taut as new rope. There could be no more kissing. He was having a devil of a time forgetting the one they'd shared.

All the women except Deborah asked after

his family, glad to hear how well his uncle and cousin were progressing.

Deborah rose to help Jordan clear the table while Michal brought in a pecan pie from the kitchen. The sweet scent of sugar and nuts made Bram's mouth water.

"Deborah made pie," Marah said.

Whether she had remembered how or someone had helped her, Bram knew it would be excellent.

He took the dessert served by Jordan, waiting until all the women sat before asking, "Any word from Jericho?"

"We had a wire from him a couple of days ago telling us that he and Catherine had left New York City," Mrs. Blue said.

Jordan's eyes sparkled. "They should be home in another week or so."

"They've been gone so long," Marah said. "I hope Evie still remembers me."

"S-she will," Michal reassured her.

"Better than I did," Deborah quipped.

Bram chuckled, irritated when her smile faded. He bet she had smiled all day for Orr. Were any of these females going to mention the store clerk's visit?

He knew Deborah wouldn't, so he would bring it up himself.

He took a sip of coffee. "Anything happen today?"

"Mitchell came out," Marah said.

"That right?" Bram kept his gaze on Deborah, who stared at her pie. She wouldn't look at him.

Her sisters' gazes went to her expectantly, but it was Jordan who finally answered, "Yes."

"Was he making a delivery?"

"No," Marah said.

Jordan glanced across the table at her older sister, who took a dainty bite of her dessert. "He just came to see Deborah."

"I thought he was sweet on somebody." Bram barely kept from growling the words.

"A widow in Merkel," Marah supplied. "Mitchell said they had decided to go their separate ways."

Which meant Orr was free to make his *separate* way to Deborah. Bram gripped his fork tight enough to bend it. Was the store clerk planning to court her? What were his intentions?

Last night Bram had told her that he hadn't forgotten how she'd planned to leave him. That their kiss never should've happened. Still, he couldn't seem to dismiss the burning need to know everything that had passed between Deborah and Orr.

He tried to make his voice casual, which was

difficult since he spoke through gritted teeth. "How long did he stay?"

"A couple of hours," Jessamine answered.

Two hours!

Marah wiped her mouth with one of Mrs. Blue's fancy cloth napkins and said indignantly, "He almost stepped on Felix."

"That was an accident," Deborah said, still not looking at him. "He apologized."

She hadn't made eye contact with Bram once since he'd arrived. It went all over him. Determined to change that, he pushed away his empty dessert plate. "You outdid yourself on the pecan pie, Deborah."

"Thank you." She aimed a smile his way, a polite blank smile that made him want to haul her outside and kiss her until she got mad or gave in.

He had questions for her, questions he didn't want to ask in front of the others. The conversation turned to a wounded bird Marah had found, then to illustrations Jordan had drawn for the youngest of Deborah's future students.

Bram ground his teeth. He didn't know if she still planned to teach in Abilene.

After supper she excused herself to help her mother clean up. She obviously intended to make sure he didn't have a chance to talk to her.

Blood boiling, he thanked the women for

the meal and stepped out into the fading sunset. Questions about Orr burned in his brain. Bram told himself he had no business asking her anything, no business wondering about the other man's intentions. It didn't stop him wanting to know.

He checked on Scout and the Blues' mare, Addy, as well as their milk cow before he looked for signs that someone else might've been there. He found boot and hoofprints. The fact that they were on the road that led straight here from Whirlwind and back told Bram they belonged to Orr.

By the time he made one last pass around the house and the yard, night had settled in. He headed for the barn and the bunk that had been set up for him. Pulling his shirt over his head, he hung it on a peg beside one that held two bridles. He left his boots and pants on, then lay down.

On the other side of the barn wall, he heard the horses grazing. A puff of wind blew across Bram's sweat-dampened chest and he shifted against the scratchy sheet at his back. The crickets seemed particularly noisy tonight. In the far distance, he thought he heard the howl of a coyote.

Moonlight filtered through a crack in the wall and he stared at it as the conversation at supper

circled around in his head—as well as the fact
that Deborah would barely look at him. When
she finally had, it was as if he were a damn
stranger. He guessed he practically was.

Bram wished he could just forget her the way
she'd forgotten him.

He was about to doze off when a new sound
from outside caught his attention. Propping himself up on one elbow, he listened hard, trying to
identify it. The noise came from the direction
of the house.

The creak of a board had him reaching for
his Peacemaker and quietly getting to his feet.
Thumbing down the hammer, he sidled up to
the open doorway and peered right, then left.
And froze.

Deborah stood on the stoop, resting against
a porch column. Her face was tilted up toward
the clear starry sky, her eyes closed. Silver light
skimmed her delicate profile and the dark silky
braid hanging down her back. His gaze moved
over her slender curves, taking in her loosely
belted wrapper, the pale cotton of her nightgown
in the vee of the robe.

The slight breeze molded the lightweight fabric to her full breasts and flat belly, causing him
to curl his free hand into a fist. A pair of fancy

slippers peeped out from under the hem of her wrapper.

Why was she out here? Had she experienced another nightmare like the one she'd had at the cabin when he'd first found her?

It hit him that he had no idea if she'd had more bad dreams since returning home. He hadn't asked. Tightness stretched across his chest.

Bram told himself to go back inside the barn, but he was already moving toward her. He released the hammer on his revolver. "Everything okay?"

She jumped, her eyes flying open, her hand going to her chest. "You scared the daylights out of me!" she whispered harshly.

"Sorry." Closer now, he could see how the pale light turned her eyes a silvery-blue. And he could smell the clean musky scent of her skin beneath that of the prairie grass.

"Are you okay?" he asked again.

"I'm fine." She pulled the belt of her wrapper tight, taking a step back. Her gaze slid across his bare shoulders, lingered on his chest.

The flash of hunger in her eyes had his entire body going hard. He wanted to pin her against that column and kiss her silly. Instead, he focused on his original concern.

His attention locked on the pulse tapping frantically in her throat as he asked quietly, "Night-mare?"

Surprise flashed across her features. "Just... couldn't sleep."

"Neither could I." What had kept her awake? It damn sure better not have been thoughts of Mitchell Orr.

She pushed away from the wood support post. "Good night."

He should let her leave. He had every intention of doing just that; instead he stepped up on the porch, blocking her way. "Did you invite Orr out here?"

"What if I did?"

"Did you?" It drove Bram crazy to think so.

She glared. "As you reminded me last night, things between you and me are over."

His jaw nearly snapped in two. *"Did you?"*

"No."

The tension across his shoulders coiled tighter. He should drop it, but he couldn't seem to shut up. "What in the Sam Hill could you possibly talk about with him for two hours?"

"He asked if you and I were courting."

Bram stilled. "What did you tell him?"

"I started to say no. Absolutely not." Her voice was like velvet-covered steel as she stared him square in the eye. "But I recalled that he did see us together in town."

Bram was glad for that. Whether he should or not, he didn't want Mitchell or any other man sniffing around her.

"When he saw Duffy helping Mother with some chores, he asked if you'd sent him here. Mitchell offered to lend a hand so Duffy could go home."

Bram knew good and well Orr would have lent a lot more than that, given the chance. "What else did he offer?"

Her mouth flattened. "He asked if he could take me for a drive sometime."

"Well, he can't." The words shot out of Bram's mouth so fast, he was surprised they didn't burn his tongue. Savage emotion knotted his gut. Emotion he had no place feeling.

She angled her chin in that stubborn way she had, the action so much like her old self that he blinked.

"Not that it's your place to dictate anything," she reminded him coolly. "But I told him I wasn't sure."

"You can't go unless one of my men or I go with you."

"I believe that would defeat the purpose." The

sweetness in her voice belied the sharpness of her gaze.

The thought that the other man might get her alone and try to kiss her or touch her or do anything Bram was aching to do made his finger twitch on the trigger. "It's not safe."

"He's not a danger."

"He's not the one I'm worried about. It's Cosgrove."

"Which is all that matters, isn't it?"

His eyes narrowed. "To your safety, yes."

"To your revenge," she snapped. Pulse beating frantically in her throat, she curled her hands into fists. "Don't pretend the reason you're concerned about Cosgrove is because you care about me."

He did care, dammit, and wished he didn't. Still, he didn't want to hurt her again, although apparently he had. He could see pain in her eyes right now. "Deborah—"

"I'm as ready for this to be over as you are." Her voice cracked as she moved past him and let herself back into the house.

The soft scuff of her slippers faded. He wanted to slam his fist into the wall. After a moment, the haze of anger cleared and Bram headed back to the barn, biting off a curse.

He was the one who had put this distance between them and she was giving him exactly what he wanted. Didn't mean he had to like it.

She was Bram's bait for a trap. Nothing else.

Deborah repeated that to herself a hundred times over the next several days. Sometimes she sensed more between them, a connection. The truth was they didn't really have one.

He wanted distance. She'd given it to him. Which meant he had no business asking her questions about Mitchell Orr or any other man.

She had been careful to have only minimal contact with him. Still, she hadn't stopped thinking about that kiss they had shared.

No. It seemed that was one thing she couldn't forget.

You may have forgotten what happened between us, but I haven't.

The words still stung. She should be glad he was making it so easy for her to stay away from him. Even so, he had given no sign that he even noticed she was avoiding him. That was fine with her.

A week after their midnight discussion on the back stoop, she woke just before dawn and dressed, then headed out to the barn to milk Bossy. The cow stayed in one of the far stalls, so Deborah intended to use the back entrance in case Bram had risen. She had no desire to see him.

It wasn't until she was feet away from the barn that she realized milking was one of her normal chores. She had automatically gotten up and dressed, grabbed the pail from beside the sink and come outside.

Another memory! She wondered who had taken over the duty. As glad as she was for another small piece of her past, Deborah wanted to remember something significant like her life or what she'd been doing with Cosgrove.

The golden light of a lantern glowed inside the barn. As she reached the open doorway, she heard her sister's halting voice.

"Th-thank you."

Deborah smiled. Was Michal thanking the cow? On the rare occasion when Bossy became vexed, Deborah had sometimes talked to the animal, she remembered.

Just as she started to tease her sister, a deliciously sleep-husky masculine voice said, "It's not a problem."

Bram. She froze, peering carefully around the door frame into the barn. He was leaning over the cow's back talking to her sister, whose boot-shod feet and plain tan skirts she could see beneath the animal.

"Until Deborah remembers, I can help you."

Help with what? She should make her presence known or leave, but she couldn't make herself do either when she heard his next words.

"Milking is Deborah's chore, isn't it?"

"Y-yes, b-but I don't mind."

"How are things going with all of you and your sister?"

What did he care? Deborah thought hotly.

"F-fine."

"You still wanting to work for Josie in her sewing shop?"

"Yes, b-but I...I—"

"Take your time, Michal," Bram encouraged softly. "The way Deborah taught you."

She stilled. What had she taught her sister? Something to help her stuttering?

After a long moment the other woman said slowly, "I...want...to work there, but I...will put off the customers."

Deborah's heart squeezed hard.

"What does Josie say?" Bram asked.

"S-she doesn't think so."

"I'll help you practice."

"Y-you will?"

He would? Deborah inched closer to the doorway, aware of the smells of earth and hay and animal flesh. Thank goodness Bram wore a shirt.

She hadn't forgotten the sight of that wide bare chest and she would just as soon her sister not be treated to the same image.

"Sure, I'll help."

Deborah could hear a smile in his voice.

"I know Deborah used to work with you. I don't mind doing it until she's ready to take it up again."

"Thank you."

Yes, thank you. Deborah was grateful, although this wasn't helping to keep her guard up with him.

"What services do you offer in the sewing shop?"

A pause. "Everything from…"

Bram waited patiently.

The younger woman continued, "Making complete garments to mending."

"That was good. Do you replace buttons?"

"Yes."

"Ever made a man's coat before?"

Another pause. "I'm…making one for my brother for Christmas. It's a surprise. Don't… tell."

"Promise. How long would it take you to make me a couple of shirts?"

Deborah's chest swelled with emotion.

"Two days," Michal said. "If you're willing to pay extra."

Bram laughed, sending a shaft of pure warmth through her.

This was the man she'd fallen in love with. Deborah knew it deep inside. The realization that he was also the man she had planned to leave sobered her.

"You wouldn't sew someone's sleeves closed so a body couldn't get their arms through, would you?" he asked her sister.

What? Deborah's eyes widened.

"That was…years ago," Michal answered. "I only did that to Jericho because he wouldn't take me to town with him."

"He still likes telling the story."

Michal laughed. "I guess it's kind of funny."

"It is," Bram said warmly.

It hurt to hear the two of them share a memory she didn't have, and Deborah admitted to a little resentment. Still, the sting was lessened by what Bram was doing for her sister.

"Do you think you and Deborah might ever patch things up?" Michal asked quietly.

Deborah's heart kicked hard. Probably not if he had his way. She waited for him to laugh harshly or snap at her sister.

Instead, his voice was low with regret. "I don't know, kiddo."

A painful lump rose in her throat and she blinked back tears.

Michal said, "I wouldn't mind having another brother."

He gave an exaggerated groan. "I'm not sure I'm up for three more sisters on top of the females I've already got at home."

The knot in Deborah's throat spread to her chest and she eased back against the barn wall, fighting resentment and sadness.

The pounding of hooves made her look up. Though the pink light of dawn told her it was probably Amos coming to relieve Bram, her pulse spiked anyway—then took off racing when Bram appeared in the barn doorway.

Weapon in hand, muscles coiled, he had his gun aimed at her. She gasped and he immediately lowered the revolver.

Expecting him to dismiss her, she was surprised when he didn't, though his gaze clearly questioned why she stood there.

"I heard a horse." His eyes narrowed on her. "Were you eavesdropping?"

"Yes." She curled her fingers tightly over the milk pail's handle. "I— Thank you."

"For what?"

His gruff voice sent a shiver through her. "For being kind to my sister."

He stared at her for a long moment, his hot gaze trailing down her body. It was the first time in a week that the chill in his eyes had thawed. Deborah fought the urge to move nearer.

"You're welcome," he said gruffly.

There it was again. The closeness she'd felt to him the other night. Right on its heels came a sudden flutter of panic.

She was falling for him all over again and that was the worst thing that could happen. Because the connection Deborah felt to Bram might be new to her, but it was over for him.

That afternoon, Bram was being tossed and yanked around on the back of a black-and-white paint he was saddle breaking. Sweat trickled down the side of his face and he could feel the late-day heat roasting his back as if he wore no shirt.

The horse twisted and reared, trying every awkward angle she could to throw him. The muscles in his arms burned and the strain worked through his legs as he fought to keep his seat. His teeth snapped together every time the mare threw back her head with a powerful lunge of her body.

He barely managed to avoid getting his leg crushed when she tried to slam him into the side of the corral. Together with his brother, he had been working with the mare for over a week.

Finally she began to calm, bucking only occasionally. In a low voice, he said, "Whoa." He matched the directive with a smooth pressure on the reins.

Once the mare stilled, he walked her around the corral until she responded immediately to his commands and the pressure of his knees.

When he finally dismounted, she stood quietly as he ran a hand down her sweat-soaked neck and slipped the bridle over her head.

The horse's sides heaved just as Bram's did. Her black-and-white hide was dark with perspiration. As battered as he was, he still didn't feel as bruised as he did any time he looked at Deborah.

She thought all he cared about was revenge on Cosgrove. That should've been all he cared about, but if that were the case, he wouldn't want her clear to his back teeth.

And he wouldn't still be thinking about apologizing for telling her he'd kissed her only because she had asked. His conscience had gotten all stirred up this morning when she had thanked him for being kind to Michal.

Pushing away the thoughts, Bram dragged off the paint's saddle and blanket. She tossed her head and wheeled sharply, loping to the far corner of the corral. Hefting the saddle and tack over his shoulder, he let himself out, shut the gate and returned everything to its place in the barn. Then he headed for the pump.

After carrying a pail of water to the horse, Bram removed his hat and peeled off his shirt. Holding a piece of toweling in the same hand he used to operate the pump, he stuck his head under the cool gush of water.

Ever since their heated discussion on the back porch, he had been careful not to spend much time with her. He needed to let her go. That's what he had to do.

After a good dousing, he released the handle. He grabbed the towel and wiped his face, then rubbed the cloth over his head to dry his hair.

A low quiet voice sounded behind him. "Ross."

Bram turned to see Deborah's brother, Jericho. Holding the reins of his Appaloosa mare, the man stood there with a scowl on his stern features. The former Texas Ranger was tall, lean and deadly with a gun, despite one lame hand.

Bram shoved his wet hair back with one hand,

offering the other. They shook hands. "Didn't know you were back from New York."

"We arrived last night."

So why was the big man here instead of with his mother and sisters? Unless... "Did you already stop to see your family?"

"Yeah. Catherine and the baby are still there."

"So what brings you here?" Bram was afraid he knew.

"I have some questions, starting with what the hell is going on with you and my sister?"

Chapter Nine

Bram froze. "You stopped in town on your way out to see your family."

Jericho nodded. "And I'm not likin' what I heard."

Jake had mentioned there being talk in Whirlwind. Because Bram knew the likely source was Millie Jacobson, he had discounted it, thinking people would do the same. Evidently he'd been wrong.

He swiped the towel across his wet shoulders. "Want to go in the house?"

The man's blade-sharp gaze panned the yard, then shifted to the house. Bram could hear his family's voices inside.

"Let's talk in the barn," Jericho said.

Bram nodded. The former lawman wanted

to keep anything about his sister private. Bram wished he could've done the same, but short of hobbling Millie's lip, he didn't know how he could have.

Jericho left his horse at the water trough and followed Bram into the shade of the barn, palming off his light-colored hat.

Figuring this would take a while, Bram leaned against the corner of a stall. "How much do you know?"

"My ma told me what's going on." He stood with his arms folded, his feet planted wide. "I want to hear it from you."

Bram fingered the bullet graze on his right cheek. "Starting with me chasing Cosgrove from the shoot-out at Theo Julius's ranch?"

"Start with when you found my sister at your cabin."

Bram nodded. "I tracked Cosgrove's horse there from Monaco, but he wasn't there. Deborah was. I had no idea she'd been anywhere near him. No one did, because she'd left a note for your family saying she was going on to Abilene for her meeting with the school board."

"But she was forced to write the note."

"That's what your ma and sisters believe."

"Was she hurt when you found her?"

"She had cuts and bruises."

Jericho paced to the next stall. "Was she... Had she been—"

"No," Bram said quickly.

A pained look crossed the other man's face. "Could that be another thing she's forgotten?"

"Maybe, because she can't recall anything that happened in Monaco, but Annalise believes that Deborah wasn't hurt that way."

"Annalise checked her out?"

"Yes."

"Good." Jericho exhaled loudly. "When you found Deborah, she had no memory?"

"That's right," Bram agreed.

"How does that happen?"

"I don't know. And neither does Annalise. She's waiting on a letter from a doctor friend of hers in Philadelphia who's had a patient like Deborah before."

The other man was quiet for a moment. "Talk about the money."

"She had forty thousand dollars with her, the same amount Cosgrove robbed from the bank."

Jericho moved in front of Bram, a dangerous glint in his eyes. "So, you decided to bring the money home with her and use her as bait to draw out Cosgrove."

"It started out that way," Bram admitted.

"And now?"

"It's still the one thing that I know will get that bastard here."

"And what about my sister's safety?"

"She has protection twenty-four hours a day. Me and two of my ranch hands, both excellent shots."

A muscle bunched in Jericho's jaw. "Where's the money now? Here at your ranch?"

"No. It's been returned to the bank and they've agreed to keep silent about it. In exchange, I promised them Cosgrove."

"I don't know if that's better or worse." The other man ran a hand through his hair, then re-settled his hat on his head. "Has there been any sign of him?"

"Not yet. My men and I check the area hourly for new footprints, any signs of a presence other than ours. Davis Lee wired all the law-men around about the lowlifer being on the loose and he hasn't had any news."

"I plan to talk to him, too." Jericho leveled a look at him. "Why didn't you let me know what was going on? You can imagine how I took it coming from Millie Jacobson."

Bram straightened. "That wasn't an attempt to hide anything. Everything was after the fact. By the time I found out Deborah had been grabbed by Cosgrove, she was safe with me. The only other thing I could've told you was that she had no memory of herself or anyone else. There was nothing you could've done."

"Has she recalled *anything?* She didn't know me, Catherine or the baby."

"She's recalled a couple of things, but none that even hint at what went on between the time she left and when I found her. Something happened to her, but she still doesn't know what."

"I can understand why you didn't contact me, but I don't like that you're using her to bait a trap for that bastard."

"She's as safe as she can possibly be. The rest of your family, too. She won't get hurt. None of them will."

"I hope you mean that."

"I do." Bram frowned, slinging the towel over his shoulder.

"Good, then you can tell me what you plan to do about compromising her reputation."

"What do you mean? Yes, we spent the night together in a cabin, but nothing happened. There was a dust storm. What were we supposed to do? If we hadn't taken shelter together, we could've died."

Jericho nodded. "I agree there was no alternative."

"Well, then?"

"Millie isn't going to let this go. I suspect it's already spreading like wildfire. When I told Ma that the gossip wouldn't hold water because you and Deborah are engaged, she said that was no longer the case."

"That's right." Bram shifted from one foot to the other. "We broke things off the night before she left home."

"So you can see why your night together is damaging to her?"

Yes, Bram saw it. "Short of stringing Millie up, what do you think I can do about it?"

Jericho nailed him with a look. "There's one way to stop the gossip."

It took a moment for Bram to grasp the meaningful look on the other man's face. "You can't mean marriage!"

"Not at this point, but—"

"But what!" Bram shoved a hand through his still-damp hair. "Get engaged? Some old biddy is not going to dictate to me like that."

Jericho took a step toward him. "We aren't only talking about you."

"He's right," a familiar voice said.

Bram glanced over to see his brother in the doorway. Inwardly, he groaned.

Jake walked in, greeting Jericho with a nod

before his black gaze homed in on Bram. "An engagement would at least hinder the gossip."

This was a bad idea all the way around. "Y'all don't know that I asked Deborah to marry me and she said no. She was going to teach. That was the night before she left with that bastard Cosgrove."

"It's doubtful you'll have to go through with a wedding," his brother mused as if Bram hadn't spoken. "Just stay together long enough to shut Millie up."

"That could work," Jericho said quietly.

There suddenly seemed to be no air in the barn. Feeling cornered, Bram looked from one man to the other. "This is plumb crazy."

"Maybe so," Jericho said. "But my sister's reputation is being ruined."

"That's not my fault."

"It's no one's fault," the former Ranger said.

"But it's on you as much as it is her," Jake added.

Bram glared. "Has it occurred to either of you that she might not be willing to go along with this?"

Looking frustrated, Jericho pinched the bridge of his nose.

Jake folded his arms. "You need to at least talk to her, Bram. See what she thinks."

Hell! He wanted to flat-out refuse, but he couldn't dismiss the fact that this gossip could ruin her. Might already be doing so. Still, a fake engagement, no matter the duration, would tangle him up even more with her. He was trying to let her go. But he didn't want Deborah to pay for something innocent that was being turned into something ugly. And she would bear the brunt of the damage, Bram knew.

Even so, neither her brother nor his had any idea how prickly things were between Deborah and him. Recalling the argument they'd had the night he had called it quits, he shook his head. "She's liable to refuse and I can't force her to become my fiancée."

"Just talk to her," Jake urged.

Jericho nodded. "My sister is a practical woman. She'll see the merit."

Feeling completely whipped, Bram closed his eyes. "Fine. I'll talk to her. That's all I can promise."

"Thanks." The former lawman shook his hand. "I knew you'd do the right thing."

Bram nodded.

"You can add me to guard duty," Jericho said. "That will knock everyone back to six hours."

"All right, thanks."

"Noon shift?"

"Whatever you want."

"I'd like to know when you talk to Deborah."

"Okay." He watched as Jericho walked out and rode off. He wasn't convinced this was the right thing to do, but he didn't know what was.

Jake studied him. "It's obvious you still care about her."

"That's the damn problem," Bram muttered, tension coiling through him.

"If she's your fiancée, the talk will die down."

"I know that's the hope. She won't be my real fiancée. I'm not proposing to her again."

"You don't have to. Just tell her what's going on. This really is the only way to salvage anything of her reputation."

He needed to let her go, not yoke up with her again.

Oh, hell. He might as well get this over with and talk to her, see what she had to say.

She'd said no. Again. Bram still couldn't believe it. The next morning he dismounted near the church and tied Scout under a copse of trees with several other horses.

Last night he'd tried to explain to her the thinking behind his not-real proposal.

Her blue eyes had sparked with a temper he hadn't seen in a while. *Absolutely not. You nearly had apoplexy over that kiss. We are* not *getting engaged.*

Apoplexy was going a bit far, Bram thought. He'd liked that kiss, wanted to do it again, but that would be going backward. No matter what he had said, there was no reasoning with her. Jericho had said Deborah was practical. She was a mule-headed woman, was what.

Other horses grazed on the slope alongside his, and empty wagons lined up on Main Street. The singing inside confirmed that he was late for services.

He slipped in and sat in the back next to Quentin and Zoe Prescott, automatically seeking out Deborah. There she was, near the front with her family—and Mitchell Orr, whose blond hair stood out like cotton next to all the raven-haired Blue women. Bram clenched his jaw tight until he registered that Orr sat next to Michal, not Deborah. It wouldn't surprise Bram if her sisters had maneuvered things that way. He couldn't help a smile at that.

His attention shifted back to Deborah. A wispy white dress with blue stripes molded to her trim back and tapered in at her small waist. A waist he knew he could span with his hands.

Tiny sleeves bared the slender arms that had slid around him for that kiss. Her hair was swept up high in the back to fall in a midnight-black curtain to her shoulders, revealing the elegant line of her velvety neck. His gaze was riveted on the tender patch of skin behind her ear where he had put his mouth plenty of times.

Hmmph. Thinking like that only stirred him up, so he quit.

When services ended, he waited as people filed by. He spoke briefly to Zoe and Quentin, then Zoe's brother, Zeke. Chesterene Eckert gave Bram a pretty smile. When the redhead walked by with a young woman who was new to town, he saw her look back at Deborah.

"With one man a month ago," she said in a low voice to her friend. "And now she's with a different one."

Bram stiffened, glancing back. Orr wasn't even next to her. The store clerk was sandwiched between Michal and Jordan.

Frowning, he caught Deborah's gaze on him. Her eyes narrowed, which didn't stop him from looking his fill of her, from her flat-brim hat, over her full breasts and down to the black shoes peeping out from her skirts. Her features turned cool and challenging. That only put a throb of desire in his blood, which he doubted was her intention.

Stay away. Her message was clear and Bram was happy to oblige.

Last night she'd made him mad. He'd made her mad. Nothing he had said could sway her. Neither could anything her brother or mother said.

Well, Bram had done what her brother and his had wanted. That was the end of any engagement talk.

He made his way outside and helped Emma unload the hampers of food she'd brought for the all-church picnic. After setting the baskets in the shade of a sprawling oak his sister-in-law chose, he returned to the wagon for quilts to spread on the ground.

As if Deborah were a lodestone, Bram's gaze was drawn back to her. He admired the classic lines of her profile and her thick midnight-black hair. He wanted to put his hands in that mass of raven silk and mess it up. She looked so pretty as she stood talking to Josie and Davis Lee.

Mitchell Orr stopped to speak to her and Bram's eyes narrowed as he was hit with a savage sense of possession. Maybe one day he would stop feeling that she belonged to him. Because she didn't. Not anymore.

It took effort to look away from her. When he did, he caught Millie Jacobson with her eyeballs fixed on him. He tipped his hat to her and her two young daughters as they walked past with a woman Bram didn't know.

Millie's husband, Verle, didn't attend church. Bram couldn't blame the man, he thought darkly as he caught Millie's words to her friend.

"Deborah Blue." She pointed surreptitiously at Deborah then made a small gesture toward him. "Alone."

"Overnight?" The other woman sounded scandalized.

"Yes."

Bram's temper started to boil. If that gossipy hen were a man, he would call her out. He hoped Deborah hadn't seen the women whispering and pointing.

She stood holding her niece, Evie, when two little girls ran up to her. Millie's daughters.

They hugged Deborah, one of them having to stretch to reach her waist. With a surprised smile, she handed Evie to Marah and bent to speak to the children.

One of the little girls twirled, showing off her pinafore. The other fluttered a handkerchief in front of Deborah. She made a fuss over them, smiling warmly even though Bram knew she had no idea who they were.

She really would make an excellent teacher.

He wanted that for her. He just wanted her to do it here, where he could see her without an hours-long ride.

His smile faded when Millie marched up to her daughters, snapped out something and dragged them off with her.

The raw hurt on Deborah's face had Bram moving before he even realized it. What had that woman said? Why had she hurried her daughters away? Bram was afraid he knew.

The woman swept past him, towing the little girls in her wake. "You can't associate with her," she said to them.

"Why, Mama? I like Miss Deborah."

"She has low moral character."

Bram stopped dead, his hands balling into fists. Had he really just heard that? He started to turn and call to Millie, but he noticed Mrs. Blue and Jordan standing only feet away.

The pallor of their faces and the fury in their eyes told Bram they'd heard the woman's poison.

Catching Deborah's name again, he glanced around to see Chesterene and her friend under a nearby tree. Both were staring at Deborah and whispering.

Anger ripped through him and he thought his head might explode.

The gossip Jericho and Jake had mentioned

was worse than Bram had realized or would even have believed. At this rate, Deborah's reputation would be completely ruined by day's end. And at church, no less.

Had anyone ever done murder in a church-yard? He might be the first.

You could nip this in the bud, a little voice said. *Propose the fake engagement again.*

No! How many times did he have to be hit in the head with that board?

Still, he was the only one who could help her. Fully aware that she wouldn't welcome his assistance, Bram strode over to her anyway.

She had turned away, but he could see fury on Jericho's stern features. The big man's gaze was directed at Millie. Catherine's beautiful face was drawn and sad. She squeezed Deborah's hand.

Just remembering that comment from Millie to her daughters set Bram off all over again. Before he could talk himself out of it, he boomed, "I've come to claim my fiancée for lunch."

He slid an arm around Deborah's trim waist.

She went rigid, as he'd expected, and tried to pull away. "What do you think you're doing?"

His hold tightened as he bent to her. "Later you can cuss me out all you want, but for your sake, go along with this."

Approval glinted in her brother's eyes and

Catherine gave Bram a grateful smile. Behind her, Marah's and Michal's eyes went wide.

"We talked about this last night," Deborah said tersely.

Bram squeezed her waist. "Look around. People are staring and talking. This is more serious than I realized."

"He's right," Jericho said, his eyes as hard as steel.

Deborah tried again to step out of Bram's hold. He put his lips to her temple so anyone looking would think he was brushing a kiss against her skin. She froze.

"Millie's not the only one talking, Deborah. Chesterene is also taking you apart."

She looked up at him, blue eyes dark with hurt. "I thought it was just Millie."

The woman had done plenty of damage on her own. "Sorry."

"But I don't want to be engaged." Her voice trembled. "And neither do you."

"This is way past what either of us want." Her soft fresh scent drifted to him. "Unless you mean to send me packing in front of everyone, you're now my intended."

"You have to do it, Deborah," Catherine urged. "It isn't fair to either of you, but Bram's right. This is the only thing that will help your reputation."

Deborah's gaze sought her brother's.

The dark flush on his face showed he was still enraged, but he spoke in his usual calm tone. "I'm afraid so."

Bram felt the fight drain out of her.

"All right," she said quietly.

"I'll get a blanket and some food and meet y'all for lunch."

"Just come on, Bram." Catherine gave him a wobbly smile. "We have a quilt to sit on and plenty of food."

"All right." He moved his hand from Deborah's waist and would've stopped there if he hadn't seen Millie gaping.

He clasped Deborah's hand as they followed her family past the church to an ancient oak. Along the way, they passed Jake and Emma. His sister-in-law looked completely poleaxed at his announcement, but Jake nodded to show he understood what was going on.

Bram helped Deborah take her seat on the quilt not far from where his family sat. He eased down beside her, but she wouldn't look at him. He couldn't even get mad at her. She didn't deserve any of this.

And Bram had just done what he'd sworn he wouldn't.

The harder they tried to steer clear of each other, the closer they got.

And now they were engaged.

Which neither of them wanted.

Well, she couldn't be mad at him now. An hour later, after they had eaten lunch with her family, Deborah wavered between gratitude and irritation. Last night, Bram's duty-like proposal had angered her, but she couldn't be cross this time.

He had just announced to the entire town that they were again a couple and he'd done it because some women were saying bad things about her. She hadn't realized the damage that was being done to her reputation until Bram had told her.

First they were engaged. Then they weren't. Now they were.

She needed a headache powder.

Sunlight filtered through the spreading branches overhead and Bram's shadow stretched over her as he stood and held out his hand. "Let's go for a walk."

She looked around nervously. "I think I've been the topic of conversation enough today."

"That's exactly why we're going." He bent

and cupped her elbow, helping her to her feet. "To show Millie Slack Jaws and her friends that we've—*you've*—done nothing wrong."

She searched his blue eyes, not protesting when he tucked her hand in the crook of his arm. She glanced down at Jericho, who leaned back against the tree with Catherine. Jessamine had taken the baby to their house for a nap.

"Bram's right," her brother said. "If you hide, Mrs. Jacobson will just have more to talk about."

"Ooh, that woman makes me so mad," Catherine said.

She made Deborah mad, too. "Very well."

She nodded at Bram and they began their walk by heading toward the church. He settled his hat on his head and she adjusted hers, too. The blue ribbon matching the stripe in her dress fluttered from the flat brim.

The sleeves of his white shirt were rolled up to reveal strong hair-dusted forearms. Beneath her touch, Deborah felt his hard muscles and the heat of his body.

No one would've blamed him for not caring what the gossip might do to her. Last night she had been clear about not wanting a fake engagement. She knew her brother had played a part in Bram's suggesting it, but Jericho had nothing to do with what had happened earlier.

Bram's actions weren't driven by a burning desire to be with her, but because that was the kind of man he was. Wishing he might change his feelings about her was fanciful. And dangerous. Still, she couldn't let his action go unrecognized.

They walked past Lizzie and Cal Doyle, and his brother, Jed.

Deborah took a deep breath. "I wasn't gracious about it, but I appreciate what you did. And what you're doing."

"You're welcome." He smiled down at her, and for a moment she went dizzy.

Every time he flashed that dimple, it chipped away at more of the distance she'd put between them. Made her start thinking that things between them were something that they weren't.

"I didn't know the gossip was this bad," she said quietly.

"It's vicious." His handsome features hardened into a cold mask as he glanced in Millie's direction.

"Maybe this will be the end of you rescuing me."

"That's not how I look at it. You didn't do anything wrong. You shouldn't have to suffer for it and I'm not going to let you twist in the wind."

"Thank you."

He walked her past Millie and Chesterene, all but daring them to say something. Deborah adored him for that.

Adored? No, she corrected. She appreciated him for it. That was all.

They approached a dark-haired man who was lunging for a toddler and a blonde woman sitting on a quilt holding a baby.

"Do you recognize them?" Bram asked in a low voice.

"No."

"It's Riley and Susannah Holt."

"He's my cousin."

Bram looked at her in surprise.

"Jordan reminded me. And Davis Lee is his brother."

"Yeah." His eyes were soft on her face.

Riley scooped up the curly-haired toddler, her golden hair gleaming in the sun.

"Papa, don't drop Margaret!" the little girl shrieked as a rag doll fell from her chubby fingers.

The rancher caught it. "Here she is. She's okay, Button."

The child hugged the doll tight.

Bram smiled at the nickname Riley had called his adopted daughter since the day she was born.

Stepping into the shade of the pecan tree

where the Holts sat, Bram tugged at one of the little girl's curls. "Howdy, Miss Lorelai."

She buried her face in her father's neck, peeking out with big blue eyes.

Chuckling, Bram gestured to Susannah and the dark-haired little boy asleep on her shoulder. "Looks like Ben is tuckered out."

Deborah knew Bram was naming everyone for her benefit and she lightly squeezed his arm in gratitude.

Susannah stroked her son's hair. "He's had a full day. Learning to walk is hard work."

Riley shifted his daughter to his other arm. The little girl's curls were the same shade of gold as her mother's. The rancher's shrewd gaze moved from Deborah to Bram.

"I guess congratulations are in order."

Deborah felt Bram tense, but his tone was easy. "Thanks."

"Yes, thank you," she added.

Susannah looked up. "Have you talked about when you might have the wedding?"

Deborah almost choked.

Bram pressed her arm tight into him. "Not yet."

Riley's piercing blue eyes settled on Deborah. "Aunt Jess said you leave soon for your position in Abilene."

"Yes, in several weeks." Her mother had told her. That was why her family had found it so odd when Deborah had left a note saying she was going on to Abilene almost two months early.

She had yet to share with her family that she wasn't sure she still wanted to teach. And she would have to notify the school board. She felt like such a fraud. With a fake fiancé and a job she would probably quit.

"Good luck to you," Riley said.

Susannah nodded. "You'll do well."

"I hope so."

Nodding goodbye, Bram drew her away.

Deborah could feel Millie Jacobson's gaze boring into her back. "I think she heard every word."

"Well, I don't see how she could make anything bad out of that."

She hoped not. "How long have Riley and Susannah been married?"

"A little over two years." He grinned. "Her brother sent her to Whirlwind under the assumption that Riley wanted to marry her, but he knew nothing about it. And he didn't want to marry again."

"Again?" It was hard to picture the rugged rancher with another woman.

Bram sobered. "His first wife died in a dust

storm. That's another reason why I didn't think twice about both of us staying in that cabin. I'd do it the same way again."

She glanced back at Riley and Susannah. "They seem very happy."

"I think they are." He guided her up the slope behind the church. "Have you let the school board know you've changed your mind about the teaching position?"

"Not yet."

"You could always report for the job and still do it."

"Even if I wanted to, who would keep someone with no memory?"

"You're a good teacher."

She looked at him in surprise. "You don't have to say nice things just because we're alone."

Something flickered in his eyes. Irritation? "I'm not. It's the truth. You are a good teacher."

"But I don't know anything about myself. The only life I remember is what happened after you found me. I have no roots, no history."

"The board members don't have to be told that. Who knows? By the time school starts, you might have your memory back. Besides, you've recalled some of your education knowledge. If you had to, you could study up and probably learn it all again, double-quick."

She tilted her head. "Why are you encouraging me? You don't want me to teach."

He stopped, his gaze leveling on hers. "I didn't want you to leave in order to do it. There's a difference."

They both quieted as they approached his brother and sister-in-law.

A tow-haired toddler clomped over to them, green eyes sparkling. She lifted her arms expectantly. "Bwam, hold."

"Yes, ma'am, Molly." He swung her up, flipping her upside down. She gurgled with laughter.

Seeing him with the little girl made Deborah's breath catch. She swallowed past a lump in her throat to ask Emma how Bram's uncle and cousin were doing.

"On the mend," Jake's wife said with a quiet smile.

As they visited, Deborah noticed how Jake seemed to always be touching his wife. Or she was touching him. The adoring looks they shared made Deborah wonder if that had been the way she used to look at Bram.

Jake took a wiggling Molly from Bram. "Welcome to the family, Deborah."

"Thank you," she murmured, catching the curious gaze Jake shot Bram as they took their leave.

No doubt Bram would fill his brother in later. For a few moments, neither of them spoke.

Her gaze was caught by the way Bram's hair curled slightly at his bronzed nape. As they walked, the powerful length of his legs brushed against her skirts.

His dark hair made the blue of his eyes even more noticeable. The Sunday shirt he wore stretched across wide shoulders and tucked neatly into the lean waist of his dark trousers.

Every woman at the picnic, married or not, gave him at least one look.

For every person they saw, he gave her a name and a fact about them. He held her hand curled over his arm. She inhaled the deep male scent of him, fighting a sudden urge to rest against his solid muscled chest.

Occasionally he would look at her with a teasing warmth in his eyes. If she hadn't known better, she would have believed they were a couple.

She could follow his lead, pretend they were a couple in order to shut up Millie Jacobson and that girl Chesterene and anyone else who cared to gossip.

Still, Deborah's nerves stretched taut as they made their way around the church. They spoke to Ef Gerard and his wife, Naomi, as well as Russ and Lydia Baldwin. Deborah caught sight of the other Baldwin brother, Matt. Just as big as Russ, he stood between the church and the Whirlwind Hotel next to his fiancée, Annalise Fine. It was a great relief to Deborah to know someone by face and name.

The doctor came over to ask how Deborah was while Bram spoke to Matt. After a brief visit with the couple, she and Bram made their way back toward the church.

She was keenly aware of the weight of Millie Jacobson's disapproving stare.

She wanted away from the scrutiny and overly curious gazes, but the worst thing she and Bram could do right now would be to disappear from sight.

A sturdy red-haired man walked by, calling out his congratulations on their engagement.

"That's Hoot Eckert," Bram explained.

At Deborah's quick look, he nodded. "Yes, Chesterene's daddy. He runs the newspaper, *The Prairie Caller.* He's generally good at keeping things to himself, so I don't know where his daughter gets her leaky mouth."

The term startled a laugh out of her.

Bram grinned. "Haven't heard that one before?"

"Well, I don't *remember,*" she said smartly.

He chuckled, squeezing her fingers.

Several more people wished them well, making Deborah squirm inside. "We're lying to everyone."

"Because someone told lies about you," he reminded her with a scowl. "We're justified."

No matter how gallant he was, she knew he didn't really want to be here with her. "How long do you think we'll need to stay engaged?"

"I don't know. What Millie's done makes me want to burn some powder."

Was he this angry on her behalf? Deborah wondered. It was no small thing he had done for her.

They stopped at the side of the church beneath the overhang so they were out of the sun. He looked down at her, smoothing a thumb over the furrow between her brows. "Stop fretting."

"I can't help it." She still held his arm with one hand. His eyes were dark and intense. "When you came to church this morning, you didn't know you'd be leaving with a fiancée."

"Neither did you."

"True, but it's so unfair to you."

"It'll be okay." He grazed her chin with his thumb, his gaze locked on her mouth. Anticipation hummed inside her. Was he going to kiss her?

She wished he would, but not out of duty or

because someone might be watching. She wanted him to kiss her because she was his…. Just *his*.

The thought startled her and she glanced away. No. No, no, no. She couldn't forget this relationship was only pretend.

"Surely our walk has satisfied even that Millie woman. You've done your duty and I thank you, but I'm sure you'd rather be somewhere else, probably with your family. We don't have to be together every minute, do we?"

"No," he said slowly, studying her face. "But it will look odd if you can't bear my company longer than this. We're supposed to be in love."

"But we're not." Her nerves twanged. "You made your feelings about us quite clear the other night."

His eyes narrowed. "You mean when we kissed?"

"When *I* kissed *you*. I believe that's the way you put it."

He didn't reply or stop her when she slid her hand from his arm. She turned to start back toward her family.

He snagged her wrist, his touch gentle yet firm. "Deborah, what I said that night? It wasn't true. The reason I kissed you wasn't because you asked. I wouldn't have done it if I hadn't wanted."

She faced him. "Then why did you tell me differently?"

"I just don't think I—" He broke off, visibly struggling with his words. "I don't think we should get involved again. That's what I should've said. When you get your memory back, you'll leave. That was your plan anyway."

She noticed that he didn't say his reason for keeping her at arm's length was that he didn't want her. A little thrill of excitement went through her at that.

"When things return to normal, I don't want you to feel that you have to stay in Whirlwind."

"Do you really think my life will ever return to normal?"

He was quiet for a long time, then said, "I don't know, but if it does, I want your choices to be your choices. I want you to be able to do what you want."

Her heart clenched tight. Right now she wanted to stay here with him. She knew she wasn't thinking clearly, because for the first time she wondered if she wanted to remember at all.

Chapter Ten

Deborah knew the magnitude of what Bram had done for her. So did her family, as evidenced by the fact they now believed he could walk on water.

Having attended church together two Sundays in a row, shopped together at Haskell's and dined at both The Pearl and The Fontaine, Bram and Deborah were getting good at acting like a couple.

Their appearance together earlier today at the wedding of Annalise Fine and Matt Baldwin had gone a long way toward convincing anyone who might be doubtful. The nuptials had also forced Deborah to admit she wanted another chance with Bram. She had no idea what he wanted, so she tried not to let her desire show and she checked herself every time she wanted to touch him.

A few hours after the wedding, she and her sisters were in the bedroom she shared with Jordan. A warm breeze came through the open window, making the lamplight flicker and swirl. Beneath the smells of prairie grass and dirt was Jessamine's rosewater fragrance.

Michal lay on the bed beside Marah, chin propped in her hands. "That was the most beautiful wedding," she said dreamily.

Jordan sat on the edge of the mattress, brushing her hair. "Annalise just glowed."

"Probably because it was hot as blazes," Marah said matter-of-factly.

Deborah laughed along with the others.

Michal tugged their youngest sister's braid. "You're so romantic."

Marah stretched out on her stomach beside Michal. Like the rest of them, she wore her sleeveless summer-weight nightgown.

Deborah moved in front of the mirror, removing the pins from her chignon and shaking out her hair.

She picked up the brush just as Jordan asked, "Do you ever think anymore about marrying Bram? I mean, I know you two aren't really together, but he still looks at you like you hung the moon."

Deborah certainly hadn't noticed that. She glanced in the mirror, noting that her sisters were watching her curiously. "He isn't interested in that any longer."

"If he said so, he's lying," Michal said.

Deborah paused in braiding her hair, glancing at her sister.

Marah pushed herself to a sitting position. "What if he was interested?"

"I don't know." She turned back to the looking glass and continued plaiting her thick tresses.

Jordan moved up beside her and Deborah eased to the left to make room. When she glanced at her sister's reflection, she was taken aback at how much alike they looked. Enough so that she was disoriented for a moment.

They had the same slight widow's peak, the same blue eyes, the same arch to their eyebrows. Yet Deborah's hair was straight, while Jordan's had a wave. Her sister unwound the white ribbon she wore in her hair, the one Deborah had lent her. The one Jordan had given her this past Christmas.

Before Deborah could get excited about remembering something new, a crush of images flooded her mind. The first time she'd walked Jordan to school, her family's trip from Uvalde to Whirlwind, the day Jericho had left home.

Almost dizzy, she sat down on the edge of the bed, hard.

"What is it?"

"What's wrong?"

Her sisters' voices jumbled together, sounding as if they were coming from a distance. Deborah was bombarded with flashes, pictures, words. They were all indistinct and fuzzy. More impressions than recognizable pieces. None seemed to fit together. Were they memories or just cast-off bits of the life she'd forgotten?

Slowly the images came into focus, began to slip into place like a puzzle. Entire pictures formed. They felt familiar, filling her with relief. They weren't random images! They were memories. *Her* memories.

Overwhelmed, she felt her chest tighten. She became aware of concerned voices and realized they belonged to her sisters. Gradually their anxiety penetrated her spinning thoughts and she looked up, trying to steady herself. She recalled her entire life before and after falling in love with Bram—the first time she'd met him, their first kiss.

"Deborah?"

Her mother had come in. She bent and gave her a little shake. "Honey, what's wrong?"

"Nothing." Still dazed and disbelieving, she gave a small laugh as her sisters gathered around. "I think I'm remembering."

"What?"

"Really?"

"Wonderful!"

Her siblings all spoke at once. Their voices grew louder as Deborah's own excitement rose.

"When's my birthday?" Marah asked.

"August ninth."

Michal leaned in. "Where did we live before Whirlwind?"

"Uvalde." Heart racing, Deborah stood. "I was going to teach school there. Until Sean."

Jordan squeezed her hand. "How old were you when Pa died?"

"Five. Jericho was twelve. You were all under four."

Marah let out a loud whoop. "You really do remember!"

Jessamine hugged her tight as the girls continued to pepper her with questions. Deborah laughed from sheer joy.

Suddenly her mother stilled, her head turned toward the wall as she listened hard. "Oh!"

Not until Jessamine left the room did Deborah hear a heavy pounding on the door.

"What's going on in there?"

Bram. She grabbed her wrapper, shrugging into it and tying the belt as she hurried into the front room.

Her sisters followed.

Jessamine opened the door and motioned the big man inside.

Taking off his hat, he stepped over the threshold, his sharp gaze checking each of them. One big hand rested on the butt of the revolver hanging low on his hip. "What's all the ruckus? Y'all about made my heart stop!"

"Deborah remembers!" Marah exclaimed.

Surprise flared in his blue eyes. "That right?"

His gaze was so intent on her, so piercing that all she could manage was a nod.

Despite the leashed energy vibrating from him, he moved his hand away from his gun. "Do you recall how you came to be with Cosgrove?"

"The day of the shoot-out at Theo Julius's ranch, he showed up here." She cleared her throat, her voice growing stronger. "He threatened to hurt Mother and the girls if I didn't go with him. He wanted to use me as a hostage."

"In case I caught up to him," Bram said flatly.

"Yes. He said it was also because anyone look-

ing for a lone male rider would pass him by if he
had a woman along."

"See, Bram," Marah said. "Deborah *was*
forced to write that note and go with that polecat."

"Sure enough." He smiled, but it didn't reach
his eyes.

Jordan eased up beside Deborah. "She's remembered all kinds of stuff from before we
came to Whirlwind."

"What about after?" Tension coiled in his
body as he searched Deborah's face.

His intense regard had her nerve endings
stinging. "We arrived here two years ago for
Jericho and Catherine's wedding. You and I met
at their wedding."

One side of his mouth hitched up in a half
grin. "I remember."

She smiled at his teasing tone, aware of the
other women laughing softly. He had later told
her he had been smitten the first moment he'd
talked to her. Her heart clenched hard at that.

In the flickering lamplight, his eyes glittered.

"That was also the night Ian McDougal escaped from jail and Davis Lee went after him,"
she said. "So did Josie, because Ian killed her
family."

Bram nodded, his expression pleased and concerned at the same time.

Her mother hugged her. "Do you remember the first time you accepted an invitation from Bram?"

"Yes." Deborah watched him as closely as he watched her. "We went riding. To the creek behind your house."

"We had a picnic," he said gruffly.

They had also shared their first kiss.

They had taken off their shoes and socks to wade in the water. She had slipped and almost fallen, but Bram had managed to catch her. He swung her up in his arms, and after making sure she was all right, he'd kissed her. They had become so caught up in the moment that he had nearly dropped her and fallen himself.

Her mouth tingled at the memory. And the look on his face sent a shiver through the rest of her body. The searing desire in his eyes let her know he remembered, too.

She couldn't stop staring at his mouth as her sisters named other things she and Bram had done together. They had attended the grand opening of The Fontaine, Russ and Lydia Baldwin's hotel. Gone to J. T. Baldwin's wedding to Cora Wilkes, a widow from Whirlwind. Buggy rides, supper in town, horse races.

She recalled when her niece was born, when Bram's brother, Jake, married the woman he'd hired to take care of the baby abandoned on his doorstep.

"Remember the tie party at this year's Founder's Day celebration?" Marah asked.

Because Bram had managed to end up with the tie that matched Deborah's dress, they had spent the whole day together. That night, behind The Pearl restaurant, they'd gone further physically than ever before.

With unsettling clarity, she recalled the feel of his mouth on her neck, the swell of her breasts. Her gaze shot to his. He was staring at her with a raw hunger on his face that he quickly masked. Her stomach dipped.

After an hour of reminiscing, she noticed her mother and sisters hiding yawns. Bram noticed, too.

He bid them good-night and with one last heated look, he left and closed the door.

As she climbed into bed with Jordan, Deborah smiled. She'd remembered at last! Well, she knew her life before and after Bram. Not one thing about what had happened in Monaco. Which dragged at her relief and excitement over the progress she had made.

While that worried her, what kept her awake

was the argument she'd had with Bram the night he had proposed. An argument she recalled in full detail. An argument she still didn't understand.

He had never explained why he was so dead set against her leaving to teach. That night, he had made her so mad that she hadn't asked why, but she wasn't mad now and she wanted an answer.

Bram was mostly happy that Deborah had finally regained her memory. Only mostly, because he fully expected now she would leave as she'd planned all along. He was glad he hadn't let himself get involved with her again. Betrothal aside.

Two hours after the women finally quieted down, Bram made one last pass around the house and barn. He stripped off his shirt and lay down, but he couldn't sleep. It was too hot and he was too wound up over Deborah.

He rose and stepped outside, staring up at the stars sprinkled across the clear dark sky. The moon hung fat and low, veiling everything in silver.

The muffled sound of a door opening and closing made him slide his Peacemaker from the holster hanging off the stubby bedpost. Gun leveled, he turned toward the house.

Gasping, Deborah stopped midstep, holding her hands up. "It's me."

"Don't sneak around." He lowered his weapon. "You know I'm armed."

"Sorry. I wanted to talk to you."

"Did you remember something else? Something about Monaco?"

"No."

He couldn't tell if she was anxious about that. "You'll probably recall things soon."

"I hope so."

He eyed her curiously as he returned his gun to his holster.

She stepped down and moved toward him. In the moonlight, her skin shone like polished ivory. Midnight-black hair draped over her shoulder in a thick braid. The wrapper she wore was loosely belted, drooping to the side to reveal the strap of her nightgown. The shadowed swell of her breasts showed in the vee of her robe.

Her gaze did a slow glide over his chest, then the rest of him.

Body going tight, he swallowed hard. His words came out unintentionally harsh. "What did you want to talk to me about?"

"I remember the fight we had the night you proposed."

Bram wanted to get his hands on her, his mouth. It was a good bet she hadn't come out here for that. He focused on her face. "And?" he demanded impatiently.

"Why were you so set against me leaving for that teaching job?"

He didn't want to dance this dance again. Now that she remembered, what was the point in dragging everything back up?

"Go back inside. I can't look at you half-dressed like that without—"

"Without what?"

He moved closer, looming over her, trying to intimidate her into going back inside. "Without wanting to peel you out of those nightclothes."

"Oh," she breathed, looking interested. In the pale light, he saw a slash of color darken her cheekbones, but she didn't step away. She didn't look as if she was going to budge at all. "Don't try to distract me. Why were you so set against me leaving for that job?"

He folded his arms. "Seems normal to me that a man would want his fiancée to stay near him."

"It was more than that, or at least something besides that."

"Sounds like you have it figured out." He turned to go back inside the barn.

"Please don't do that," she said quietly. "Don't dismiss me."

He glanced over his shoulder and the plea in her eyes tugged hard at him. Damn. After a long moment, he faced her. "All right."

"Your not wanting me to leave had something to do with your mother, didn't it?"

He shoved a hand through his hair. "Why does it matter? You're leaving anyway, aren't you? Have you resigned from that job yet?"

"No. Please answer my question. I've asked you twice."

"We're not even together anymore." He read the protest on her face, figured she was fixing to bring up their present "engagement." "Not in truth anyway."

She angled her chin at him. "This is how you were that night, too. Stubborn. Cutting me off."

"Me! You'd just agreed to marry me, then in the next breath you said you were leaving. I wanted you to be my wife." He gritted out the words.

"But not enough to wait for me."

"That cuts both ways, sweetheart. You wanted to be my wife, but not enough to stay."

"I had already given up my dream for one man. I wasn't going to do it again."

"Don't talk about other men." Bram narrowed his eyes, hands clenching into fists. "This is between you and me."

"I know that." Though anger flashed in her eyes, he could tell she was trying to calm herself. "Keeping our relationship together would've required sacrifice on both our parts, but we could've done it. We could have written to each other and I would've come home at Christmas."

"And what about when your contract was up?" He braced his hands on his hips. "Would you have stayed another school term? Then another?"

"No. I contracted for two. That was all. You knew that." She paused, looking stricken. "That's it, isn't it? You believed I wouldn't come back even though I gave you my word. How could you think that? I'd never broken your trust before."

"You'd never wanted anything that badly before either," he muttered. "You sure never wanted me that badly."

Sadness flickered across her face. "You think I wanted that more than I wanted to be your wife?"

"I proposed. You planned to leave."

"Did you only ask me to marry you so I wouldn't go to Abilene?"

"No, but even if I had, it didn't work, did it? You still planned to run off."

"I wasn't running off!" She threw up her hands. "I would've come back."

"My ma never did." Though the words were true, Bram immediately regretted saying them.

Deborah let out a big sigh that sounded like relief. "I knew she had something to do with this. Maybe she was a victim of circumstances and she couldn't come back."

He barked out a laugh. "Frannie Ross wasn't a victim of anything."

"How do you know?" Deborah took a step toward him, hurt flaring in her eyes when he moved back.

"Because I tracked her down when I was fifteen."

Deborah's eyes widened. "And you spoke to her."

"Yes." For all the good it had done. "She didn't even know who I was. When I told her, she said she didn't want to see me again *and* she was never coming back here."

"Oh, Bram." Tears filled Deborah's eyes.

"Save your pity," he growled.

"It's not pity, you oaf. It's— How could you think I would do that to you? How could you think I would break my word?"

"You wouldn't, not at first anyway, then things would slowly change."

"You're saying you think I would abandon you." Her voice cracked. "You don't trust me."

His chest felt as if it were splitting wide open. "Doesn't matter now. After I catch Cosgrove, this pretend engagement will end. We'll both be free to do what we want."

She was quiet for a moment. "What if I don't want it to end? Don't want *us* to end?"

The words were so soft Bram thought he heard wrong. "Why wouldn't you want that?"

An odd look crossed her face. "Here, there or anywhere."

Bram's knees nearly gave out. "What?"

"You said we would love each other here, there or anywhere. The phrase has been floating around in my head, but I didn't know what it meant until now."

When she had repeated those words, he'd been struck dumb. "It doesn't really change anything."

Hurt flared in her eyes. "It wasn't true, was it? You could only love me if I was here, nowhere else."

"You didn't even talk to me about taking that job! Just announced that you were leaving five minutes after you accepted my proposal."

She stared straight at him. "I think it might be a mistake to walk away a second time."

"What're you saying?" This woman turned him inside out. "That you want us to give it another go?"

"What if I am?"

He couldn't imagine it. She didn't even sound like herself. "You have most of your memory back now. Before long, you'll be itching to go to that job."

"I'm not sure I want to do that now."

"What? Leave?"

"Or teach."

He froze. "Teaching is the most important thing to you."

"Maybe not any longer."

He knew he hadn't heard that right. "That's crazy. You don't know what you're saying."

"Yes, I do." She turned and walked back to the house. "And I want to stay here."

Bram's jaw dropped and he stared after her. What the hell?

Teaching was no longer the most important thing to her.

Deborah's words circled around in his head. That was what she had said, wasn't it? Either she didn't realize what she'd expressed or Bram had heard wrong.

She drove him plumb crazy.

For so long, teaching was all she had wanted. Enough to leave him to get it. He couldn't see her giving that up. Not for long anyway.

Two days later, Bram was still turning her words over in his mind. He'd given up trying not to think about it. The possibility of her staying was there all the time, buzzing around in his brain.

Which was why he went into town to see Annalise. Maybe Deborah's declaration was another symptom or side effect of this memory-loss issue. Bram was hoping Annalise had heard from her doctor friend in Philadelphia.

He refused to consider that Deborah did mean what she'd said. It only sent his mind in all kinds of wrong directions.

Could memory loss make her act out of character? Because that's what she was doing.

She had only just gotten her memory back, and not even all of it. It was likely she was confused. That made sense to him. Hell, it didn't sound far-fetched at all, not like someone losing their memory.

Until he had some answers, all he knew to do was give her a wide berth. Which was what he'd planned to do until he left Annalise's office and was stopped by Tony Santos. The rotund man who ran the telegraph office that also served as the post office asked Bram to deliver a letter to Deborah.

Seeing that it was from the school board in Abilene, Bram's heart kicked hard. It probably contained details about where she would live and how many students she would have, but even as he told himself that, apprehension knotted his gut.

And the dread didn't go away when he gave the letter to Deborah that evening. He wanted to watch her read it, but all she did was stare at it, then slip it into her skirt pocket. Mrs. Blue began putting food on the table, so he washed up for supper.

As they all sat down to eat, the older woman asked, "Bram, did you come from town?"

"Yes, ma'am. I rode in to ask Annalise if she'd heard back from her doctor friend yet and she hasn't."

He glanced at Deborah, who gave a small smile. "Maybe soon."

Did he imagine those shadows he saw in her eyes? Everyone was silent as they ate. As hungry as Bram was, he hardly tasted the fried chicken.

"Michal," he said, "Josie asked if you were still interested in working for her."

"Oh…yes." Deborah's younger sister smiled broadly.

"She said she might have some sewing to give you at church on Sunday."

"Okay."

As supper progressed, Deborah added to the conversation here and there. She wasn't unusually quiet, but Bram knew something was wrong and he knew it had to do with the letter he'd delivered, because she didn't mention it to anyone.

Maybe the school board wanted her to come early and she was uncertain about saying so after her declaration that teaching wasn't as important to her as it had once been.

Bram could drive himself crazy trying to guess. He saw no sign of tears or even that she was distracted.

Once supper was over, she rose and began clearing the table. When she reached for his plate, he touched her hand. "Come take a walk with me."

She glanced at her mother, who nodded her permission.

The sun was sinking below the horizon when he and Deborah stepped outside.

He waited until they rounded the corner of

the house, keeping his voice low because the screened windows were open.

"Are you okay?" he asked.

"Yes."

He studied her profile, frowned at the anxiety coming from her. "Something's wrong."

"I'm fine." She kept her attention on the ground.

"It has something to do with the letter I brought, doesn't it?"

Her chin trembled. "Bram…"

He tugged her into the barn. "What is it? They want you to come earlier?"

"They don't want me to come at all."

"What?" He paused in lighting the lantern.

She burst into tears, burying her face in her hands. She said something, but he couldn't understand because she was crying so hard.

Turning up the flame, Bram stared dumbly at her. "Deborah?"

She only cried harder.

Maybe he should fetch her ma or one of her sisters, but Bram couldn't leave her like this. He wouldn't turn away from her. Hell, he didn't care if he regretted this the rest of his life. He pulled her into him and wrapped his arms around her.

Chapter Eleven

She latched onto him as if she was planting roots, and Bram held her just as tightly. A spot on his shirt was damp with her tears. "Deborah? Sweetheart?"

She lifted her head, her lashes spiky.

"Tell me what the letter says."

"It says—" She broke off, more tears streaming down her face. She fumbled in the pocket of her skirt and brought out the piece of paper, pushing it at him.

He couldn't stand seeing her like this. When she laid her head on his chest again, he held her to him and began reading. She slid her arms around him, causing a funny ache in his throat.

Though she still cried, her sobs were quieter,

less frequent, but he could almost feel her heart breaking. And he could see why.

The further he read, the more blistered up he got. In the flickering amber light he scanned the words—*release you from your contract* and *already looking for a replacement.*

Bram's gaze returned to one sentence. *We don't hire women of low moral character.*

Low moral character. The phrase exploded in his head.

That was exactly what Millie Jacobson had said about Deborah at church that day. Deborah hadn't heard it, but Bram had.

Black fury slashed at him. Although he didn't know how Millie had done it, he knew that viper was responsible for this. He wanted to ride into town and take a whip to her, but Deborah needed him right now. He wasn't going anywhere.

She sagged against him as if her legs were about to give out. He swung her up into his arms, eyeing the bunk where he slept. The narrow bed didn't look as if it would hold both of them, so he moved to a bale of hay several feet away and eased down, settling her in his lap. The feel of her soft curves against him had his body going tight.

Night sounds filtered in through the partially open barn door. The occasional murmur of a voice from the house, the chirp of crickets, the call of a hawk.

The fresh scent of her skin teased him as she looked up, her eyes deep blue and wet. "It sounds as if the school board knows about the night we spent in the cabin. How is that possible?"

Bram knew how.

"Oh!" Looking horrified, she covered her mouth with her hand. "Somebody from here had to have said something. Don't you think?"

He damn sure did.

"Do you think it was Millie?"

"Yes." He couldn't keep the edge out of his voice.

Fresh tears rolled down Deborah's cheeks. "I've never done anything to her and neither have you. Why would she be so vindictive?"

That same question burned in his gut. With one knuckle, he wiped away the wetness on her face. "I've never understood gossips or why they don't mind ruining someone's reputation. The school board should've at least asked to hear your side."

Deborah exhaled a ragged breath then sat up, swiping furiously at her cheeks. "I don't know why I'm so upset. Earlier, I said I wasn't sure I wanted to teach anymore."

But she obviously did. Why else would she

be so distraught? The short-sleeved dress she wore bared most of her arms and his thumb made small circles on a silky path above her elbow. "And that would've been a decision you made. Not one that someone made for you based on rumors and gossip."

Her mouth was close to his, close enough that he could feel the flutter of her breath. "I think I'm more angry than disappointed."

Bram wasn't so sure about that. His fist clenched on the crumpled piece of paper and he tried to ignore the desire pounding through him. "This isn't right. You can fight it. You have a signed contract with them, don't you?"

"Yes."

"Well, then."

"If I challenge their decision, I might have to tell them that you were there, too."

"I don't care about that!" Why was she thinking about him when it was her good name at stake? She amazed him. "It isn't my reputation they're trying to ruin. Even if you decide you don't want this job, you should meet with these people."

"What would be the point?" she asked sadly. "It's obvious they've already made up their minds about me."

That went all over Bram. "I'll go with you and speak to them, as well."

"Maybe this is a sign that I should stay here."

The anguish in her eyes grabbed at something deep inside him. Was she trying to convince herself that was what she wanted? Bram wasn't convinced. One damn bit.

"There are other schools you can try."

Her face fell. "You want me to leave?"

Hell, no. He closed his eyes against the brilliant flare of pain in her eyes. "What I want is for you to be able to do what you've thought about for so long, what you studied for. Nobody should take that away from you." Including him.

"I told you I wasn't sure any longer."

"I know you did." The feel of her in his lap was starting to affect his body. She had to feel his arousal. He tucked a stray lock of hair behind her ear, smoothed her gray skirts. "But I also know how much you want to teach. That's why you didn't resign. Don't give it up because of me. Because of anyone."

"Even if I want to?" Her fingers grazed the scar on his cheek.

The need on her face echoed the need throbbing inside him.

She fixed her gaze on his mouth and Bram knew she was going to kiss him. If she did, he knew he wouldn't be able to refuse her. Knew he wouldn't even try. "Deborah."

"I'm so glad you were here when I got that letter."

The trust on her face, the vulnerability there, unlocked something inside him. Her finger touched his lower lip an instant before she brushed her mouth against his.

He froze, trying to muster up some common sense. The savagery of the desire rising inside him startled him. His muscles trembled with the effort it cost him not to pull her under him, strip off her clothes and have at her the way he wanted. Hard, fast.

It didn't matter that he told himself to put her away from him. Or that he could probably stop this with a word. He wanted her even though he knew it wasn't smart. Right now he didn't care about smart. He cared about the sweet, soft woman in his lap.

The first kiss was tentative and all her. But the instant she drew away a fraction, he moved his hand to cup the back of her head and keep her in place. His mouth covered hers.

When she opened to him and her arms slid around his neck, his common sense went up in smoke. All he cared about was getting her closer and keeping her there.

Aching, he took the kiss deeper, wanting her complete surrender. When she melted into him, a primal need to claim her clawed through him. The broken sound she made deep in her throat destroyed every thought in his head.

The only thing that existed was this woman, her fresh teasing scent, the warmth of her body, the press of her full breasts against his chest. Short nails grazed his nape as her fingers delved into his hair, her hip shifting right over his arousal.

He needed to touch her, all of her. Bram moved his lips to her neck, up to the sensitive spot behind her ear. She shuddered against him. Her soft hands tugged his shirt from his trousers and pushed the fabric up so she could flatten her hands against his bare back.

Remembering the sweet-cream taste of her skin, he angled her to him so he could reach the buttons down the front of her bodice. The glide of his hand over the unrestrained lines of her torso told him she wasn't wearing a corset.

Sliding his mouth down her elegant neck, he unfastened her. The backs of his fingers skimmed her heated skin as he drew in the scent of her purely feminine musk. Once her bodice was undone, he slipped the buttons free on her camisole and spread the undergarment open, lifting his head to look at her.

The sight of taut dusky nipples and ivory skin made his mouth go dry. Savage need punched him. Compelled by the rush in his blood and feelings he'd spent too long denying, he curved his fingers around the full weight of her naked flesh. He felt her pulse hitch when he stroked the tender underside of her breast.

Next to her fair skin, his hand looked dark and big. He stared down at her in rapt silence, entranced by the play of smoky light on her body, until she squirmed on his lap.

"I could look at you forever." He bent and ran his tongue along the inner curve of her smooth, warm flesh and up to the swell of her breast before he closed his mouth over her.

The ragged sound of his name spilling from her went straight to his heart, then lower. Pure burning desire drove through him like a spike. And a savage need to claim her. Here. Now.

He took her mouth again, hard this time. Demanding. She held him tighter.

Focused on getting her under him, he moved to her other breast, curling his tongue around her. Just as he started to lay her down, something sharp jabbed his arm. It took a moment for his hazy thoughts to clear. Hay had poked him.

They were sitting on a hay bale. In a barn. A barn, for cryin' out loud.

Reason finally surfaced. Their first time couldn't be like this. He wasn't even sure they should have a first time. Oh, yeah, he wanted it, wanted her, but this wasn't some woman he could just take and walk away from. Not Deborah.

Dragging in a steadying breath, he lifted his head, his breathing as rough as hers. She opened her eyes, the desire in her smoky blue eyes tempting him to make love to her here anyway. No.

He withdrew his hand, rested it on her waist.

"Bram?" Her shaking voice had him tightening his hold on her.

He was breathing hard and she was, too. "We can't do this, Deborah."

"But I want to be with you."

Touching her face, he swallowed hard. "Not in a barn. Not like this."

Her lips were swollen and red. She blinked as if only now recalling where they were. Well, at least he wasn't the only one who'd been completely swept under.

"The barn," she mouthed, shifting on his lap so that she sat up.

Right on top of his arousal. Even in the dim

light, he could see color flush her cheeks. The sight of her breasts, pushed high, moist from his mouth, nearly did him in. Blood pounded in his groin and he literally hurt from wanting her. He bit back a groan.

Her raven hair was tousled, some of it escaping her chignon to rest on the delicate spot where her shoulder met her neck. He'd done that. Bram hadn't even realized he'd put his hands in the thick silky mass.

Seconds passed as he tried to still the ruthless desire swirling through him. It didn't help that she was an inch away or that the subtle musk of her skin made him ache to put his mouth back on her. All over her.

Looking half-dazed, Deborah fastened her camisole and began closing her bodice, hiding her satiny skin bit by bit.

He clenched his hands into fists. "I'd help, but I couldn't make myself button you up."

She gave him a wobbly smile. Once she was finished, he set her on her feet and stood.

He noticed a piece of paper on the dirt floor behind her and realized it was the letter. He didn't remember dropping it.

She stooped to pick it up and stuffed the missive back inside the pocket of her skirt. The sorrow on her delicate features only reinforced for

Bram how much she wanted that teaching position.

Now that his brain seemed to be working again, he realized the mistake he'd almost made. If he claimed her the way he wanted, he would be committing himself to her and he didn't know if he could.

Because it didn't matter how much she insisted that she had changed her mind—the devastation in her eyes when she'd shown him that letter told a different story.

After the ups and downs of losing her memory then regaining it, how could she be sure of anything? Hadn't he said he wasn't going to touch her?

She must have seen something on his face, because when she finished straightening her clothes, she said, "Please don't apologize for what just happened."

"It would be a lie if I did, but I think we lost our heads. If we make love, it won't be in a barn."

She flushed, looking away as she asked hesitantly, "So, you didn't stop because you don't want me?"

He took her hand and laced her fingers through his. "You felt every inch of my body. Did that feel like a man who doesn't want you?"

"No."

"We just need to take it slowly. Make sure it's what we both want."

"I'm sure that I want to be with you." She tilted her head, searching his eyes. "Maybe you aren't sure you want the same."

He wasn't. He kept seeing the devastation in her eyes when she'd read that message.

It made him furious that Millie's gossip had traveled all the way to Abilene. And it had to be Millie because of the phrase used in the letter. He wasn't going to stand for it. Nothing untoward had happened in that cabin, yet he and Deborah had been forced into a pretend engagement. Although because they had, everything was proper now.

He'd bet good money Millie hadn't spread *that* word.

If Deborah changed her mind about teaching, he didn't want it to be because of him or because she'd been forced by someone else's decision.

He fumed about it all night, and near dawn he came up with a plan.

When Duffy showed up for his shift, Bram didn't go home. Instead, he rode to Whirlwind. He wasn't going to be the one who took that job from her. And he wasn't going to let anyone else either.

* * *

Upon reading the letter from the school board, Bram had been furious on her behalf. He had looked murderous. That meant he still had feelings for her, didn't it?

After what had happened in the barn, Deborah caught him watching her with frank sexual intent. Several times she felt his gaze on her, searing through her clothes to all the places where he had put his mouth. But he didn't kiss her again. In fact, he was careful not to touch her.

She didn't understand why. Things had changed for them that night. She knew he felt it, too, even though he hadn't responded in kind when she had told him she was sure she wanted to be with him. Why wasn't he sure? Did he regret what had happened between them in the barn?

She was still wondering that two days later when Annalise Fine Baldwin arrived in a buggy driven by her dark-haired husband. Deborah walked out onto the porch with her mother and sisters. Easily one of the biggest men she had ever seen, Matt Baldwin reined the buggy up in front of the Blue home.

Jericho rode beside them, his Appaloosa mare keeping easy pace with their bay.

When Deborah saw Annalise, her pulse jumped. If the doctor was here, maybe that meant she had news. She shaded her eyes from the noon sun. As her brother swung his tall lean body out of the saddle, he hollered at Amos Fuller, who was riding off because his shift had ended with Jericho's arrival.

Her brother had taken responsibility for the noon to 6:00 p.m. shift and Bram had begun staying from six at night until six the next morning. The other shift rotated between Amos and Duffy.

Amos turned back, Jericho meeting him halfway. She couldn't hear what the men said, but the red-haired ranch hand nodded, then urged his sorrel mare into a flat-out run.

Jericho walked over to them as Matt helped his wife from the buggy.

Jessamine looked up. "Son, has something happened?"

"Nothing bad, Ma," he said. "In fact, Annalise may have some good news."

About her, Deborah hoped.

The doctor smiled and fluttered a piece of paper. "I heard from Dr. Hartford."

Deborah hoped the letter contained something encouraging.

"Come in, come in." Jessamine opened the front door, glancing back at Deborah's sisters. "Marah, you and Michal water the horses."

Marah took Cinco's reins and led her brother's horse around the house. Michal followed with the Baldwins' animal and buggy.

Annalise stepped up on the porch, but Matt hung back. The big rancher tipped his hat to Mrs. Blue and Deborah. "I'll let y'all talk privately with my wife."

After giving her a quick kiss, he disappeared around the house.

Mother motioned everyone inside. "Let's go into the parlor."

Jericho palmed off his hat as he let the women precede him. "I sent Amos for Bram."

At the questioning look Deborah shot him, her brother said, "He needs to hear this. It's better if he gets the same information from Annalise that we do."

As Deborah and Annalise followed her mother into the parlor, Jordan returned from the kitchen with a silver tray of lemonade. After serving everyone, she left with a glass for Matt.

Situated off the front room, the parlor was small and windowless yet provided a quiet meeting place. A deep burgundy rug covered the floor in front of the dusky green sofa.

As Deborah took a seat on the sofa beside her mother, Annalise settled across from them in the leather chair the same green as the couch.

They'd brought both pieces from Uvalde along with Jessamine's silver service.

The sound of pounding hooves had Deborah turning toward the door. Boots thudded across the floor and Bram appeared. The open placket of his shirt revealed the hollow at the base of his throat and a smattering of dark hair on the wide expanse of his chest.

Fatigue creased his rugged features, showed in his blue eyes. He didn't look as if he'd slept any more than she had last night, yet he had come anyway.

He removed his hat. "I hope I didn't hold you up."

Annalise shook her head. "We haven't even started."

He crossed to the opposite wall where Jericho stood next to a picture of his parents. The two men shook hands.

"Thanks for sending word," Bram said.

Her brother nodded, his silver gaze shifting to Annalise. The doctor looked from Deborah to Jessamine, then to the two men.

"Is this everyone?" she asked.

"Yes," Jessamine answered.

Anticipation stretched Deborah's nerves taut. Feeling Bram's gaze on her, she looked past the doctor to the big man who studied her with a perplexed expression. As if she were a puzzle he was trying to solve. She didn't understand that look.

Annalise opened the letter and Deborah's attention shifted to the woman in front of her.

The doctor scanned the first page. "Deborah, when I saw Bram in town a couple of days ago, he told me you'd regained most of your memory."

"That's right."

"Are you still unable to remember the time you spent in Monaco?"

"Yes." Looking over as her mother squeezed her hand, she tried to keep the frustration out of her voice. "Bram and I both thought it would come back to me, like the rest of my memories, but it hasn't."

The other woman nodded, thumbing through the letter. "When you regained most of your memories the other day, was there any pain?"

"No."

"That's good."

Bram cleared his throat. "Doc, is it possible that people who suffer from memory loss would act out of character? Did your friend say anything about that?"

Deborah glanced at him. What was he talking about? And why wouldn't he look at her?

Annalise nodded, her green gaze scanning a

page. "Hartford writes that he's observed such a thing in quite a few patients."

"So, it wouldn't be unusual for a patient with Deborah's problem to suddenly change their mind about something they've always wanted?"

Deborah frowned. Did he think that was why she had changed her mind about teaching? She glared at him, but spoke to Annalise, "It doesn't happen in every instance, though, does it, Annalise?"

"Not according to Dr. Hartford, who's certainly seen more cases than I have."

"Still," Bram persisted, "such a thing is probably pretty common, right?"

"I don't know if I would say common."

See? Deborah pinned him with a look.

Jericho's curious gaze went from her to Bram and back again. So did her mother's.

Annalise indicated her current page. "Dr. Hartford does write that he has observed such behavior in more patients than not."

See? Bram shot a look right back at Deborah.

Ooh, she wanted to tell him to hush. She narrowed her eyes.

Looking amused, the doctor shifted in her chair, her gaze going from Bram to Deborah. "Have you experienced any flashes, like you did at Jericho's house? Anything, even if you aren't sure or think it's nothing?"

Deborah shook her head. "Is that bad?"

"Not necessarily. At least we know you were in a specific place during the time you're missing."

"Do you think I should try to remember? Not just wait for it to come to me? When I asked before, you said I shouldn't force any memories."

"That was at the beginning. You had no recall at all. Now that you do, it could be a different story."

"So it might help if I do try to make myself remember?"

Bram's disapproval lashed her from across the room.

Annalise turned her attention back to the letter. "Ah, here it is. Dr. Hartford believes that it sometimes helps the victim to try and re-create what they think happened."

Deborah's heart sank. "I don't know enough to do that, but I could go back to Monaco."

"No." The word shot out of Bram like a bullet.

Four gazes jerked to him.

Deborah held on to her temper with an effort. Didn't he want her to remember? "Why not? It might help."

Bram shook his head, his jaw going anvil-hard.

Jericho shifted from one booted foot to the other. "What's the problem?"

Bram looked at Deborah. "Have you forgotten how badly your head hurt when you tried to remember before?"

"It hasn't happened in a while." Did he really need to tell her brother about that?

"How bad?" Jericho asked.

Bram folded his arms. "It was painful enough that tears were rolling down her cheeks."

Her brother frowned. "Maybe Bram's right."

"No." Deborah stood. "I need to know what happened in Monaco, and if there's a chance that going there might help me remember, then I'm going."

"Not by yourself," Jericho and Bram said in unison.

Her brother glanced at Bram. "I can't go until next week."

"I can go in a couple of days."

Impatient and finally encouraged that there was something *she* could do, Deborah spoke up. "Maybe someone else could take me."

Bram's eyes narrowed. "You can get that notion out of your head right now."

Instead of feeling pleasure that he didn't want anyone else accompanying her, she was irritated by his attitude.

"There's no telling how you'll react to anything," Annalise cautioned as she got to her feet. "Going back there might have a negative impact."

"I have to try." She wanted her life back. Her entire life.

"Since you and Bram are engaged now, the two of you can go without a chaperone," Jericho pointed out.

Bram got a pained expression on his face, almost as if he were afraid to be alone with her. What did that mean?

Her temper flared. "Are you sure you're willing to take me?"

At her caustic tone, he gave her a flat stare. "Yes. Until Cosgrove is caught, you sure aren't going anywhere by yourself."

Half an hour ago, she would've been happy to go alone with Bram to Monaco. To anywhere.

Annalise folded the letter and walked to the door. "If I come across anything else helpful, I'll let you know."

"Thank you." Deborah hugged the other woman. "And thanks for driving out."

"We really appreciate that," Jericho said in his quiet voice.

As the Baldwins drove off, Bram and Jericho began discussing the upcoming trip.

"What if you run into Cosgrove?" her brother asked.

"I'll be armed and so will Deborah."

"If you decide you want someone to ride along, I can ask Riley or Davis Lee."

"Jake's another possibility, but I think we'll be okay."

The two men finished their conversation and shook hands. After bidding everyone goodbye, Bram started toward his horse.

Was anyone going to ask Deborah's opinion? Of course not. Her *fiancé* thought she didn't know her own mind.

Picking up her skirts, she hurried after him. "Bram?"

He turned, his gaze moving over her face before dropping to her mouth. A shiver rippled through her.

She knew now why he wasn't sure about being with her. He didn't believe she knew what she wanted. Or meant what she said. "You seem determined not to believe that I know what I want."

"You did a complete turnaround!"

"Yes, because I changed my mind. Are you afraid that I'm not thinking straight because I haven't regained my full memory?"

"I don't know. I just know you stood in that barn and told me you suddenly didn't want something that you've wanted your whole life. That makes no sense, Deborah."

"People change their minds all the time."

"Not you." He slapped his hat on his head. "Not about this."

He made her want to scream. "You don't want to believe me."

"I didn't say anything like that."

"You don't want to want me either."

He closed the distance between them, his blue eyes glittering like steel. "I sure as hell didn't say that."

She angled her chin at him. "Why did you stop the other night? When we were kissing and…stuff?"

"Because we were in a barn," he said in a low rough voice, looking around to make sure no one could hear them.

"There was another reason, too."

He pinched the bridge of his nose, closing his eyes briefly.

"Ever since then, I've been trying to figure out why you aren't sure you want to be with me. I think it's because you don't trust me. That's the real problem, isn't it?"

His nostrils flared, a flush darkening his cheeks.

"Even though I told you differently, you think I still want to teach."

Stone-faced, he leveled a stare at her.

"And if I have to leave in order to do it, you don't expect me to come back. That's it, isn't it?"

He didn't say anything. He didn't have to.

She inched closer to him, until her skirts brushed the tops of his boots and she could feel the line of his thighs against hers. "I'm not going anywhere."

As he rode off, she knew he didn't believe her. But he would.

Chapter Twelve

Deborah was excited about the trip to Monaco. She was glad Bram was the one taking her. Not only because he was able to make the trip sooner than her brother, but also because she wanted to spend time alone with him. The morning was well under way by the time he drove the buggy out of her yard and headed west.

She wore her lightest summer traveling suit, a white bodice and a pale blue split skirt that matched the ribbon of her bonnet. His revolver lay between them and his rifle was tucked under their seat. Deborah carried a pocket pistol in her skirt pocket. Years ago, Jericho had built one for each of his sisters and their mother. And he'd taught each of them how to hit what they aimed for.

As the buggy bumped along the wagon-rutted road, Deborah slid a look at the big man beside her. Though the top of the buggy was up, Bram wore his cream-colored Stetson low. Large calloused hands held the reins loosely on the palomino mare that pulled the cart.

The summer sun was hidden behind a fat bank of clouds, which slightly cooled the boiling temperature. The sleeves of his white shirt were rolled back to reveal corded forearms dusted with dark hair. Her gaze took in the burnished skin of his neck and face, the black hair curling damply against his strong nape.

He glanced at her, giving her a slow smile that sent her heart tripping.

They hadn't kissed since that night in the barn. Had barely touched, she realized. Because her family was around all the time? She had hoped that once she and Bram were away from Circle R land, he might try to steal a kiss or two. Or at least act as though he wanted to, but he hadn't.

There was an easy silence between them as the buggy rolled along. Deborah couldn't seem to stop staring at the carved line of his jaw, the high crest of his cheekbones. The mouth that had been so hungry on hers.

She was the first to speak. "Thanks for bringing me. I know you don't like the idea."

"I want you to remember." His voice rumbled out. "I just don't want it to cause you pain."

She laid her gloved hand on his knee. Beneath her touch, she felt the flex of a powerful thigh.

"Maybe that won't happen this time," she said.

"I hope you're right."

"This will be a good trip. I can feel it." She smiled. She expected to remember everything, fill in all the blanks in her memory.

What would be more difficult and would take longer was getting Bram to trust her.

The thought of the letter from the school board still slashed at her—she didn't like being falsely accused—but that didn't mean she regretted her decision.

Bram needed to know she had no intention of changing her mind. "Did I tell you that Catherine asked me to tutor Andrew when school begins?"

He slid her a slightly surprised look. "That's good."

"And Annalise asked if I would be willing to help her with her patients now that Catherine is occupied with Evie. I said I would."

His gaze, speculative now, settled on her. "You're good at being a nurse. You'd be a good doctor, too."

He'd told her that before. Now, as then, pleasure warmed her, but she wanted him to understand what she was really doing—making plans for the future. A future in Whirlwind.

He was quiet for a moment, then turned to her. "And what about teaching? Have you thought more about that?"

After their conversation two days ago, she'd thought a lot about whether she really meant what she said. "Yes, I have."

"If you agreed to tutor Andrew, you obviously don't want to give up teaching."

"There's no sense in letting my studies go to waste. I also told John Tucker I would substitute for him in Whirlwind if he ever needed someone, but that will be enough to keep me happy." She waited until he looked at her before adding deliberately, "And in Whirlwind."

He soberly searched her face.

She hoped he could see she meant it. Hoped he could see and accept it.

Before long, Bram reined up on top of a small rise that looked down on a bustling town. The wide main street was sand, not red dirt like Whirlwind.

Horses and wagons waited in front of a long line of attached buildings. On the south corner was a bank, a tall stately structure with four white columns.

"Anything look familiar?" he asked.

Deborah scanned the limestone and terra cotta building fronts, her gaze pausing on a hotel at the north corner. "Not really."

She couldn't stop looking at the hotel. It felt almost familiar. Trying to place it in her memory, she ignored the stab of pain in her temple.

"You keep looking at that hotel. Want to go there first?"

"I...guess so."

When Bram stopped the buggy in front of the whitewashed brick structure, she was able to read the sign hanging out over the street. The White Hotel.

He hopped out and came around to help her down. As she studied the two-story building with its tall arched windows and wide porch, unease snaked through her. She didn't want to let go of Bram's hand, but she did.

"Anything?" he asked quietly.

"Not really."

"Maybe if we went inside."

"Okay."

Shooting a narrow-eyed glance at the people crossing the street and a group of boys loitering down the way, he pulled Deborah's valise and his saddlebags from beneath the buggy seat. "Don't fancy leaving our stuff out here where somebody could make off with it."

"I agree." He had suggested they both bring a bag in case they had to stay overnight.

He slung his saddlebags over his shoulder, switched hers to his other hand and with his free one, steered her into the hotel.

Stepping inside out of the sun, Deborah savored the slightly cooler air and immediately caught the faint scent of roses. Something flashed through her mind and her attention automatically went to a basin of water on the corner of the long walnut registration desk.

She pointed toward the bowl. "That's rose water. For guests to wash their hands. I've been here."

"Yeah?" There was a cautious optimism in Bram's voice.

"Be right with you," a man said from behind the counter. After a few seconds he stood, waggling a pen. "Just looking for this."

A round barrel of a man, he had a thinning halo of brown hair. He placed the pen in the open registration book before turning his attention to them.

His friendly gaze moved to Deborah and his eyes widened. "Well, hello. I wondered what became of you."

"You know me?" Her heart skipped a beat.

"I remember when you were here before."

Bram stepped up beside her. "So she stayed in your hotel?"

The man gave them a considering look. "Yes. With an older woman and a man. Then one day all of you were just gone, your things left behind. I kept your valise. All of your things are in there."

An older woman and a man? A strange feeling came over her. Something hovered in the back of her mind. What was it?

Bram asked another couple of questions.

"The three of you were here a few days," the manager said. "Had a bank robbery around here the time y'all left. Witnesses said the thief was the man you were with."

She froze, her head pounding. "But I wasn't there?"

"No, ma'am. Not you or the other woman." He stroked his chin, his hazel eyes kind. "I don't think you realized what a no-account that man was."

"I didn't," she said. "Would it be possible to see the room where I stayed?"

The man frowned. "I suppose, but the room's been cleaned. If you're thinking you left something behind, we put all of your things in your valise."

She and Bram hadn't discussed how much, if

anything, to tell people about why they were here in Monaco. She gave the manager an apologetic smile. "I'm having a hard time remembering. I thought being in the room might help me."

"It hasn't been all that long ago." The older man clearly didn't understand why she would be having trouble.

"She's been sick," Bram put in. "We thought coming here might help her recollect things."

"Hmm." The manager took a key from under the counter. "It's on the top floor, room 212. Last door on the right. If you folks want to go up, I'll fetch the bag you left."

"Thank you." Deborah took the key and started up the stairs with Bram.

The gold-and-white flocked wallpaper wasn't familiar. Nor were the few gaslights that were posted on each floor or the green rugs at the top of the stairs. Her head throbbed, but she kept searching her memory. Nothing.

When she and Bram reached the room, her hands began shaking so hard she couldn't get the key in the lock. He set down their bags and closed his big hand over hers, managing to open the door. It looked like other hotel quarters she'd seen. Nothing stood out.

She took a step inside, then another. The room was clean with a nice-sized bed, a washstand

and a basin, and a narrow walnut wardrobe in the far corner. White lace curtains fluttered at the half-open window.

She walked across the room. As she neared the window, she began to tremble all over, completely unsettling her. "I remember being here, Bram."

"Do you remember the woman or Cosgrove?" he asked from the doorway.

"No." She glanced out the window, then moved closer to look down on the alley behind the building and the back of a wood frame structure.

An image flashed. Two people hugging? Fighting? Deborah couldn't tell.

Without warning, a paralyzing terror swept over her. Black, frigid, suffocating.

Unaware she'd even moved, she was suddenly back beside Bram.

"Deborah?"

"I'm okay."

"You're chalk-white and you're crying," he said gruffly.

She reached up and felt wetness on her cheeks. The fear faded, so she tried again to recall something. All she got was pain and a blank in her mind, just as it had been since Bram had found her in his cabin.

"Are you sure you're okay?" he asked.

"Yes." She didn't want to tell him about the throbbing in her head. He already didn't like the idea that they were here.

With a hand at the small of her back, he guided her down to the lobby. Away from the room, his touch helped dispel the horror.

After recognizing and identifying the valise as hers as well as the dress, petticoat and brush inside, she and Bram thanked the manager and left. They stopped at the building's corner and Deborah stared into the alley.

The ache in her skull grew sharper and that choking terror rose up again, but there were no images, no ideas to explain why.

"Anything?" Bram asked.

Starting to fear she might not recall anything, she shook her head. "I really thought something would come to me."

He reached out as though he might touch her, then shoved his hands into his jeans pockets. "The hotel manager recognized you. Other people in town might, too."

"Like who?"

"Someone at the bank maybe. We know Cosgrove was there. Maybe you were, too."

"The hotel manager said I wasn't involved in the robbery."

"You still might've gone into the bank with Cosgrove, maybe when he was learning their schedule."

"Okay."

"We can stop and see the sheriff, too."

"Do you think Cosgrove would've gotten anywhere near the sheriff? Or let me?"

"Only one way to find out."

They walked down the planked walkway connecting the buildings. They passed a drugstore, a general store that also served as a post office and a newspaper office before they reached the bank. They went inside the gray stone structure with its Greek columns.

Deborah took in the mosaic tile floors, wainscoting of oak paneling and leaded glass windows. Three tellers' cages lined the counter in front of her; a gold plate above each station bore the name Monaco Bank.

Deborah and Bram greeted each of the male clerks, but none of them acted as if she were familiar. Neither did the trim young man coming out of an office marked "Manager."

She tried not to be discouraged, but her hope of recalling what had happened was quickly dwindling and the throb in her head was growing.

Bram must have noticed her face. "We can still talk to the sheriff."

Pasting on a smile, she nodded. They crossed the street and went into a redbrick building with a sign over the door that read "Jail and Courthouse."

She got a brief impression of pine floors, a polished oak desk and a gun cabinet against the wall as a wiry, craggy-faced man wearing a badge stood. "How may I help you folks?"

Bram removed his hat and stuck out his hand. "I'm Bram Ross and this is my...fiancée, Deborah Blue."

Even though it wasn't a real engagement, there was a flutter of excitement in Deborah's stomach anyway.

"Bram Ross?" The lawman's dark gaze sharpened as he stepped around the desk to shake Bram's hand. "From Whirlwind?"

How did the man know Bram? Deborah shot a look at him.

He nodded. "That's right."

"Sheriff John Hayden. Pleased to meet you. Sheriff Holt said that returning the stolen bank money was your idea. Clever plan." His gaze went past them and out the window as though looking for something. "Seeing as how you have the lady with you, I guess you don't have Cosgrove?"

"No. Haven't spotted him yet, but I still believe we will."

"Then what brings you here?" the man asked pleasantly.

Bram explained how Deborah had been in Monaco with Cosgrove against her will. "Another woman, an older woman, was with them. The three of them stayed at The White Hotel. Deborah thinks something may have happened there."

The lawman's gaze shifted to her. "When were you in town?"

"Almost two months ago," she answered.

"Something did happen at that hotel around then," Sheriff Hayden said. "We found a woman's body stuffed in the crawl space."

Deborah inhaled sharply, causing a burst of agony in her head.

The man walked around his desk and opened a drawer, then pulled out a stiff piece of paper. When he returned, she could see it was a photograph.

"This is the woman we found. Do you recognize her?"

As he held the picture so she could see, Deborah looked down at the grainy black-and-white image. The woman's eyes were closed, her face severely bruised. Her neck lay at an awkward angle. She was shockingly thin with a pointed chin, a long jaw, tight mouth. A wide streak of white cut through the right side of her dark hair.

The longer Deborah looked at the photograph, the more intense the pain in her skull grew. And that was the only thing in her head. No memories. No sense of familiarity. "I don't think I know her. I'm sorry."

"Well, I'll keep trying to identify her."

Deborah rubbed her temple. "I wish I could help."

"Are you planning to stay the night?" the sheriff asked.

Bram glanced out at the late-day shadows. "Yes."

"You should have your supper at The Star and Crescent Hotel. They have an excellent cook there."

"Thank you. We will."

The lawman shook Bram's hand and tipped his hat to Deborah. "I'm happy to have met you."

"As soon as I nab Cosgrove, you'll hear from me."

"Looking forward to that day."

Not as much as Deborah was.

After bidding the sheriff good-day, she and Bram stepped into the street. She turned to him. "You and Davis Lee returned the money? When?"

"A few days after I got you home."

"Then why would Cosgrove still come looking for it?"

"The sheriff and the banker have both kept quiet about the stolen money being recovered. Besides Davis Lee, you and me, those two men are the only ones who know it was returned."

"So as far as Cosgrove knows, I still have it."

"That's right."

"And you think he'll come for it."

"He'll come."

Deborah was very afraid he would.

Bram touched her arm. "I'll be there. He won't hurt you."

She nodded, trying not to wince at the pain stabbing the backs of her eyes.

"Goodness," she said. "I haven't thought about that money once since we left the cabin."

"Well, you've been concentrating on getting your memory back and nothing else."

That wasn't true, she thought. She had also thought about Bram and her. A lot.

He frowned. "How's your head?"

Realizing she was rubbing her temple, she lowered her hand. "It's fine."

He leveled a look on her.

"I'm not ready to give up. There may be someone else who remembers me or something that
might be familiar."

"All right." Bram's reluctance was plain.

Deborah's head was pounding so hard she felt
it in her neck, but she was determined to remember something. She had to.

"I just knew I'd recall something. I'm so sorry
I haven't."

"It's fine, Deborah." It was hours after they
had continued their trek through town and Bram
knew her head hurt, no matter what she said.

She was wan and lines fanned out in tight
creases from her eyes—eyes dulled by discomfort. One of the reasons she was trying so hard
was to help him, and Bram couldn't stand it.

"Where else should we go?" She scanned the
buildings on the back of town where they now
stood. "Maybe if I looked at the picture of that
woman again."

"Enough," Bram said firmly, yet gently. "No
more. I can't force you to stop thinking about
it, but try to leave it be for the rest of the night.
Let's go eat supper at the hotel Hayden recom-
mended."

"All right." She gave him a tired smile.

Fifteen minutes later, he had arranged for

them each to have a room at The Star and Crescent. After a delicious meal, he cajoled her into a walk beside a creek that ran along the outskirts of town. The water was just a trickle. Like Whirlwind and the rest of the area, Monaco was suffering from a drought. If they didn't get rain soon, the creek would dry up.

He and Deborah discussed books and music and Marah's pets. Bram thought she was finally relaxing. The shadows in her eyes had eased, as had the cruel lines around her mouth. A mouth he'd wanted to kiss more than once today. But he hadn't.

Since that night in the barn, he had kept his hands to himself and it was becoming a real struggle, especially today. The more pain he saw in her eyes, the more he wanted to hold her, soothe her, help her.

When they finally returned to their hotel, Bram walked her to her door. A gaslight at each end of the hall spread a hazy curtain of yellow over the area, glinting off the oak woodwork and door. "My room is just across the hall. I'll leave the door unlocked in case you need anything."

"Like…you?"

Hell, yes. Her half-whispered question drew his muscles up tight. Sweat broke out on his neck. "Like if you remember something or get spooked."

"Oh." She looked up at him, her features soft in the dim light. Tears welled in her eyes. "I'm so sorry, Bram. I know I've disappointed you."

"No, you haven't. Stop apologizing." She was clearly torturing herself and he wanted to give her a little shake. "It'll come when it's supposed to. I don't want you making yourself sick over this. Especially for me. It's not worth it."

"But—"

"No buts."

All day he'd watched her struggle, watched her features grow more pinched, her blue eyes cloud with anguish. He just couldn't stand there and let her hurt.

He pulled her into him and wrapped his arms around her, murmuring, "Please try to relax. I know your head is paining you."

He slipped one hand under her hair and stroked the taut muscles in her neck until he felt the tension in her body start to ease.

She melted against him, her breasts pressed to his chest, her arms tight around his waist. His body clenched tight. "You're a good man."

"Because I'm rubbing your neck?" he asked wryly.

She lifted her head. "No. Because you care

even if you don't want to. In that way, you're like my brother and my cousins. You're a good man, Bram."

Aching with need, he knew good was not what he felt at the moment. He wanted to get her clothes off. Plastered to him as she was, she had to feel what she did to him.

The rosy flush on her cheeks said she did. He knew she was turning that sweet pink all over.

"You haven't touched me since that night in the barn."

"Because I don't trust myself to stop when I should."

Desire flared in her eyes. "What if I don't want you to stop?"

Her voice was so low Bram figured he hadn't heard right. Her next words proved him wrong.

"I want you," she said quietly. "I've wanted to be with you since that night."

What was she doing to him? When he'd said he wanted her to relax, he hadn't meant by using sex. It would only muddle things further. Still, the tantalizing idea and the feel of her breasts against his chest, her hips against his, chipped away at his common sense.

"Stay the night. Please."

When she looked up at him with those liquid blue eyes, how was he supposed to refuse her?

Refuse himself? He cleared his throat. "I don't know if that's a good idea."

His body thought it was a fine idea.

She pulled back to look at him, sadness clouding her eyes now, not pain. "I've been assuming that if I stayed in Whirlwind, you and I would be together again. Together in truth. But you may not want that. You may not want *me*."

Not want her? Bram couldn't imagine it. His arms tightened around her as he huffed out a laugh. "I want you. Surely you can feel it."

She flushed. "Is it that you still believe I'll leave?"

He took a moment to answer. "You've told me your plans and they all include Whirlwind. I know you're serious about staying."

"And about you."

She sounded so sure. Bram wanted to believe the way she did.

But the image of her sorrow-ravaged face when she'd shown him that damn letter wouldn't leave him. Thanks to him, he knew there was a possibility she might get that job back. Which meant she would leave.

And she might not *get the job,* said a voice in his head.

She toyed with a button on his shirt. "I'm offering you all of myself, Bram. If that doesn't prove I intend to stick around, I don't know what will."

"Deb—"

"Stay with me. Please."

Her eyes were deep and hot with need. The same need that burned in him. All he'd done since their argument after his marriage proposal was push her away. He couldn't do it any longer.

He framed her face in his palms, his thumbs grazing her cheekbones. "Are you sure? You need to be certain."

"I am." Her hands curled over his wrists.

The smoldering heat in her eyes set him off and he kissed her hard. Too hard. He tried to gentle his mouth, his hands.

He could've stood there kissing her all night, but a tiny bit of his brain still worked. "Not out here. Need to move."

She reached behind her and opened the door to her hotel room. Bram backed her inside, closing it as he moved her toward the fluffy bed.

Tugging his shirt out of his jeans, she slid her hands to the bare skin of his back. He made a rough sound, yanking off the garment and dropping it to the floor.

With frank appreciation on her face, she skimmed her hands up his chest, flexing her fingers in the dark hair there.

He wanted to taste her, feel her naked flesh against his. Savage, rioting need raced through him and Bram struggled to calm it. This was her first time. He needed to slow down so he could make it good for her.

Watching her face, he slid the pins out of her hair. The thick raven silk fell around her shoulders.

"I want to see you," he said hoarsely. "All of you."

"I want to see you, too."

He settled his mouth on hers, kissed her slowly and deeply. Anticipation pulsed inside him, raw with an edge he'd never felt. He toed off his boots, yanked off his socks and knelt in front of her. "Hold on to my shoulder."

She did and he had her button-up shoes off in a flash. His gaze moved to her face as he bunched her skirts in one hand and began pushing them up.

"What are you doing?" she asked breathlessly.

"Stockings. Off." The moon gave enough light that he could tell a flush darkened her cheeks as he uncovered her calves, then her knees. He lifted her skirts higher. "Hold this for me."

Legs trembling, she held the bunched fabric. He moved his palms up the back of her legs, up her firm thighs then around to the front. He

nudged up the loose hem of her drawers and un-
rolled her left stocking, dropping it beside him.
Then he did the same to the other one.

She put one hand on his head, her breathing
ragged. "Bram."

"Right here, sweetheart." In the muted light,
he could barely make out a jagged scar on her
right knee. He kissed her there. "What happened?"

"I gashed it on a rock when I was a girl."

He wanted to see the rest of her in the light.
Rising, he walked to the small table beside the
bed and lit the lamp there. Smoky amber glow
filled the room.

She shifted, her uncertain gaze going to the
lamp.

"Don't be nervous," he said softly. "I just want
to see you, okay?"

After a long moment, in which he was afraid
she might say no or stop things altogether, she
nodded. "Okay. I want to see, too."

He hadn't thought he could get any harder, but
he did. When she began unfastening her bodice,
he went to her.

"Let me." His voice sounded as if he had
gravel lodged in his throat.

The fabric parted as he worked his way down
the buttons, revealing creamy flesh, the delicate

low-cut neckline of her chemise. He helped her out of her dress, hung it across a straight-backed chair behind him.

His mouth went dry at the sight of her breasts swelling over the top of her chemise. She took off her petticoat, then unhooked her corset; he deposited those things on the chair, too. Finally she stood before him in only her chemise and drawers.

The nearly sheer fabric clung to her full breasts and skimmed her hips, her flat belly. The sight of her made his breath back up in his throat. The faint bite of kerosene smoke hung in the air, but it was the scent of soft warm woman that filled his lungs.

With a slightly unsteady hand he pulled the tie of her chemise and pushed the garment off her shoulders. It fell to her hips, then slid to the floor.

Bram dragged in a gulp of air at the sight of her full breasts. Her nipples were dusky and taut, her velvety skin brushed with amber lamplight.

His chest tightened as he reached out and cupped her. "Now, that's pretty," he murmured.

Her fingers slid beneath the waistband of his jeans and she lightly scored his belly with her nails, making his muscles clench.

"You've seen me before," she said, blushing.

"It gets better every time." He bent to take her in his mouth.

She shifted restlessly, her fingers undoing his buttons.

He didn't remember shucking off his jeans or getting rid of her drawers, but finally they were skin to skin. He laid her back on the bed and she touched his face, bringing him to her for a kiss.

She shifted against his erection, driving a hard-edged need through him. When she closed her hand around him, his muscles coiled as he struggled for control.

He gently moved her hand away. "In a minute, honey."

"I'm hot," she said on a ragged breath. "Do something."

He smiled down at her. "You want me to just get it over with?"

"Yes. No!" She slid her arms around him, arching up against him. "You know what I mean."

He dragged a hand up her thigh, then slipped a finger into her silky heat. He added another, his thumb circling the sensitive knot of nerves at her center. She gave a small cry, her muscles tightening around him.

He levered himself over her and widened her legs with his. She stared up at him, flushed and rosy. The look on her face—the love—went straight to his heart.

Knowing he was her first released some savage primitive urge in him and his arms quivered as he fought the need to bury himself in her completely.

After a moment, he smoothed back the sweat-dampened hair from her forehead. "It's gonna hurt this first time."

She nodded, tensing as he eased inside. Her hands coasted down his back to his flanks and when she pulled him closer, he thrust hard. She flinched slightly, making a sound deep in her throat.

He froze. "Are you okay?"

"Yes."

Brushing kisses across her eyelids, her cheek, he held himself still until she relaxed around him. He slid his hands beneath her hips and began to move.

"Oh!" She blinked up at him.

He smiled. "Still okay?"

"Oh, yes." She drew a finger down the scar on his cheek, then curled a hand around his neck, bringing him to her for a kiss.

He watched her, forcing himself to go slowly. Her body shifted beneath his and he surged inside her. Hard. "Sorry."

"Bram," she whispered.

When she caught his rhythm, the lock on his control snapped and he fought to hold on until she broke apart.

He buried his face in her neck and followed. For long moments they lay there, then he rolled to the side so as not to crush her. Taking her with him, he held her close and kissed the top of her head.

The slender arm resting across his chest tightened on him as she asked drowsily, "Are you going to stay the rest of the night?"

"Yes." He stroked the silky skin of her arm, her hip.

She pressed a kiss right over his heart and his throat tightened. He loved this woman. He'd never stopped.

"I'm not going anywhere, Bram," she said into his chest. "Everything I want is in Whirlwind. We have something wonderful."

He thought so, too. He just wasn't sure it was enough.

Chapter Thirteen

Blood. Blood on the ground. Blood on her.

The slightly metallic smell filled her nostrils. Two shapes then three, hitting, punching.

She was outside. The sun was overhead, but it was dark where she was. Menacing.

Suddenly someone was in front of her, their features indiscernible in the shadows, hard hands grabbing her. It was a man, she saw now. His face was cold and his dark eyes gleamed with malice. Those hard hands came toward her, twisted her arm. A woman cried out and Deborah tried to go to her. The man turned where she could no longer see his face.

A sickening thud had her racing toward him, lunging. A meaty fist swung, then again. She grabbed his arm. Her head snapped back and hit something hard. She heard a crack. Pain exploded in her skull, her shoulder, and she tried to move, but her feet wouldn't work.

The man loomed over her, his features distorted by rage, eyes flat and cold like a snake.

It was Cosgrove, fist raised to strike. A scream lodged in her throat.

"Whoa." Strong arms slid around her. "Deborah, wake up."

She fought, scrambling to get away, but was trapped by cloth wrapped around her hips, her legs. Struggling fiercely, she pushed against an immovable wall, pounded it. The arms around her tightened.

"Deborah?" The voice was low and soothing, whittling away at the horror. "Please wake up. Come on, sweetheart."

Soft words, deep voice. A hand stroked her hair, soothing. Reassuring.

She was lifted and settled into a hard lap, against a wide hairy chest, hot male flesh. Bare flesh. One muscular arm was still curled around her waist; the other moved to her head, fingers sunk deep in her hair to cradle her skull.

Restraining her. No…sheltering her.

The suffocating sense of danger eased and she stilled. She slowly clawed her way out of the black terror clinging to her, sucking at her like pitch. She was surrounded by quiet strength. Steadiness.

Sobs tore out of her, her breath hitching.

She blinked open her eyes, trying to breathe and stop the panic. Orient herself. Moonlight streamed through the window, wove across the foot of the bed. A solid wall of man protected her.

"Deborah?" The concern in the voice penetrated.

It was Bram.

Panting, fighting to drag in air, Deborah huddled into him. "Wh-what happened?"

"You had a nightmare. A bad one." He shifted her on his lap and tipped her chin up. "Are you okay?"

"Yes." Despite the warm temperature of the room, the dampness of her flesh and his, she shivered. "No."

"You're safe." He brushed a kiss against her temple. "You're here with me and there's no one else. We're still in Monaco. In the hotel."

A fine trembling seized her body. Strong fingers threaded through her hair, soothing until the panic retreated. Shoving her tangled hair out of her face, she rested her head on his chest.

"Are you all right?" he whispered.

She nodded.

He let out a deep breath. "You scared the hell out of me."

"Me, too."

He gave her a soft kiss. "Want me to light the lamp?"

"Yes, thank you," she said hoarsely.

He reached over and though it was awkward in his position, he kept one arm around her while he struck a match against the wall and lit the burner.

Quaking, she struggled to level out her breathing. "Did I disturb anyone?"

"No. You didn't scream, sweetheart. Just kicked and punched."

Her gaze moved over his face, halted on his neck and the red, raw mark there. She gasped, her touch gentle. "I scratched you. I'm so sorry."

"I'm fine. You aren't." He took her wrist, placed a kiss in the center of her palm. He brought his other arm around her, angling her toward him. "Do you know what you dreamed about?"

Throat burning, she closed her hands on Bram's steel-hard shoulders. "I remember," she said hoarsely. "I remember everything."

Using one finger, he nudged a stray wisp of hair away from her mouth. "It must be bad."

"He killed his mother, Bram. Cosgrove killed

his mother. That woman in the picture—" She broke off, bile rising in her throat as the memories unfolded one after the other like an accordion fan.

He rubbed her back. "The woman in the picture Sheriff Hayden showed us is Cosgrove's mother?"

"Yes. Her name is Elda." Tears flowed down her cheeks. The more she scraped at them, the faster they fell. "She was in on the robbery with him."

"Are you sure he killed her?"

She shuddered, her gaze meeting Bram's. "I saw him."

He cursed under his breath, holding her closer. She shivered against him, chilled to the bone despite the summer heat. His steady strength calmed her enough to continue.

The memory happened in slow motion. "I tried to stop him," she said haltingly. "That's why he hit me."

Bram went rigid against her, tension coiling in his body. The bruises on her face, her body, *had* been inflicted by that bastard. Fury blazed through him in a white-hot flash. Bram could barely get the words out. "He hit you?"

"Yes." Her voice shook.

"Can you tell me all of it, honey? Or is it too much?"

"I want to get it all out." She shuddered against him. "Cosgrove kept me in that hotel room with his mother. He stayed down the hall."

A vicious darkness Bram had never felt before rose in him. Trying to keep his touch gentle, he rubbed her back.

"I tried to find out anything I could from them."

"They'd robbed banks before?"

"A train. In Missouri. And they scammed a rancher out of the profit from his cattle sale."

"How did you learn all of this?"

"I stayed quiet, hoping they would decide I was no threat so I could attempt an escape. It didn't work."

So, she *had* tried to get away from the murdering cattle thief.

"I didn't know he had robbed Monaco's bank until his mother hurried me to the alley behind The White Hotel. Two horses were saddled and waiting."

"How did the woman keep you from running?"

"She held a gun on me."

A hush came over Bram's body. "Did she hit you? Hurt you?"

"No." Deborah massaged her temple. "We hadn't been there that long when a commotion broke out. People were screaming. There were gunshots, the sound of people running. Cosgrove came rushing into the alley, yelling for us to mount up and ride."

Bram did his best to focus all his attention on her voice. But she was naked in his lap. There was no way she couldn't affect him, but he ruthlessly willed down the desire. That wasn't what she needed right now.

"He crammed all the money in his saddlebags. His mother grabbed a flour sack full of it and suggested they each take half and split up then meet later. Cosgrove refused."

Deborah closed her eyes, her next words slow as if she didn't want to miss any details. "He said he was sick of following her plans and that the last time he'd gone along with her suggestion, he hadn't seen a dime of the money.

"She slapped him and he just…erupted. I don't know another word for it. He hit her. He kept hitting her. I didn't even think, just grabbed his arm. He threw me off, shoved me into the hotel wall and slammed my head into the brick—" She broke off, chin quivering.

Bram's entire body shut down for a heartbeat. Then a molten, seething rage filled him.

He thought his jaw might snap in two. The bastard could have killed her.

With an unsteady hand, he stroked her shoulder, her hair, trying to keep his touch gentle.

"When I came to, he and his mother were gone. Now I know where they were."

"He was hiding his mother's body under the hotel."

"Yes. There was blood on me and on the ground. I was terrified," she whispered, that damn pain flaring in her eyes again. "Something told me to run, to get away as quickly as I could, so I took Cosgrove's horse and rode out. He saw me. He yelled after me. Even though I didn't remember who he was or what had happened, I knew I couldn't go back."

"From there, you headed home."

"Yes." The wet tracks of her tears were silver in the moonlight. "Although I didn't realize that was where I was going. I just wanted to get away."

"Then you took shelter in my cabin."

"And you found me." She cupped his cheek, the realization of how close she'd come to maybe never seeing him again a sharp pain in her chest.

What if she hadn't gotten away from Cosgrove? What if she hadn't come upon the Ross cabin? "I'm so glad it was you who found me."

"Yeah, I found you and accused you of all kinds of things." His face was full of self-loathing. "I assumed the worst about you. When I found you gone from your house and saw that note, I was so damn mad that you'd promised to think about staying with me then disappeared that I didn't care about anything else."

"I hurt you terribly." She cupped his cheek. "And I apologize."

"That goes both ways," he said huskily. "How's your head? Still hurting?"

"A little, yes."

He blew out the lamp, then eased them down to the mattress, twitching the sheet over them. "Close your eyes and try to empty your mind."

She snuggled into his side, one hand on his chest, her head resting on his massive biceps. He was solid. Steady. She wanted to never let go.

A breath shuddered out of her. He held her close, her soft leg twined with his hair-roughened one. The room was warm and sweat slicked their bodies, but Bram showed no sign of moving away in order to sleep.

His heart beat strongly beneath her ear. After long moments, she settled—her thoughts as well as her racing pulse.

"Bram?" she asked drowsily.

"Hmm?"

"Don't let go of me."

His hold tightened on her hip. "I won't."

She knew he wouldn't. She knew everything would be fine.

She was completely in love with this man. Why would she ever walk away from him? She'd meant it last night when she told him she was staying.

On their way out of Monaco the next morning, Deborah slid another look at Bram. She couldn't seem to stop looking. Or stop wanting to touch him—his hand, his face, that broad muscled chest.

As he'd promised, he had held her all night and Deborah had slept better than she had in weeks. Except for the unfamiliar delight of waking up in bed with Bram, she felt like her old self.

As the buggy rolled along the prairie, she laid a hand on his knee. "Thank you for last night."

"I didn't do anything." He gave her a crooked grin.

"You did. That nightmare was terrible." Her throat tightened. The way he had listened to the awful details she'd given him had helped her get through the horror of the memories.

"I would've screamed that hotel down if you hadn't been there."

His eyes darkened with concern. "I'm glad I was there, too."

"And I'm very grateful that you were with me this morning when I had to repeat it all to Sheriff Hayden and show him where everything happened."

"Knowing the name of Cosgrove's ma will help the sheriff find out anything else she and her son might've been up to."

"He's going to prison for a long time," she said fiercely.

The lean muscles beneath her touch flexed. "I don't plan for him to make it to prison, honey."

The steel in Bram's voice gave Deborah a little shiver. "You're going to kill him?"

Bram nodded, his face grim and unyielding.

"What if he turns himself in?"

"He won't. And I won't stop until he pays for what he's done. Especially for using his fists on you."

Her brother would feel the same. Tears burned her eyes and she brushed a kiss against Bram's cheek. "Thank you."

His big work-roughened hand covered hers.

"Your family will be glad to hear that you remembered everything, though I imagine they'll be concerned about what you saw. That's an ugly thing to have witnessed." He played with her fingers. "Are you going to be okay?"

"Yes." A quick flicker of Cosgrove beating his mother made Deborah tense. "Though it might be awhile before I can keep it out of my mind, I'll be all right. I don't like that the image is in my head, but I liked even less that I had a big black hole in my memory. It was awful not knowing what had happened."

"With any luck, this whole business will soon be over." He gave her a soft kiss, then another. He drew back. "Better not do too much of that or we'll never get back."

"I wouldn't mind."

Desire flared in his eyes, but all he did was squeeze her knee then drive on.

Before Deborah knew it, they reached Whirlwind. Coming in from the west, she could see The Fontaine's laundry building, the back of the hotel itself with the smithy on one side and the livery on the other.

"We're home," he said.

She laughed. "You sound disappointed."

"I liked having you all to myself. Wish it had been longer."

So did she.

He squeezed her hand. "We'll stop in and talk to Davis Lee to tell him what you know."

She nodded, her heart swelling. Home. Now that her memory was complete, she finally felt the full connection to the town she had adopted as her own. As much as she loved this town and most of its people, it was the man beside her who made it home.

The man who'd found her. Who had protected her even when he didn't want to. Bram hadn't said he loved her, not since his marriage proposal almost two months ago, but she'd seen it in his eyes last night as they'd made love, felt it in every gentle touch of his hands on her body.

Bram pulled the buggy to a stop between Ef Gerard's blacksmith shop and the sheriff's office. The low hum of people's voices was broken by the clop of horses' hooves and the occasional shriek of a child.

The side awning of Ef's smithy was empty. As Bram helped her down, she saw Millie Jacobson go into the mercantile. Thank goodness the gossipy old hen didn't take any notice of her and Bram.

A few minutes later, they stood in the jail. The smells of pine and soap mixed with that of Bram's clean sweat.

After Deborah told Davis Lee what she had remembered, he rose from the corner of his desk where he'd been since she and Bram had arrived.

He hugged her. "I'm sorry you had to witness that, cousin, but I'm glad you finally have some answers."

"So am I."

He looked at Bram. "You still keeping to the same plan to trap that bast—uh, Cosgrove?"

"Yes. As they promised, the banker and sheriff in Monaco kept quiet about the return of the money. There's no reason for Cosgrove not to come for it."

"There haven't been any sightings reported."

"I'm glad." Deborah looked at Bram. "But it makes me wonder if Cosgrove will show. What if he's dead or hurt or something?"

"If he's dead, we'll hear about it at some point because Davis Lee got the word out about him to all the lawmen in the area."

The other man nodded before asking Bram, "Do you want to put more men at Deborah's house? I can take a shift. Riley probably can, too."

"I don't want to make any changes. If Cosgrove has been nearby at any time, he'll get suspicious."

"If he's been around, why do you think he hasn't made a move or tried to get to Deborah?"

"The odds are against him."

Deborah nodded. "Bram has plenty of men protecting me."

"And," Bram said, "his best bet for getting to her would probably be anywhere in this town and she has only one man with her."

Davis Lee nodded. "I'll still patrol in and around town."

"Thanks."

Davis Lee hugged Deborah again, his blue eyes somber. "Hopefully, this will be over soon."

"I'm ready." Impatience edged through her. She couldn't wait to have back the life she had finally remembered. Without Cosgrove.

They bid the sheriff goodbye and went down the steps of the weathered pine building.

Cupping her elbow, Bram turned her slightly toward him. "We can eat dinner at The Pearl or The Fontaine—"

"Unca Bwam!"

He and Deborah turned toward his niece's voice to see the entire family in a wagon driven by his brother. Molly waved, wiggling in Emma's lap. Ike and Georgia rode in the second seat.

Jake braked the wagon in front of the smithy and hopped out to help Emma down.

Bram strode over to assist. He lifted Georgia down as Uncle Ike clambered out, favoring his shoulder. Bram steadied his cousin, admiring how well she managed with her withered hand even when injured.

"What are y'all doing?" he asked. "Is there a problem?"

"Just that we're about to grow roots," Ike groused. "We haven't been out of the house in a month of Sundays."

Deborah smiled. The lanky man's bluster was the typical reaction of anyone who wasn't used to being inactive.

Georgia's brown eyes twinkled. "We're going to see Annalise later, just to make sure we're fine to do what we want."

"Or need," Ike said to Bram. "I don't take too kindly to letting you and your brother do all the work on the ranch."

"Neither do we." Bram grinned, making Deborah's stomach take a dive.

As Emma joined them, Molly launched herself out of the woman's arms, squealing for Bram. He barely caught the squirming child and shifted her to one arm.

"How was the trip?" Jake asked.

"It went well. Very well."

The way Bram lowered his voice had Deborah flushing. She hoped it wasn't evident in the sunlight. "I'm looking forward to telling my family."

"I'm looking forward to nabbing Cosgrove," Ike said.

Georgia nodded. "Our family has suffered enough because of him."

Bram juggled Molly to the other shoulder. "Deborah and I are planning to eat in town before we head home later. Why don't y'all join us?"

"Yes, please do," Deborah invited.

The others accepted. Jake hitched a thumb toward the smithy and the strapping black man who came out of the house and ducked under the awning with a wave. "I have some business with Ef, but can meet y'all later."

"Sounds good," Bram said.

"Deborah," Georgia said, "you can go with Emma and me to Haskell's."

She wasn't sure she wanted to risk a meeting with Millie Jacobson. But she had done nothing wrong, she reminded herself.

Bram must have thought her hesitation stemmed from concern about Cosgrove or something else. "I'll go with you."

Deborah glanced at him. "It will be a good chance for me to see if Josie's there and find out if she has any sewing to send to Michal."

"Your sister's helping Josie now?" Emma asked.

"She just began." She turned to Bram. "Stay and talk to your brother and uncle."

There was still a shadow of doubt in his eyes.

"I'll be fine, Bram. I won't be alone. Emma and Georgia will be with me."

"And me!" Molly sang from Bram's shoulder.

Deborah smiled at the toddler. "And Molly."

He hesitated. Deborah saw a look pass between his brother and sister-in-law. Both of them smiled.

"It's only across the street. I have my gun." She patted her pocket. "What could happen?"

Looking more reassured, he reached for her hand in the folds of her skirt and squeezed it. "All right. I'll see you in a bit."

Emma looked at Jake. "What time should we meet you?"

Before he could answer, Bram said, "Jake will finish well before you ladies."

Amid their indignant protests, he laughingly said, "We'll just come to the store."

After Jake kissed his wife, Bram returned Molly to her.

Deborah and the other women waited for a wagon to pass, then they angled across the wide main street toward the general store.

Georgia smiled at Deborah. "I think something happened in Monaco."

Though there was no way either of these women could know what had passed between Bram and Deborah, Deborah's gaze jerked to the older woman's.

"It does seem that way." Emma glanced over her shoulder. "Bram hasn't taken his eyes off you since we walked away."

Deborah chanced a look back, too, and saw him watching. "That's because he's nervous about Cosgrove."

"I don't think that's the only reason," the blonde said impishly.

Georgia chuckled. "Maybe your fake engagement could turn real."

A blush heated Deborah's cheeks. "Something did happen," she confirmed.

"Oh?" Georgia sounded hopeful.

"I remembered. Everything."

"That's wonderful!" both women exclaimed.

"It must be a relief." Emma switched her half sister to the other hip.

"It is. I didn't realize how much until my memory returned."

Georgia gave her a quick hug. "Was it bad? If it involves Cosgrove, I can't imagine it's good."

"It was…bad."

"Do you want to talk about it?"

Recalling that Millie Jacobson was nearby, Deborah shook her head. "Not here, please."

"I saw Millie in town earlier," Emma said quietly.

Georgia's face darkened. "Then later it is. Or if you'd rather, we can ask Bram. Or not, I guess."

"I don't mind if you know." Reminded of how he'd been there for her—naked, in bed— while she relived the horror she'd endured with Cosgrove, Deborah's face went hot.

A mischievous grin spread across the older woman's face. "I think more than one thing happened in Monaco."

Emma laughed. "Deborah, your face gives away a lot. I think you and Bram will be able to make things work this time."

"Once Cosgrove is taken care of," Georgia said.

Deborah agreed. The sooner, the better. As they passed the newspaper office, Quentin and Zoe Prescott stepped out. The couple stopped for a quick chat.

Deborah loved recognizing and knowing these people without having to ask Bram or anyone else for help. Haskell's was next door and she followed the other women up its pine steps.

Mitchell, who stood unloading crates from a

wagon in front of the store, rushed over to open the door for them.

"Thank you, Mitchell," Georgia said.

"Tanks," Molly echoed.

Deborah smiled at the little girl. Before she could follow the others inside, she heard someone call her name.

She turned to see Reverend Scoggins hurrying toward her. Telling Emma and Georgia she would catch up with them, she waited on the landing. "Hello, Reverend."

She liked Able Scoggins, but didn't know why he would wave her down.

A broad smile spread across his boyish face as he reached her. Hazel eyes twinkled. "I was just fixin' to ride out to your place."

"Why is that?"

"This just came." The slender balding man handed her an envelope.

Frowning at it, she looked back at him.

"It's from the school board at Abilene and they want to apologize."

"Apologize?" The word felt strange on her tongue.

"They also want to offer you the job again."

"Wh-what?" Stunned, Deborah could only stare at him. "But how...why?"

Emotions rushed through her, but the only

ones she recognized were shock and the little flip-flop of excitement in her stomach. "I don't understand."

Why was the reverend delivering the letter? For that matter, if it was for her, why had he opened it? Barely aware of what she was doing, she turned over the envelope and saw that it was addressed to him. That only confused her more.

She struggled to make sense of what was going on.

He smiled. "I believe they want you to arrive one week before the term begins so they can draw up a new contract and finalize everything."

His words buzzed in her ears. She stared down, trying to read the letter, but all the ink seemed to run together. "I'm sorry. I don't understand. Why would they change their minds?"

The preacher gave her an odd look, then glanced over her shoulder. "Ah, here comes Bram. I'll let him explain everything."

She wished someone would! Wait a minute. Bram? Why would he know? It was the reverend who had received the letter. The school board wanted to offer her the job they had wrenched away from her. Bram knew about the letter in her hand. He could explain what was happening. The thoughts tumbled around in her mind, barely more than nonsense. She could hardly grasp the sudden suspicion that sparked inside her.

Bram reached them. As if through a tunnel, she heard him greet the other man.

His gaze searched the street before coming back to settle on hers. Concern darkened his eyes. "Everything okay?"

No. Even though Deborah wasn't sure exactly what was happening, she knew things weren't okay. With a sick feeling in her stomach, she held up the letter. "What have you done?"

Chapter Fourteen

***

Wariness flashed across Bram's rugged features. "About what?"

The reverend frowned. "This letter came for Deborah today from the school board in Abilene. They've apologized and want to offer her the job again."

Deborah couldn't look away from Bram. He watched her carefully, his gaze measuring.

"I thought this would be good news," Able said. "Have I spoiled a surprise?"

Deborah arched a questioning brow at Bram.

"You haven't spoiled anything, Reverend," he said. But he was starting to wonder if he had. Focused on her and the confusion in her beautiful blue eyes, Bram was barely aware of people passing them. Pearl Anderson and her daughter, Violet. Pete Carter who owned the saloon.

The preacher stepped aside for Penn and Esther Wavers from the Whirlwind Hotel. He glanced at Bram. "Maybe the two of you would like to talk in the church? It's empty and available."

"Thanks, Reverend."

With one last puzzled look at them, he tipped his hat to Deborah and squeezed Bram's shoulder on the way past.

Her expression perplexed, Deborah eased closer to Bram. "I know you thought I should challenge their decision, but I didn't. Did you?"

"Not exactly," he muttered.

"I don't understand why they would change their minds. The letter they sent releasing me from my contract was clear and to the point. It sounded nonnegotiable."

Once he explained, she would be glad. And he would be forced to let her go, damn it.

Snagging her hand, he tugged her toward the church. "Let's go talk in here."

She walked up the church steps with him and preceded Bram through the open door. Though out of the sun, it was still hot. Pulling a handkerchief from her pocket, she dabbed at her sweat-dampened forehead and chest.

Things were starting to fall into place and she didn't like where they were landing. She sank into the nearest pew. "Please tell me what you did."

"It wasn't anything bad." She turned toward him and he sat in the pew behind her where he could see her face. "The night you showed me the letter from the school board, you looked as though part of you had died."

"Yes, but then I was fine with their decision."

"No, you weren't," he said tightly. "The school board had no way of knowing you and I had become engaged, which likely would've kept them from calling your character into question in the first place. I knew there wasn't much I could do about it, but I thought a letter from the reverend might at least clear your name."

She frowned. "So you asked him to write?"

"Yes."

"Did you think they would offer me the job again? Did he ask them to do that? Is that what you hoped for? That I would leave?"

Yes, he started to say, but he sensed a trap. "It shouldn't have been taken from you."

"I made a decision, Bram. Yes, it came from a bad circumstance, but I made the choice I wanted to."

"And I know you did that for me."

"For us." She shook her head. "We lost a lot of time together because I was so hardheaded about it to start with."

"I made you choose."

"You didn't. You proposed."

"Then demanded you decide whether you would take the job or stay with me. Two months ago, you chose what you really wanted and I think you should have it. The look on your face…" The pain in his eyes touched her. "I never want to see you like that again."

She huffed out a breath. "First you don't want me to go. Now you do."

"I wouldn't say I *want* you to go."

"Well, you're trying to talk me into taking the job that came between us in the first place."

"It might be fine for you not to teach at first. Maybe for a month, maybe for a year. But, Deborah, you *are* a teacher. Even if you say you want to walk away from it, you don't."

"I guess I know what I want." She angled her chin at him.

"You'll miss it." He surged to his feet and went to the front door, staring blankly at the wagon parked in front of Haskell's. "Then you'll start to wish you could do it. Then you'll start to resent me because you'll feel obligated to stay with me. I don't want that."

It was a nice thing for him to have done. A selfless thing. But something just didn't fit for Deborah. "You don't trust me to know what I want. Haven't we talked about this before?"

"Of course I trust you to know what you want." He slashed a hand through the air, turning back to her. "I think you want to teach and you won't admit it. That's what makes you happy."

"You are what makes me happy, you crazy man."

"For a while, maybe. I just don't want you to be unhappy."

"What do you think this conversation is doing to me? I thought you wanted us to be together. After last night, I thought we *were* together. Do you not want that?"

He scowled. "That's loco."

"Is it?" She thought about last night and how special it had been for her. She'd thought it had been special for him, too. He'd said last night that he wanted them to be together, that he wanted…

She mentally replayed their conversation in the hall. She'd asked him to stay the night. When he hesitated, she'd realized he might not feel the way she did.

I've been assuming that if I stayed in Whirlwind, she'd said, *you and I would be to-*

gether again. Together in truth. But you may not
want that. You may not want me.

Deborah's breath backed up in her chest. All
he'd said was he wanted *her*. He'd never said he
wanted them to reconcile. He had never once said
he wanted a future with her, never once said he
believed they had one.

She was the one who had said those things
and her mind had jumped ahead, assuming he
wanted them the way she did.

He didn't want to tie himself to her. He was
waiting for her to leave, just like his mother.

Deborah realized he'd spoken and she dragged
her attention to him.

"I'm not trying to hurt you. I thought what I
did was a good thing."

"Even if I don't want it?"

"I don't think you'll be able to live with the
choice you made."

"You mean *you* won't be able to live with it."

He went still, just stared at her.

"You'll always be wondering if I'll leave,"
she said, getting to her feet. Her heart felt as if
it were being carved out of her chest. "Waiting
for me to go. So instead of trusting me to stay,
you're getting rid of me yourself."

"I did this for you."

"You did it for yourself," she snapped. "This

way, you won't have to wait and wonder if one day you'll wake up and I'll be gone."

He yanked off his hat, shoving a hand through his hair. "Why can't you understand?"

"I do understand. Regardless of what I say or do to prove differently, you think I'll leave. You *expect* me to. That isn't trust, Bram.

"I've given you all of myself." She realized tears were running down her cheeks and she swiped at them angrily. "But you haven't done the same for me. Why can't you just admit you don't trust me?"

"Why can't you admit what you really want?"

"I have admitted it," she yelled. "And you think it's a lie!"

"I'm not having you give up a life you've wanted. Not for me. I don't want you resenting me for that someday."

"The real crux of the matter is that you think I'll leave you. This way, you won't have to wonder."

She started out the door.

"Where are you going?"

"Home. I'll ask your brother for a ride or rent a buggy from Pete."

"You can get that notion out of your head right now. I said I wouldn't let Cosgrove hurt you and I meant it."

"There's no way he could hurt me as badly as you just did." She walked out the door, not caring whether he followed or not.

What the hell had just happened? For a moment Bram stared after her, his head spinning. His teeth clenched so tight he thought he might break a tooth.

Seeing her march past Annalise's clinic and go in the direction of the livery jolted him into action. Right now they both wanted space. Unfortunately, neither of them was getting it, because she wasn't going anywhere without him.

He stalked out the door and down the church steps, easily catching up to her with his long strides. A faint whiff of her fresh scent reached him.

The sun beat down, glinting almost blue in her raven hair. She looked straight ahead, her face flushed with anger, her jaw set. Little puffs of red dust swirled around her skirts.

From the corner of his eye Bram caught a movement and glanced over. Jericho was walking down the hill from his house, coming into town between the Whirlwind Hotel and the church.

Deborah saw him, too, and angled back, making a beeline straight for him. Bram groaned inwardly. He reached them in time to hear Deborah ask her brother to drive her home.

The former Ranger frowned, shot a look at Bram. Before he could say anything or explain, Deborah tugged Jericho down to her and spoke.

The man straightened, his silver gaze leveling on Bram's. "Whatever's going on is between the two of you and I won't interfere, but she's pretty upset."

Bram expected Jericho to demand an explanation. Instead, he added, "It would probably be better if I drove her home."

Bram wanted to argue. He didn't cotton to the idea of not taking her himself, but Jericho was the one man Bram trusted to protect her as vigilantly as he would. Besides, he knew by that stubborn locked angle to her jaw that she wasn't coming with him, no matter what.

His fists clenched at his sides. "All right."

"I'll check in with Duffy. Make sure he has nothing to report."

"Okay." His focus shifted to Deborah. "I'll be at your house for my shift at six o'clock."

Jericho acknowledged the words with a nod. His sister said nothing.

Which went all over Bram. This whole thing went all over him. Dad-burned female!

* * *

Still fuming an hour later, Bram drove into his barn and unhitched the palomino from the buggy. Last night he and Deborah had been in bed together. Reconciled. Now they were nothing.

Between their trip to Monaco and the way they'd spent last night, Bram hadn't slept much in the past twenty-four hours. Still, he knew he wouldn't be able to close his eyes. He was too blistered up.

Removing the horse harness and collar with jerky angry movements, he returned the tack to its place on the wall. He didn't understand and he sure as hell didn't appreciate being accused of trying to get rid of her when his aim had been to help her.

She wouldn't help herself. Hell, she wouldn't even admit what she wanted.

All he'd done was try to fight for her, challenge the unfair actions of the school board. They should've at least let her defend herself against what they'd heard. She wouldn't do it, so Bram had. Evidently he was an idiot, because he couldn't fathom how she viewed his good deed as bad.

A little voice chided him, but he ignored it.

The smells of hay and dirt and horseflesh

calmed him somewhat. Just as he began brushing down the mare, he heard the rattle of wagon wheels. His family was home.

Back in Whirlwind, Bram had told Jake that he and Deborah had changed their minds about eating in town and were going home. He'd left in the buggy. She had gone with her brother. Everyone in the Ross clan—hell, probably the whole town—knew something was wrong; they just didn't know what.

As Jake braked the wagon in front of the barn, Bram tossed the horse brush into the nearby bucket and went to help.

Georgia made it out of the buckboard on her own. All Ike needed was a shoulder to balance on as he carefully planted his feet on the ground. Bram took Molly so Jake could help Emma down. When he returned the little girl, she snuggled into the blonde's neck, her eyes sleepy.

His sister-in-law put a hand on Bram's arm. "Are you okay?"

"Sure," he said gruffly.

He could feel the others watching as her green eyes searched his. "Is everything going to be all right between you and Deborah?"

"I don't know." The calm words belied the churning in his gut.

"It was obvious the two of you had words," Ike said.

"Yes, sir." He didn't trust himself to say more.

"I'm sorry, Bram," Georgia said. "I thought things would work out this time."

He didn't know what he'd thought.

"What happened?" Jake asked.

Bram hesitated. He wasn't exactly sure.

"Jake, he may not want to tell everyone." Compassion filled Emma's eyes. "Just know that we'll be here if you need anything."

"Thanks." He gave her a quick hug, watching as she followed Ike and Georgia out the barn door and to the house.

Temper barely in check, he helped Jake with the wagon. As they backed the horses up, guiding the buckboard into its spot against the outside wall of the barn, his brother didn't speak. Didn't say anything when they unhitched the animals and took off their collars and harnesses. Bram led both bays to the water trough just outside the barn door.

He left the horses to drink as he went back inside. He dragged his forearm across his perspiring brow and moved to the mare's other side with his brush, his strokes smooth and long.

Jake hung the leather collars on their pegs

along the wall. Sliding a look at Bram, he asked quietly, "Wanna talk about it?"

He paused in midstroke, his fury gathering again. "I tried to do something nice for Deborah and she took it the wrong way."

"Nice like what?"

Outside Bram and her family, no one knew about her losing her job, but Bram trusted Jake to keep the information to himself. "Last week, she told me she wasn't sure she wanted to teach anymore."

His brother frowned.

"I didn't believe it either," Bram said ruefully. "Two days later she received a letter from the school board in Abilene, breaking their contract with her because they don't hire women of low moral character."

Just saying the words spurred his temper higher.

In the process of draping harness straps over the rail that ran the length of the wall below the collars, his brother stopped.

Jake stared at Bram with the same disbelief he had felt upon seeing the letter. "Where'd they get that fool idea?"

"They learned that she recently spent the night alone with a man."

"From Millie." His brother's dark eyes hardened.

"It had to be." Bram rested his brush on the palomino's back. "You should've seen Deborah's face, Jake. I've never seen her like that. She looked hollow, like…all hell come undone."

"I imagine so."

"She cried hard for a bit, then pulled herself together and told me she didn't know why she was so upset, since she wasn't sure she still wanted to teach."

"Just like that?"

"Yes. What the school board did was wrong. I told her she should challenge it, but she didn't agree. You know why she didn't want to?" Yanking off his hat, he shoved a hand through his hair. "Because she might have to name me as the man who'd been with her in the cabin and drag my name through the mud!"

His brother's eyes widened.

"I wanted to ride straight for Abilene, but being as I was the man who *ruined* her, I knew anything I said wouldn't have much weight."

Jake studied him. "Still, you did something."

Crushing his hat, Bram paced to the other side of the barn. "I asked Reverend Scoggins to write the school board and tell them that the man Deborah had spent the night with was her fiancé. That the reason we were in the cabin was because of the dust storm. Scoggins was happy to write the letter, although he didn't know if it would help."

Bram walked back and forth in front of the ladder leading up to the loft. The mare turned her head, watching him warily.

Jake leaned one shoulder against the wall. "I take it you didn't tell Deborah you'd done this."

"No. What was the point? There was no way to know how the school board would react. Or if they would even read the letter."

"True."

"Today she received another letter from the school board." Bram jammed his hat back onto his head. "They've rescinded their decision. They apologized and offered her the job again."

"And she's going to take it?"

"We didn't get that far, but I thought she'd *want* to take it. That sure isn't how she acted." He braced his hands on his hips. "Hell, I tried to do something special for her and she threw it back in my face. She wasn't one bit grateful."

"What was she?"

"Mad." The sadness in her eyes, the disappointment, had taken him by surprise, but the betrayal in her blue eyes had reached in and twisted his heart. "Hurt."

Jake was silent for a moment. "Maybe she really doesn't want to teach."

"Two months ago, she wanted it badly enough that she was ready to leave me in order to take that job." Bram shook his head. "Right now we're both focused on Cosgrove. What happens after he's been dealt with? I don't think she'll be able to live with the choice she's made."

"Did you tell her so?"

"Yes. The woman is a born teacher and she wants to do it. She wants it more than anything."

"Even more than she wants you?"

"Yes, although she won't admit it." Bram knew she had feelings for him. There was no way she could've faked the love that had been in her eyes when he'd been deep inside her. But he didn't believe she was being honest about the job she'd spent so much time preparing for.

"She accused me of meddling in her affairs and said I'd only done it to get her out of town."

A shrewd light flashed through his brother's eyes. "Did you?"

Bram stopped short, frowning. "What kind of question is that?"

The other man chose his words carefully.

"Ma left and never came back. Are you afraid Deborah might do the same?"

"I just told you—"

"Answer me."

After a long pause, in which he wanted to tell his brother to leave it be, he finally nodded. "Yes."

Deep down, where only Deborah seemed to know him, Bram couldn't deny that as much as he hated the thought of her leaving, he also would've accepted it. Because then he would have known for certain that she was out of his life. He wouldn't have had to wonder if she would abandon him.

Was she right? Had he tried to protect himself by getting her out of town before she could leave him?

Maybe so. He could admit now that he had proposed marriage to her two months ago because he thought it would make her stay. It wasn't that he hadn't meant the proposal—he'd meant every word, and would've done it at some point. But when she'd said she was taking the teaching job and leaving, he decided if he didn't keep her here with him, she would never come back.

"What if Deborah really isn't sure she wants to teach anymore?" Jake pulled off his worn leather gloves and tucked them into the back pocket of his jeans. "People's priorities change, Bram."

"From something she's wanted and worked for her whole life?"

"She says she wants to give you what you want."

She'd shown him her intent to stay, her commitment to them by telling him of the future plans she'd made. Recalling what she'd said about tutoring Andrew and working with Annalise dimmed Bram's anger. He didn't want to let go of his anger.

She'd been shocked upon receiving that letter. And confused. Learning he was behind it had hurt her. She had looked at him as if he'd violated her. A man didn't just forget that.

Even if he didn't understand why, it was obvious he had caused her pain and handled the situation badly. Had he ruined what was between them?

If she really had feelings for him, very deep feelings, wouldn't she have understood what he did?

"You need to talk to her. Try and set it straight. Don't wait."

"And what do I do if she decides to take the job?"

"Y'all work it out. She might not even have to leave in order to teach."

"If she wants a classroom right now, she does. Unless Tucker is fired or something happens to him, she can't teach in Whirlwind and there's no reason for Tucker to get fired."

"You have to decide if you're going to trust her. That's what being together is about. It's a decision."

A decision?

Jake clapped him on the shoulder. "Just remember she's never given you a reason to think she'd do anything like Ma."

She hadn't done anything *yet*. As Bram watched his brother step outside and move the horses into the corral, he realized trusting her *was* a decision.

He just wasn't sure it was one he could make.

Chapter Fifteen

Bram wanted her gone? Well, she would be happy to oblige him.

When they'd fought the night he had proposed, Deborah had thought nothing could hurt that badly again. Finding out that he would rather she leave than trust her to return made her feel as if her chest were cracking open.

Her temper hadn't cooled even an hour later after she'd told her family what had happened. In the emotional aftermath, she almost lost sight of the fact that she'd remembered what had happened in Monaco.

During the drive home, she had shared with Jericho that she had witnessed Cosgrove killing his mother. She also confided in him about what had happened with the school board in Abilene and the set-to with Bram.

Once they arrived home and were settled in the parlor with the rest of the family, her brother helped her explain everything, including why Bram didn't trust her. After everyone had calmed down, Jericho asked the question she had yet to ask herself.

"Are you going to take the job, Deborah?"

"Truth be told, I haven't thought about it. This business with Bram knocked it clean out of my head."

Just last night they'd been as close as a man and woman could be. She didn't regret the intimacy they had shared and she was angry that he'd ruined what was between them.

In less than a day, she had gone from experiencing the best thing that had ever happened to her to the worst, both involving the same man.

Rising, she went to the window and looked out over the rippling prairie grass. "I'm really not sure if I still want to teach."

"Don't give it up for a man, like you did before," Jordan warned.

She didn't want to.

Marah shook her head. "I can't believe Bram would do something so mean."

"Neither can I," Michal added.

Jericho sat forward on the sofa. "You sure you didn't misunderstand or read it wrong?"

No, she wasn't sure. Anger and hurt had been all she'd felt since learning about his part in the letter to the school board. Now doubt crept in.

Had Bram really realized what he was doing?

He hadn't denied it when she confronted him about it, but when she had accused him of hoping to get rid of her, there had been a flicker of some emotion in his face. Realization and then something she had thought was guilt. Now she didn't know what to think.

She moved to stand between the sofa and the chair where her mother sat.

Jessamine looked up. "Have you considered accepting the job?"

"Yes." The idea of leaving Bram behind definitely appealed to her right now. The man flat riled her up.

"Are you thinking about it because you're angry at Bram?"

"Yes." Which irritated her. "Even though I shouldn't base any decision on him, especially this."

"You don't have to decide this minute." The older woman patted her hand. "Take a little time and think about it."

Jericho leaned forward, elbows resting on his

knees. "If you want this job, sister, you should take it. I doubt you'll get another chance."

"Won't that just prove to Bram that he was right about me?"

"Maybe, but if you stay here to prove him wrong, you're the one who will lose." He shrugged. "Besides, both of you might be right."

"How can that be?"

"You may not want to teach anymore after you get a taste of those hellions," he said with a grin.

"Oh, Jericho," Jessamine chided.

He winked at Deborah. Though she smiled at her brother's teasing, she knew he was serious. And he might have a point.

"If you do take the job, it would give you and Bram a chance to cool off," her brother pointed out.

She wished she knew what to do. She wished the only emotion inside her was anger, but it wasn't.

After several more minutes, Jericho took his leave, hugging Deborah tight before he left. "If you need any help with Bram, you let me know."

"What kind of help?"

He tapped the butt of his holstered pistol.

That got a smile out of her. "Oh, you. Go on."

She knew he was teasing, although shooting Bram had certainly crossed her mind. Hadn't the night they'd spent together meant anything to him? He'd been her first. Her only.

At the memory of what they had shared, bittersweet pain cut her breath. She thought back to the moment she had accused him of wanting to get rid of her. The shock on his face had been genuine. So had the confusion.

Had she accused him unfairly? What if he was just as hurt as she was?

The hollowness in her chest said her suspicions about his motives showed she'd been correct. Even if he hadn't realized what he was doing, he surely knew now. Knew how hurt she was. Yet there was no sign of him.

The fact that he hadn't come after her meant she hadn't made a mistake, didn't it?

They were well and truly over.

She choked back a sob. She'd done all the crying she was going to. Being with her family comforted her, but she also felt crowded.

She stepped out on the porch. "I'm going to water the cow and the horse."

"Want some help?" Jordan asked.

"No, thanks."

Once outside, she went around the right side of the house. The pump was located about halfway between the back stoop and the barn.

Deborah picked up the bucket standing at the base of the pump and filled it with water.

Curling both hands around the handle, she walked carefully to the back of the barn, trying to keep from spilling. Bossy stood in her stall, tail flicking lazily. The heat magnified the odors of dirt and cow flesh.

Deborah placed the bucket in front of the cow and scooped up an empty one on her way out.

After pumping water into the second pail, she bent to pick it up. Just as she straightened, a hard muscular arm hooked around her throat and squeezed.

The bucket fell, water quickly soaking into the thirsty earth and wetting the hem of her gray skirts. Panicked, she struggled against the choking pressure around her neck. In the next breath, she felt a sharp prick against her neck.

"Quiet," a masculine voice ordered.

Cosgrove! Fighting to stay calm, she stood still, trying to judge the situation.

The outlaw increased the pressure around her neck, cutting off more of her air. He rubbed his bristly cheek against hers. "I thought I'd never get you alone."

"What...do you want?" she asked hoarsely.

He tightened his arm, crushing her windpipe. "You know."

Going up on her tiptoes to keep him from strangling her, she started to shake her head. The blade cut into her skin. It stung and she blinked back tears.

"You're going to take me to the money you stole from me."

"*You* stole it from the bank!" she croaked, unable to stop the words.

He pushed harder against her windpipe and she felt herself growing faint. Her pistol was still in her pocket. If she could reach it, she could at least fire and signal that she was in trouble.

He jerked around, hauling her with him to the side of the barn. She struggled to keep her feet under her, frantic for air, desperate to ease his hold. She stumbled and the blade bit into her neck again. He half carried, half dragged her with him, her skirts making a swishing noise in the grass.

A red roan gelding stood a few yards away. Spots danced in front of her eyes. Something lay on the ground near the horse. Cosgrove dragged her to the mount and she gasped. Not something. Someone!

It was Duffy—motionless, facedown in the grass. His back was covered in blood. He'd been stabbed.

Cosgrove's steel-hard arm cut off the scream

welling up inside her. Her family had no idea this murderer was so close. Was he planning to kill all of them?

"Do what I say or I'll cut you. You won't die like this old man, though. I'll keep you alive until I get that money."

She'd witnessed him murdering his mother; he wouldn't let her live any longer than he needed her. She couldn't tell him the money had already been returned to the bank.

She needed to convince him the money was hidden somewhere, but where?

One arm still around her throat, he pushed her toward the gelding. "Mount up."

She couldn't get on that horse. Fear made her wild and she swung, landing a blow to his nose. He backhanded her, snapping her head to the side. She screamed and he hit her again. Tasting the salty tang of blood, she reeled, trying not to fall.

He hauled her up and shoved a dirty bandanna into her mouth, then threw her into the saddle. Before she could blink, he scrambled up behind her.

A sudden burst of voices sounded from the house. Stunned, her jaw throbbing with pain, Deborah could barely make sense of what was happening, but she knew to fight.

She clawed at his face. He punched her and her head jerked back, light flashing behind her eyes. She sagged forward.

Cosgrove grabbed the reins and clucked to the horse. The animal lunged into motion, tossing Deborah to the side. The outlaw's free arm locked her to him as they raced off.

Her mind dazed by his latest blow, she struggled sluggishly.

Voices yelled. Her mother. Jordan. Gunfire erupted, bullets whizzing past.

Cosgrove cursed and she hoped he was shot. But if he was, he stayed upright. The horse kept moving, pounding across the prairie toward a narrow grove of trees.

The sound of gunfire grew faint. She heard a distant scream of horror and her heart squeezed. Had someone found Duffy?

Nauseous, she fought not to be sick. She wrapped her clammy hands around the pommel as they bounced along. Beneath the odors of horseflesh and earth, the smell of Cosgrove's too-sweet cologne nearly choked her.

The ride was jarring, snapping her teeth together. Grass and dirt flew beneath the horse's hooves. After long moments, they barreled down the side of a gully. Cosgrove yanked the roan to a stop at the base and seized both of Deborah's wrists with one of his hands, squeezing with bone-crushing pressure.

While he grabbed the rope lashed to the saddle, she reared back, trying to throw him off.

She managed to free one hand and made the awkward reach for her gun. Her hand closed over it and her finger found the trigger as she brought the weapon up.

He grabbed her arm, wrestling her for the weapon. She fought to hold on, but he twisted her hand back until the gun tumbled out of her hold to the ground.

She couldn't see where it fell. He lashed her hands to the pommel, causing a sharp pain to shoot up her arm. Once he had her secured, he gripped her jaw hard and turned her face toward him.

"Tell me where the money is."

"And you'll let me go?"

"Hell, no." He barked out a disbelieving laugh.

He would never willingly release her. Not alive anyway. Horror spread through her chest, a pulsing molten pain.

She'd lost her gun, but not her last chance for escape, if she was smart. Cosgrove wanted the money, which she didn't have.

Her mind raced. It would take time for her sisters to get word to Jericho. Or Bram. Despite what had happened between them, he would come. For Cosgrove, definitely. For her, maybe.

She swallowed back the hurt. It didn't matter. All that mattered was staying alive.

Shaking so hard her teeth chattered, she battled to remain calm, to think.

Cosgrove flashed the knife an inch from her face, the blade glittering in the sun. "Start talking."

She had to take him somewhere close, somewhere they could be found quickly once word got out that Cosgrove had taken her.

"Don't think about lying. You make me waste time around here, I'll cut you."

"It's a cabin," she croaked, her throat dry and bruised from the punishing hold he'd had on her. "On the other side of Circle R land."

She'd said it without thinking it through. Bram might be the only one who would think to look there.

Cosgrove pinched her arm, hard. "You take me for a fool? You think I'm going to ride past Bram Ross and his brother?"

She had to make him believe her. "That's where it is."

His normally trimmed hair was ragged and dirty. He stared at her, his dark eyes piercing.

It took everything she had to hold his gaze. She could hardly breathe.

He gripped her jaw. "Let's go. You better pray we don't run into any of them."

That wasn't all she was praying for. An hour ago, she hadn't wanted to see Bram ever again. Now he was all she wanted.

Bram chewed on what Jake had said and tried to hang on to his anger, but he kept seeing the hurt in Deborah's eyes, the betrayal. Yes, she'd been right about him.

Did it even matter that he hadn't been aware of what he'd done until she lit into him for it?

The whole reason he'd asked Scoggins to send the letter was that he couldn't stand seeing the stricken look on her face. The school board had put it there the first time. The second time was all him.

He couldn't let it stand. As much as he hated the thought of telling her she'd been right about him, hated the thought of hurting her all over again, he had to go to her. When he looked to the future, he saw himself with her. Not without her.

He didn't know if they could work things out, but he wanted to try. What if it was too late? What if she was finished with him?

What if she had accepted that job?

He muttered a curse. If she agreed to teach in Abilene, what would he do? Bram didn't know. Still, he couldn't leave things like this between them.

After telling his family where he was going, he headed for her home.

He was well away from his house when he saw a horse racing toward him. Skirts billowed behind. As the bay neared, he realized the rider was Jordan Blue.

Alarm shot through him. There could be no good reason for Deborah's sister to be riding as if she'd seen the devil. Unless she had.

"Dammit." Bram reined up as her mount danced to a stop beside him. Dread snaked through him.

"Cosgrove has Deborah," Jordan panted, eyes huge in her pale face.

A black haze blurred his vision. "How long?"

"Minutes. He stabbed Duffy."

"Let's go." Bram kneed Scout into a full-out run and Deborah's sister kept up.

They reached the house in short order and he followed her around to the barn where Mrs. Blue and the other girls were waiting. He slid off his mount and helped Jordan down before going to where he saw a man sprawled in the grass. Duffy.

As Jordan had said, the cowhand had been stabbed. He lay there limp, his face waxy, his chest moving shallowly. He was alive. Barely.

Anger made Bram's voice sharp. "What happened?"

"Deborah said she was going out to water the animals," Mrs. Blue answered. "We heard a scream and came running."

He moved along the side of the wagon to help Jordan hitch up the bay. Bram scanned the dirt and grass around the barn. He didn't see more blood, which was a relief. Beside the pump was an overturned bucket and a ring of damp red dirt where the water had already soaked into the hard ground.

Mrs. Blue lowered the end gate of the wagon and Bram returned to Duffy. It took some effort, but he managed to get the wounded man into the buckboard.

Marah climbed into the back of the wagon and carefully moved the ranch hand so that his head lay in her lap. "Cosgrove had Deborah in front of him on his horse and they were racing away."

Jordan closed the end gate and walked up the opposite side of the wagon.

Michal brought out her pistol. "I fired t-two shots."

"So did I," Jordan said fiercely.

Bram gave Mrs. Blue a hand up into the buckboard. "I don't know if any of us hit him, but we tried."

"Then we found Duffy here in this spot," Marah said. "He really needs a doctor."

Bram helped Jordan and Michal into the wagon.

Jordan looked at him. "Cosgrove wants that money, doesn't he?"

"Yes." Which meant Bram didn't have much time to get to Deborah before the outlaw realized the stolen bills weren't in her possession.

He scanned the prairie from west to north then back to the south. Where would she take the bastard? Someplace close. A place she thought would be easily found.

"Which way did they go?"

"That way." Marah pointed west.

Bram's head jerked toward her. "Back toward the Circle R?"

"On a red roan gelding."

He almost smiled. Trust Marah to give him an accurate, detailed description.

Bram strode to his horse and swung into the saddle. Deborah was taking Cosgrove to the cabin. She had to be.

It was close. Somewhere Bram would think to look. He turned to her mother. "When you reach

Whirlwind, tell Davis Lee and Jericho what's happened. Send them to the cabin on the other side of the Circle R."

Mrs. Blue nodded, appearing calm despite the distress he saw in her eyes.

"Can you ladies get Duffy to town all right?"

"Yes." Jordan took the reins from her mother.

"Just find my daughter, Bram."

"I will, ma'am." Urging Scout into motion, he rode past the barn and across the prairie. With the drought, the earth was too hard to show tracks, but he could still follow broken twigs or branches.

He saw nothing until he came to a gully. The sun glinted off something that lay in a spidery patch of grass. Bram guided his horse closer, realizing it was a gun. He slid to the ground and scooped it up. Deborah's pistol. The one she'd taken to Monaco. She'd been here recently.

He slipped her weapon into his saddlebag, then remounted and urged the horse on, taking note of trampled grass in a narrow grove of trees. Making sure to keep an eye out for anyone who might be hiding in the sparse cover of the brush that dotted the landscape, Bram galloped through knee-high brittle grass.

He came up on the back side of the cabin.

Soon the side of the barn and the rear of the house became visible.

In case someone was there, Bram halted his mount a good distance away and hobbled him to a stunted mesquite tree. He crept closer to the cabin, sliding his gun out of the holster and thumbing down the hammer.

His heart beat hard and fast. If Deborah wasn't there, he wasn't sure where else to look.

He topped a rise and saw an unfamiliar horse outside the barn. A red roan, its sides heaving, its coat dark with sweat. That had to be Cosgrove's animal.

Careful to move quietly through the dry crackling grass, Bram eased up to the window. He could hear the rise and fall of voices, both male and female.

Pulling off his hat, he peered around the window frame and through the glass. There they were.

When he saw Deborah, Bram's heart stopped for a full two beats. She stood in the center of the room, her wrists bound together in front of her. Blood speckled the white collar of her gray dress, and a raw jagged fury slashed through him.

From here, he couldn't tell if she was physically injured. The thought that she might be had him fighting to marshal his rage, to focus. He needed to be calm, think. He had to get to her before Cosgrove figured out there was no money here.

Chapter Sixteen

Deborah wondered how long it would take Cosgrove to realize the money wasn't here.

Ever since directing him to the cabin, she'd had a sick knot in her stomach. Was this the best place to have brought him? It had made sense back at the house. In fact, it had been the only idea she thought would work, but she'd been operating on fear and desperation. She probably still was.

"Check that cabinet," Cosgrove ordered.

Hands still tied in front of her, jaw throbbing where he'd hit her, she moved to the short work cupboard that sat near the dry sink. A Franklin stove squatted in the adjacent corner, covered with a thin layer of dirt just like the rest of the cabinet. She opened the cabinet, her nose twitching at the dust she stirred up. Empty.

The cabin had been built by Bram's uncle Ike when he and his late wife, Rose, first settled there. Though it sat unused for years, Jake had fixed it up last October for his and Emma's honeymoon, installing indoor plumbing.

Neck stinging from the cut Cosgrove had given her, Deborah ventured, "Where have you been all this time?"

"Waiting for a chance to get you alone," Cosgrove snapped. "Do you and your sisters ever do anything by yourselves?"

"Not often." When she had wanted to be close to Bram, she had found their constant presence sometimes annoying, but now she was thankful for it.

"Ross has had someone guarding your house twenty-four hours a day since I arrived." The outlaw's voice took on even more of an edge. "Now look in the stove behind you."

Hands and clothes grimy, Deborah managed to open the cook door with her bound hands, then looked inside. Also empty.

Cosgrove cursed, gesturing with his knife toward the bedroom. She skirted the small dining table Bram and Jake had made when they were boys and walked straight ahead. A blue-

and-white quilt lay at the foot of the mattress; light blue curtains hung at the window, all still coated with dust from the storm.

On the opposite wall sat a small heat stove. A bathtub with porcelain knobs was angled into the right corner.

Cosgrove limped in behind her. She had noticed his uneven gait just after they had entered the cabin.

"What happened to your leg?" she asked tentatively.

"Got shot by someone in Monaco when I was chasing after you." He tapped the knife against the door frame. "Back here. The wardrobe."

Deborah turned, walked to the tall narrow cabinet and opened it. Empty.

His face darkened, his cold flat gaze drilling into her. He locked a hand around her upper arm and yanked her to him, pressing the knife under her chin. "Where is it? If you're playing games with me—"

"I'm not. I wasn't here when Bram brought the money, so I don't know where he hid it. It must be in the barn."

How much time would that buy her? Not enough. Would Bram think to look here? Would Jericho?

She closed the wardrobe doors. "Have you been watching my house this whole time?"

"I almost caught you the day you ran off, but I lost you in the dust storm. It allowed me to escape the authorities, too. I hid out in a lean-to until the wind quit." He glanced down at his leg. "The gunshot became infected, so I healed up at the Eight of Hearts. Had a bed there and plenty to eat."

Deborah's gaze sliced to him. Two months ago Bram, the Baldwins and the Holts had been involved in a tense stand-off with a band of rustlers that included Cosgrove. The owner of the Eight of Hearts, Theo Julius, and every member of the murdering Landis gang, save Cosgrove, had died in a shoot-out there. He had gone back to the very place he'd escaped.

She didn't need to wonder why he was being so free with information. She knew he intended to kill her.

"Look under the bed."

She knelt, keeping him in her line of sight as she bent to check beneath the mattress. The film of dirt hadn't been disturbed. "It's not here either."

He snatched her up by one arm, hauling her into the front room and toward the back door.

"We're going to the barn. You better hope the money is there."

"It has to be." When Cosgrove discovered there was nothing in the barn except dirt and hay, he would be livid.

Once they got outside, she had to make a run for it. She was afraid to wait any longer.

He shoved her toward the rear of the cabin. Suddenly a knock sounded on the front door.

Startled, both Deborah and Cosgrove jumped. He gripped her upper arm with bruising pressure. "What the hell—"

Without warning, the door splintered off its hinges and fell into the room.

Bram stood in the doorway, gun leveled at Cosgrove. "Let her go!"

The outlaw dragged Deborah in front of him, one arm banded around her middle. He pressed the knife to her throat, the blade biting into her skin.

"Ross, you better lay down your weapon or Deborah dies. All it takes is one slice right across her pretty throat."

Bram's eyes darkened. Deborah could see he didn't have a clear shot at Cosgrove. And wouldn't have one unless she helped him.

Everything happened in an instant.

She went limp, causing Cosgrove to stumble. He quickly caught himself and shoved her at Bram.

With her hands still tied, her balance was off and she couldn't steady herself. Momentum had her careening right into him and he caught her, losing his grip on his gun when he did. It skittered a few feet away.

Cosgrove dived for Bram. He shoved Deborah behind him and clamped both hands on the outlaw's wrist, trying to keep the blade from slicing his face.

He punched the other man in the stomach, then hit his jaw. Cosgrove stumbled back, taking Bram with him. The men crashed to the floor.

Deborah searched frantically for the gun. There it was, under the dining table. Too near where the men grappled, grunting and landing blows.

Cosgrove pinned Bram and raised the knife. Bram threw him off. Deborah raced for the gun, sliding to her knees and grabbing the weapon. Her hands were slick with sweat, making it difficult to hold on.

She thumbed down the hammer and took aim, waiting for one clear shot. The two men rolled across the floor, hitting the wall. Cosgrove recovered first, raising his knife and plunging it straight toward Bram's eye.

Deborah fired, hitting him dead center. Cosgrove froze. He looked down at his chest, then at her. His eyes went flat. The knife clattered to the floor.

She shot again. And again until the chamber was empty of bullets. The outlaw fell half on top of Bram.

Shaking, tears blurring her vision, she cried out, "Bram!"

"I'm here." He shoved Cosgrove off him and slid across the floor to her. "I'm okay. Are you?"

"Yes," she sobbed. She held the gun leveled at the outlaw, her finger still on the trigger.

Bram curled an arm around her waist and covered her hands with his big one. "He's dead, sweetheart. Give me the gun."

"He's really dead?"

"Yes. All the way. You did it with your first shot."

"Good."

Dazed, she realized Bram was trying to ease the weapon from her grasp.

"It's okay. Give me the gun."

She released it and he laid it on the floor, catching her when she fell into him, crying.

"Let me look at you. Are you sure you're all right?" Bram drew back enough to run his worried gaze the length of her body. When he saw her face and neck, rage flushed his features.

"Untie me, please," she said raggedly.

With shaking hands he loosened the ropes binding her wrists.

She pushed them off and locked her arms around him, burying her face in his neck. "You came. I thought it might be Jericho."

"I imagine he's on his way. Davis Lee, too."

Sobs quieting, she drew in the reassuring scent of man and soap. Tears dampened his shirt and she held on for long moments until she stopped shaking. He stroked her hair, holding her tight. Just holding her.

When she lifted her head, he tilted her chin to the side, staring at her jaw then the cut on her neck. "Cutting you wasn't enough? He hit you, too."

"It could've been worse. For both of us." She shuddered as she again saw Cosgrove bearing down on Bram with that blade aimed straight for his eye.

Dragging in her first full breath, she ran her hands over his shoulders and arms. "Did he get you anywhere?"

"No."

"Thank goodness."

Bram stroked her cheek. "Deborah, I—"

"Ross!" a masculine voice boomed. "Deborah!"

Surprised, she felt her pulse skip then level as she turned and saw the big man standing in the doorway. "It's Jericho."

Bram helped her to her feet. Though she didn't know where things stood between them, she was glad he was here.

Her brother stepped inside and she went to him. He gathered her close and hugged her. "Are you all right?"

"Yes. We both are."

Davis Lee followed, his gaze going over Bram, then Cosgrove. "Good. He's dead."

"Thanks to Deborah," Bram said.

Jericho studied her soberly. "Did you empty your gun?"

"Yes." She gave him a shaky smile.

"That's my girl."

"Guess we'd better get Cosgrove to town and send a wire to the sheriff in Monaco," Davis Lee said.

Bram agreed, moving with the other man to the outlaw's body. He grabbed Cosgrove under the arms and Davis Lee took the man's feet. Together they carried him outside.

Shaken, Deborah stared at the pool of blood on the pine floor.

Jericho cupped her shoulder. "You sure you're okay?"

She nodded. What she cared about right now was finding out if she and Bram were. She needed to talk to him. She needed *him*.

Davis Lee and Bram returned. She couldn't stop looking at Bram, scrutinizing every inch from his wide shoulders and big arms to his powerful thighs. He looked all right. Earlier, he had felt all right, but she wanted to hold him again and make sure.

His gaze locked on her, too.

Davis Lee scanned the cabin. "Cosgrove is loaded on his horse. We can take him back to town."

"I'll get Deborah home," Jericho said.

Bram kept his eyes on hers. "Would you mind if I took her?"

Her brother glanced down and she nodded. "Yes, I'd like that."

"All right, then," Jericho said.

After another hug and a quick shake of Bram's hand, the two lawmen left.

She wanted to apologize. It was a good sign that he wanted to see her home.

He took a step and put his arms around her, pulling her into him. "Just let me hold you for a minute. I need to feel for myself that you're really okay."

She laughed shakily, resting her head on his chest. "I need to feel you, too."

Dragging in his first full breath, he buried his face in her hair and ran his hands lightly over her. "I was on my way to speak with you when I ran into Jordan, riding hell-for-leather to tell me Cosgrove had you."

She lifted her head, her lashes still spiky from tears. "You were coming to find me?"

Seeing the raw cut on her neck and the bruise forming on her jaw, he felt fury lash at him. He managed to keep his touch easy as he brushed his thumb along the uninjured side of her jaw. "To apologize."

"Really?" she asked tremulously. "I should apologize, as well."

"You don't need to." Her gray cotton dress was dirty, speckled with blood, her face smudged. His heart turned over. "If you don't let me get this out, I don't know that I'll be able to."

Her gaze searched his. "Okay."

"You were right." He took in her delicate features. She was so beautiful. "I didn't know you'd be offered the job again, but I knew it was a possibility when I went to Reverend Scoggins."

He paused, his chest tightening. Though he

dreaded what he would see in her eyes, he had to confess. "I did ask him to write that letter and if you'd chosen to leave, I would've let you go. I was trying to protect myself, although I wasn't really aware of it until you said it."

"Until I accused you."

"You had cause. I hurt you. It took Jake to make me see how much." Curling one hand gently around her nape, he took a deep breath. "I'm sorry, honey. I'd like another chance, if you're willing. I really want to try again, whether you take the job or not."

She raised a hand to his face and caressed his jaw, joy bubbling up inside her. "Really?"

"Really." He took her hand and pressed a kiss in the center of her palm. "I love you. Here, there or anywhere."

Her breath caught. "I love you, too."

His gesture gave her the confidence to say, "We need to talk about the teaching job."

He nodded, his gaze never wavering.

"If I accept the position, we'll probably have to still pretend to be engaged. Until my contract is finished."

"Well, that's going to be a problem," he rumbled.

Her heart sank. She had hoped this wasn't the end.

He lifted her chin. "Because I want us to be engaged for real."

"What?" Her eyes searched his, her vision blurring slightly from sudden tears. "You trust me to come back?"

"Yes." He framed her face carefully in his hands. "And when your contract is up and you're back here, I want you to marry me. If you want to think about it—"

"I don't need to think about it!" She threw her arms around him. "My answer is yes."

"Good." He laughed. "I want everyone to know you're spoken for, even if you don't accept the position."

She wasn't testing him, but she had to know. They both did.

"I think I'll take the job." Anxious and uncertain about his response, she studied him. "It will only be for two terms. I swear it."

"All right." His gaze was soft on her face.

Her arms tightened around him. "Are you sure?"

"I'm sure I love you." He thumbed away a tear on her cheek. "Don't plan to ever stop. No matter what."

As she stared into his blue eyes, she knew they would make it this time.

Epilogue

The Christmas party at The Fontaine was the fanciest shindig Bram had ever seen. And this promised to be his best Christmas ever. Only one more school term for Deborah. Just four more months.

Tomorrow he had to drive her back to Abilene for the beginning of the second term. But come spring, she'd be back here. With him. And they would marry. Finally.

He stood near the front door at the foot of the staircase. Music from Jed Doyle's fiddle and his brother's mouth harp swelled inside the high-ceilinged lobby lit by gaslight. Red ribbons adorned the garland that trimmed the entire length of the banister and a giant tree in the far corner.

Bram grinned as he watched the dancers whirl past. Quentin and Zoe Prescott had danced only twice. They were still mindful of the surgery that had recently given Quentin back the use of his legs.

Bram searched the crowd for his fiancée. She stood on the opposite side talking to John Tucker, her attention frequently wandering to Bram. Except for this dance, they had partnered on every one.

The whole town was here. Matt and Annalise Baldwin danced past, then Russ and Lydia. Their pa, J.T., led his new wife, Cora, out onto the floor.

Ike and Georgia were back to full health, enjoying the evening. Duffy stood across the way, talking to Ef Gerard and his wife, Naomi. Riley and Susannah Holt stood with their daughter and son, all staring in awe at the towering Christmas tree. Bram wanted to sneak Deborah off to a room somewhere, but he was too aware of Millie Jacobson and what she might spew.

Jake walked up beside him, grinning as if he had just bested Bram in a horse race. Over the noise of voices and music, his brother said, "Well, I was right."

Bram laughed, surprised at how excited he was. "Emma's expecting?"

"Yes." Jake looked truly happy. There were none of the shadows in his eyes that Bram had worried might be there.

He laughed, congratulating the other man. Jake had lost his first wife and their child several years ago. Bram had never known if his brother would want another child, even after he had fallen for Emma.

"Emma's glad, too?"

Jake nodded. "And tired. She's about to give out, so we're going to stay the night here."

Bram said good-night as Jake went to collect his wife.

Deborah caught Bram's eye and she smiled, that slow sweet smile that always made his blood hum. Impatient to get his hands on her, he motioned her over.

His chest went tight as she started toward him. Her ice-blue silk gown bared her shoulders and hinted at the swells of her breasts. Her upswept hair drew attention to her elegant neck. The dress was stunning on her, but all Bram cared about was getting her out of it.

Davis Lee and Josie paused on their way out the door. Their daughter slept peacefully in the sheriff's arms. "Merry Christmas, Bram."

"Merry Christmas."

Jericho and Catherine were next to leave. Evie

was wide-awake, looking at everything from her perch against Jericho's shoulder as he said good-night to them.

Deborah finally reached him, lacing her fingers through his. "I have one more Christmas gift for you."

She'd already given him new work gloves and a shirt, made by Michal. His gift to her had been a simple diamond ring to wear on her right hand until they married.

He leaned down so she could hear him. "If you say we can be alone, that will be the best Christmas gift I've ever gotten."

Eyes laughing, she took his hand and led him past the front door toward the less populated end of the lobby.

"Where are we going?"

"Russ said we could use his office."

Bram put both his hands on her waist and pushed her along. "That means we *can* be alone, at least for a bit."

She laughed, pulling him into the office. The soft gaslight polished her skin to the sheen of pearls.

He glanced around. "Darn, I wish I hadn't helped Russ move that bed out of here after he and Lydia married."

She swatted at him. The shaving stand remained, still across the room. A large desk with a leather chair behind it sat to their right, faced by a pair of chairs in the same dark brown leather.

Bram backed up to check the lobby. Once he was sure no one was paying them any mind, he closed the door. He grinned and curled a hand around Deborah's waist, tugging her to him.

Her eyes sparkled. "What do you think you're doing?"

"Spending some time with my intended." He covered her mouth with his, backing her against the desk. When he lifted his head, he kissed her forehead, her eyelids, her temple.

She sighed, her hands curling into the fabric of his shirt to bring him closer even as she said, "We shouldn't be doing this."

"We should." He nuzzled her neck and she tilted her head so he could kiss his way down her throat. "I'm going to need more to hold me the next four months than those little pecks you've been giving me all night."

"I need to tell you something."

Dragging his mouth over her chest to the swell of her breasts, he inhaled the sweet heady fragrance of woman. "Make it fast."

"You don't have to drive me back to Abilene tomorrow. They've hired another teacher."

"What?" He snapped straight up, his hands

tightening on her waist. "They can't do that. You signed a contract."

"They've hired John Tucker to replace me."

"Tucker!" Bram thought his head might explode. "He knows how badly you want that job, what you went through to get it."

"He'll teach there and I'll teach here."

"What is going on over there? Is it Millie? Has she been up to her nonsense— What did you say?" Bram stopped, finally comprehending what she had said.

Deborah's eyes sparkled as she rolled up on tiptoe and kissed him. "I said I'll be teaching here. The school board in Abilene agreed to accept John's contract and Whirlwind agreed to accept mine."

He searched her eyes, looking for any sign of doubt, any hint of reluctance. "Are you sure? Did you do this for me? You don't need to."

She clasped his face in her hands. "I did it for me, for us. Because I love you."

"Here, there or anywhere," they finished together.

* * * * *

So you think you can write?

Mills & Boon® and Harlequin® have joined forces in a global search for new authors.

It's our biggest contest yet—with the prize of being published by the world's leader in romance fiction.

In September join us for our unique Five Day Online Writing Conference
www.soyouthinkyoucanwrite.com

Meet 50+ romance editors who want to buy your book and get ready to submit your manuscript!

So you think you can write? Show us!

A sneaky peek at next month...

HISTORICAL

IGNITE YOUR IMAGINATION, STEP INTO THE PAST...

My wish list for next month's titles...

In stores from 5th October 2012:

❏ Two Wrongs Make a Marriage – Christine Merrill

❏ How to Ruin a Reputation – Bronwyn Scott

❏ When Marrying a Duke... – Helen Dickson

❏ No Occupation for a Lady – Gail Whitiker

❏ Tarnished Rose of the Court – Amanda McCabe

❏ All a Cowboy Wants for Christmas

    – Judith Stacy, Lauri Robinson & Debra Cowan

Available at WHSmith, Tesco, Asda, Eason, Amazon and Apple

Just can't wait?

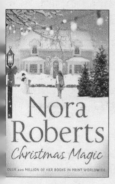  

The World of Mills & Boon®

There's a Mills & Boon® series that's perfect for you. We publish ten series and, with new titles every month, you never have to wait long for your favourite to come along.

Blaze.
Scorching hot, sexy reads
4 new stories every month

By Request
Relive the romance with the best of the best
9 new stories every month

Cherish™
Romance to melt the heart every time
12 new stories every month

Desire™
Passionate and dramatic love stories
8 new stories every month